THE DESERET RECKONING

Matthew L. Huffman

ISBN: 9798861994903

This is a work of fiction. Names, characters, businesses, places, events, locales, and incidents are either the products of the author's imagination or used in a fictitious manner. While similar to real places and people, the names and identifying details have been changed to protect the privacy of individuals who may be the inspiration for characters. Any other resemblance to actual persons, living or dead, or actual events is purely coincidental. I realize that although based in part on actual events, some real-life persons may have different memories or different opinions of the events in question. Write your own book.

The Deseret Reckoning

PART 1

Chapter 1

Susan: Washington DC, July 1982

The commute wasn't long enough most days.

Susan Kingsley secretly hoped the train to the Smithsonian complex on the Capitol Mall would take longer than the usual hour and a half. It was her best time to read. Today, she longed for another ten minutes. Susan looked down at her watch, a stainless steel banded and gold-rimmed Citizen her father had given her for her thirtieth birthday. That was five years ago. She glanced up from her book and out the window of the second car, listening for the last signal crossing to fade, and clutched the thick cardboard-bound research text. It was part of her job at The Smithsonian Museum, Historical Acquisitions Department. Collections and Acquisitions Assistant Specialist, American History. Middle management. Despite the lengthy job title, one of the perks was travel. And the acquisition of historical artifacts.

Days in the office were quieter and more productive than the days spent on the road, collecting museum pieces. And they were more productive than days spent at home preparing briefs and catalog reports. Today was like many others, tying up loose ends from a collection of black and white photographs by Egbert Fowx from the Civil War to be on permanent display in the Smithsonian's American History Wing, the hall of fame for any other history museum.

After a predictable commute and a focused walk from the train station to her office, Susan spent the majority of the morning reviewing the final cataloging process for the photos, then lunch at her desk alone. The afternoon seemed to drag on with meetings, an awkward hallway conversation with her boss, and expense reports from last week's travel. The hustle and bustle of the Northeast always put her on edge. She was just preparing to leave for the day when the phone in her office rang. She picked up on the second ring. "Acquisitions."

"Oh, hello, this is Alfred Steggeman from the Cambridge, Ohio History Museum. Is this a bad time?"

"Not at all, Mr. Steggeman. What can I help you with?" Susan was, in fact, clearing her desk and taking home a text on the War of 1812. She hoped to finish reading it on the train ride home if she could manage to leave the office on time.

"I was referred to you by a supporting member of the museum. He said you might be interested in some letters we've recently acquired."

Susan paused, set down her purse, and opened a new file to record the details of the call. She started with the date, *July 22nd, 1982,* and sat back in her chair. "What's the backstory with these letters? Tell me a little more, please."

"We're a small museum, mostly late 1830s pioneer-type stuff, a few McCormick Farmall tractors in the open-air barns, and a refurbished apple press. We put on a demonstration at the annual Pioneer Festival on the third Saturday in October. You should see the crowd. It's become a tradition to drink cider, walk through the leaves, and almost every year, a young couple gets engaged."

"That's very nice, Mr. Steggeman. About the apple cider, I mean. You mentioned some letters." Susan brushed her hair from her face and tucked it behind her ear. If Mr. Steggeman droned on much longer, she'd miss her usual 5:20 train. But if she missed the 5:20, she might miss Andrew as well. *A silver lining.*

Susan shared an apartment with her ex-husband, Special Agent Andrew Harrison, assigned to a brand new division of the FBI in Manassas, Virginia. After three years of marriage, they divorced. But they were still living in the same apartment. Susan still shared the apartment with Andrew because it was difficult to find something she could afford on her own that was walkable to a train station.

"Let me get to the point then, Susan."

"Thank you, Mr. Steggeman."

"You see, we received these letters, a series of them dated from November 1868 until the last one in October 1870. They were addressed to a local resident but don't discuss much history relevant to our area of Ohio. They are very intriguing, though, and I thought they might be of interest to someone else. Perhaps someone researching the Old Spanish Trail or the Utah Territory." Alfred took a breath and continued, not waiting for a response.

"I've never been to Utah, and that's where they originate. The letters came from the estate of one Margaret Chapman, aged 81, who recently passed at the Meadow Acres assisted living center."

"I see."

"Mrs. Chapman had a cousin, you see, a woman who lives over in Cincinnati now. She had very few living heirs and wanted them to be preserved. But as I said, this is not the right museum for these letters. We've been keeping them separate."

Susan looked at her watch. She wouldn't make the 5:20 train and could avoid Andrew for another day. And avoiding him at the apartment was a regular goal these days. Andrew had stayed in the apartment after their divorce because he'd been expecting a promotion and the transfer that came with it. Susan put those dark thoughts away and returned her focus to work.

"Can you tell me about the contents of the letters, Mr. Steggeman? The letters," Susan said, slightly annoyed but firm. Firmness that men weren't accustomed to, at least outside of the urban northeast. Tension in her neck was moving upward and threatened a headache.

"To the point then, Susan. If you're interested, we, er she, would like to donate these to the Smithsonian. But Mrs. Kowalski, that's Mrs. Chapman's cousin, and she's from Cambridge originally, has been wanting to come over to make photocopies of the letters and send them to her great nephew who lives somewhere out west."

"Got it," said Susan, changing positions in her chair as she continued making notes. Letters from the 1870s were relatively common and not especially consequential for the Smithsonian.

"We've made arrangements with the middle school to use their copier after hours," said Mr. Steggeman.

"Copies?" Photocopies were never a good idea. Damage to artifacts, historically relevant or not, was common.

"That's right, for the great nephew. He lives in one of the cities mentioned in the letters, I'm not sure where."

"If you've already made copies, maybe you could send me a few of the letters to review before I decide if they're worth preserving in the Smithsonian. Just drop them in the mail to me," interjected Susan, trying to regain control of the conversation.

"Sure thing, Susan. You'd want to run it by your boss before he decides to put them in the Smithsonian's collection anyway. And I'm sure he's busy."

Susan was annoyed, but she could anticipate the end of the conversation.

"He's very busy, Mr. Steggeman," Susan said as she bristled at the inference, hesitation in her voice.

During Susan's time at the Smithsonian, her travels across America got longer, the search for authentic history became more challenging, and she became more determined to ascend the ranks of the museum. Most of the men dismissed her or resented even the slightest advancement.

With each new acquisition, she got one step closer to setting herself apart from her male colleagues. Very few women held supervisory roles. Susan couldn't recall any within her department.

Susan wanted a supervisory position, was willing to work to get what she wanted, and was willing to wait until the political winds blew in her favor. But not forever. Chauvinism and discrimination were *modus operandi* at the male-dominated Smithsonian. Still, each year of service was another milestone for Susan and other women working for less pay than their male counterparts. But her day was coming. If she could only get off the phone first.

"Then it's settled. We'll take the copies of Mrs. Chapman's letters and put them in the mail. Should I send them directly to your boss? Either way, he'll want to review them before we decide."

"That's fine. Address them to the Assistant Director, Historical Acquisitions Department, Smithsonian, twenty-four Capitol Mall Drive, Washington DC, one oh one two four. And make sure...." Susan attempted to continue and then wrap up the call when she was interrupted again.

"Assistant? What about the director? Shouldn't he make these decisions?"

"He's overseas for the next six weeks. And he doesn't make these kinds of decisions." Susan was getting impatient.

"This could all work out. By the way, maybe you and your husband could come out in October. It's the Pioneer Festival here in Cambridge. It really is a fun time. And that's Cambridge, Ohio, not Cambridge, Massachusetts."

"Review the letters first, Mr. Steggeman. Make sure...."

"Not a problem, Susan. I'll send them next week. Hope to see you at our festival, it takes a mountain of apples to fill the press, then the drive screw needs to be assembled and lowered into place, then the clamps have to be advanced and tightened. Each of the festival marshals and usually the mayor and the county sheriff take turns at the drive screw until the cider starts flowing. It's a hoot, and every year it seems, a young couple gets engaged. You see... "

"Yes, Mr. Steggeman, I'll look for the letters and consider your offer," Susan saw her opening and went for it. "I've got to go. Thank you, sir. I'll be in touch after I get the delivery." Then, quickening her pace at the end, "Have a good day, sir. Goodbye." Susan sighed as she made a few notes in her portfolio. She didn't see the point in cautioning the donor about damage to the letters from the copier. Excessive light, rough handling, and changes in temperature and humidity were all elements of potential damage to ancient paper and ink.

It was already after five, and she wouldn't be able to make the 5:20. So she stayed at the office an extra thirty minutes, made some travel arrangements, and prepared to leave her office alone, as usual. She slipped back into her dark brown pumps and headed for the elevator. The click-clack sound of her heels echoed in the hallway as she strode through the building and out into the street. The Ferragamos were a luxury she couldn't afford, but the feeling she got from wearing them was unmistakable, the pride of being comfortable, powerful even, in her own skin.

The train commute home was quiet, and Susan was able to read four chapters about the War of 1812. It was after seven when Susan finally walked into the third-floor apartment, tossed her keys on the table in the foyer, and sat down at the table by the kitchen. She poured herself a vodka neat, downed it, and poured another, pushing aside the mail and the unread *Washington Post*. Some days she liked to take the paper on the train, but Andrew liked to read the sports section and chided her for taking it a few times by mistake. It was these kinds of situations, their busy lives, and Andrew's impatience that made their cohabitation a continuing chain of events that seemed to have no resolution.

Their divorce had been quick and not as messy as might have been, with no kids in the picture, no home, and no mortgage, and each of them hungry for promotion in their respective fields and opposite commutes. That comfortable in her own skin feeling was fading, but the vodka helped.

Perhaps if she got the promotion, she could afford that new place on Michigan Avenue, closer to work, even if the train commute time was shorter.

Chapter 2

William: Santa Fe, NM, August 1870

William Mitchell was more of a leader than most men. But he was also more cautious. It was the reason he survived the War Between the States. Although he was beaten down by the war, even on the winning side, and tired of the hardscrabble life of west Texas and the New Mexico Territory, he was ready for a new start. And he still had unfulfilled ambitions, although they were off to a slow start.

Over the past three years, he had managed to save two hundred eighty-six dollars. Savings for a wife and family and a homestead. It was a small fortune for a frontier businessman. Most of the savings had come at the expense of his health. Working with cattle and horses, his knees were not what they used to be. The bullet lodged in his back still ached, making long days in the saddle troublesome. The bullet wasn't the only thing he tried to forget about Antietam. And that was years ago.

"Gonna ask around, then I'll be back before supper," William shouted. There was no answer, then in another moment came the reply.

"Si, Señor Mitchell." Villanueva was originally from Mexico

City, by way of Torreon, then Presidio San Antonio de Bexar. His dedicated work ethic was his signature.

William sauntered out of the stables and into the blacksmith's shop and then walked toward the west side of town. *Got to find the right people. Make this venture work out.*

He paused in front of the dry goods storehouse, then continued past the hardware store and lumber yard to the livestock district. The cattle brought in were skinny, almost sickly-looking animals. They looked like they'd never seen a bale of alfalfa like was grown on the north side of the farm where he grew up in rural Ohio. But farming was not a viable option in this cactus-strewn wasteland of the New Mexico Territory. And William was a long way from home and not likely to return anytime soon.

Ready for a new start, many settlers in this part of the world wanted a chance to strike it rich in California. The gold rush had already come and gone, but the stories, the rumors, and the lies remained. The chance of riches in mining in California was a siren's song of hope, yet the dream of most, willing to make the journey. William had traveled to California twice before, via the Spanish Trail to San Francisco, and knew the truth. The siren's song of hope was an illusion for most of the would-be settlers. The dream of riches led directly through the ramshackle tents of the Chinese labor camps, the masses of penniless miners, and the charlatans hawking seeded but barren mining claims. But through the lens of time and with a dose of reality, another land had captured William's imagination. The Deseret Territory, the land of Uintah, the birthplace of the Utes and the Shoshone. Some people called it Utah.

Undiscovered valleys, untouched riches. West. He walked the dusty streets. *Maybe not mining and maybe not nearby, but somewhere. And within reach. One day I'll have a farm and some cattle. A home that*

Sarah Ann's father would be proud of.

It drove him, the burning desire to achieve more than what his parents expected in this life. He continued on to the big tented saloon and stood among the men clustered in twos and threes at scarred tables and wobbly stools. Although most of the men in the saloon were there to spend their remaining coins on the whiskey and would prefer to concentrate on forgetting the day's struggle, some were willing to listen to the voice of tomorrow.

He asked for a whiskey and turned around as most of the men were still sizing him up. He looked around the tented saloon and saw men beaten down by time, by misfortune, and by war. *Hard times make for strong men. And strong men are what the Deseret Territory needs.*

William began his address. "I'm selling passage on my wagon train west to Grand Junction..."

The men in the saloon, eyes red, and faces haunted by ghosts of bitter bargains with the land they attempted to tame, scarcely gave the stranger any acknowledgement. The saloon was dark, and the floorboards were stained with tobacco spit. But the saloon offered a resort. A distraction. Hooch.

"...via the North Branch of the Spanish Trail. Passage to Grand Junction costs six dollars per man. I have a guide who knows the route. And a man trained in the securing of game–enough venison, buffalo, and elk, enough provisions to supply us along the way." A few drunkards stumbled about the decked saloon, knocking sticks of furniture, seeking more whiskey and less talk of tomorrow.

"The journey should take forty days to reach Grand Junction in the Colorado Territory. Those willing to continue west can winter over there and reprovision before continuing across the Deseret Territory and the Uintah to California. Or the Oregon Trail if they so choose. The journey I'm offering is manageable and at a fair price. It's payable at the journey's start. Each man should be responsible for his own quarters. I've got two teams of horses pulling the pair of wagons. Each man will be expected to partner in stream crossings, in securing the safety of the group, and to maintain the schedule of forty days." While none in the vicinity immediately responded, William was certain the offer would make the circuit of Santa Fe. It was the fourth little speech he'd made offering passage on his wagon train to Grand Junction in the past three weeks. He wasn't much of a salesman, but there was safety in numbers, and every bit of money he made went to his homestead dreams.

The two men closest to him continued to pay attention, so William went on, only quieter, "Grand Junction lies in a civilized and peaceful valley at the confluence of the Green and the Grand Rivers. Winters are mild there. My horses are stabled at Klein's, across from the boarding house. Ask for William Mitchell. My associate Villanueva can help with the Spanish speakers."

William laid a coin on the bar. "Thanks for the drink." He turned and donned his hat. "Gentlemen." It was a term he used to gain respect. The union army taught him that. The remainder came from experience. And from a year at Yale. And a worn-out copy of *The Odyssey*. A man of enlightenment.

Outside, the air was cleaner and bright. The weather in late August was typical for this part of the New Mexico Territory, hot and dry. Few clouds drifted above as the afternoon sun shone down on the parched adobes of old Santa Fe. William crossed the quiet promenade and sat in the shade of the government building. He kicked at the pebbles under his bench and waited for any takers from the saloon to approach.

Surely some of these people would like a change of scenery. This was still the land of the Spaniard and the Mexican settler, with most inhabitants speaking Spanish, even what remained of the native peoples.

But English-speaking white settlers from Texas were increasingly filling the gaps among the cattle rustlers, the fugitives from Mexico, and what remained of the Jemez, the Apache, and the Navajo. This was the end of the great plains of Texas and the beginning of the Great Basin desert, nearly non-navigable. The only escape from the desert was north, through Colorado and the Deseret along the Spanish Trail to San Francisco and the rest of California.

Chapter 3

Andrew: Fredericksburg, VA, July 1982

Andrew put on his uniform, slammed the door, and walked downstairs to the Chrysler. Although he didn't have to wear a uniform exactly, he still called it that. He wore the same thing every day, black trousers, a starched white button-down shirt with a clip-on black tie, and a black jacket, the standard FBI uniform. His regular issue from the motor pool was an eight-year-old, four-door. It was mostly blue but had a replacement front quarter panel in dark green. It stood out in the suburban parking lot of shiny American sedans and newer Japanese hatchbacks. With the defrost vents open, he waited for the windshield to clear and the engine to warm up as he checked his radio.

It was nearly nine, but crime didn't happen on a schedule; that much was clear. It was an easy twenty-two-minute commute to Manassas. The Chrysler was a stripped-down model but seemed reliable enough, even if it tended to pull to the left. Sometimes the smell of vomit escaped from the vents, but not on this muggy morning.

Andrew let his mind wander. *Maybe before summer is over. Maybe if that son of a bitch wannabe Johnson retires. Maybe if there's a crime wave. Maybe.* Andrew wanted more than the Chrysler. And he wanted more than a third-floor walk-up apartment.

And he wanted more than a nine-to-five museum hostess for a

wife. *Divorce meant she'd be gone by now.* He logged in his time and started his daily report. "Bitch," he said aloud.

He wanted the Task Force Commander job in Washington, DC, where the real power brokers were. At thirty-four, some thought he was too young. But he was ambitious. He wanted the press briefings and the big cases. He wanted to nab crooked politicians and old mobsters. And he wanted more than Susan. But before he could make that leap, he had to make a big case from his current position. It was a new experimental role, supporting local jurisdictions. He needed a big interstate trafficking case, something with teeth to move up. Something that made news to gain the task force. Something he could control and keep. Blood began to flood his brain. If he could just get that one big arrest, he'd have his promotion approved and a new Ford that came along with it. Black with chrome that looked like official FBI business, even in the rain. *And then I'll make my move with what's-her-name from the deli. She'd be great at home, fixin' my dinners on late nights, makin' my thermos of coffee for the commute. And swingin' those hips back and forth, under a tiny waist. And she'd be great in the sack.*

He adjusted his ass in the cold vinyl seat. "Yeah, some regular action," Andrew said, aloud this time, as the blood pumped south. He turned the vents away from the dash, punched the gas, spun out of the parking lot, and noticed a slight vomit smell coming from the vents. His nostrils curled, his groin bulged, and his ambitions surged.

***

"Harrison, get in here," Lieutenant James Gilroy called from his office into the hall.

"Yes, sir. Yes, sir," was Andrew's automatic reply.

"It's been two months since your last big arrest. That's not gonna cut the mustard around here. Two months and what was it, oh yeah, three Puerto Ricans charged with marijuana possession. They might as well have been jaywalking. There wasn't even enough to charge them with conspiracy, cuz you fucked up the surveillance tapes. This liaison role is too good for you." Gilroy waited to see if Andrew would interrupt him. He didn't. "Yes, you, numb-nuts. I'll ship your sorry ass back to Bethesda before you can say 'crab-cake'. You're a sorry excuse for a field agent."

"I'm from Baltimore, sir."

Gilroy checked his surroundings, then muttered quietly, "You better string some arrests together in the next coupla' months. Make 'em stick or you'll be back to popping prom queens for blow jobs and arresting dope fiends for dime bags in East Butfuk, Pennsylvania." Lieutenant Gilroy always had a way of motivating his agents. He had six months left until retirement. Andrew's solo assignments were a way to support small towns and leverage the budget. Andrew understood. Arrests mattered. Charges with minimum mandatory sentences gave the prosecutor leverage to catch bigger fish. Andrew wanted to move up the chain, the same way he had back in Baltimore.

He thought back to the past that brought him to this moment. He'd made his bones in the Baltimore Police Department. It was the right time to be in narcotics, what with Reagan expanding the war on drugs and the explosion of crack cocaine in every American city. It had been easy pickings for the narcotics division, flipping street dealers and turning out neighborhood gangbangers for bigger busts. It propelled his career forward in three short years. But the streets of Baltimore were just a stepping stone. He'd gotten some breaks. And now he had five years in at the FBI. His title was Community-based Roving Awareness Liaison. CRAWL for short. It was his job to assist local police departments with multi-jurisdictional arrests. When the smaller towns didn't have a dedicated SWAT team, it was his job to contact a nearby agency and coordinate the logistics. He was the eye in the sky, overseeing cooperation.

Andrew returned to his desk without looking up at the rest of the field agents. Everyone in the interstate trafficking department took their lumps from Lieutenant Gilroy. Today was Andrew's turn. So he spent the rest of the morning reading through the requests for assistance from small-town police departments and assistant district attorneys that had piled up on his desk.

He read through the short list of possible federal assistance:

Spoiled tomatoes and a dozen dead illegals rotting in a box truck in Tucson. "Uh, No," he muttered to himself.

Failed kidnapping of a thirty-two-year-old stripper in Graysville, Oklahoma—witness cooperation will be an issue.

"No."

Seventy-one pounds of marijuana discovered in the trunk of a NYC taxi cab... in Chicago.

"Only users lose drugs. No."

Two thousand pirated VHS tapes.

"No."

Cocaine in a suburb of St. Louis.

He'd take the drug case.

Chapter 4

Susan: Fredericksburg, VA, July 1982

After a quick shower, Susan toweled off and put on her favorite flower print robe. Mondays were Andrew's regular off days, plus every other Sunday. She peeked her head into Andrew's bedroom and asked, "You want some breakfast?" Susan hoped the difficulty in being cordial wasn't obvious.

"I'll just get something on the way out."

"Oh, OK."

"Unless you have something else in mind."

"I was just thinkin' we could share a bagel and cream cheese. I've already made a full pot of coffee. Maybe we could talk for a few minutes?" Relieved at the casual responses from Andrew, Susan relaxed and planned her next move.

"OK, give me a minute," said Andrew.

"Yep."

Susan went back to her side of the apartment, the guest bedroom. They'd been divorced for nearly three years, but money was always an issue, and they somehow couldn't make the time to separate their complicated lives. Their divorce had coincided with Andrew's hire at the FBI. And he never saw it coming. She threw on some comfy jeans, a T-shirt, and her favorite blue sweater. Emotions boxed and cataloged, she tossed her hair back from the towel, returned to the kitchen, and toasted the bagels.

"Sometimes I forget what day it is. Surprised to see you," mumbled Andrew.

"That's not all you forget." There they were. Anger. Resentment.

"I'm off every other Sunday now."

"Sundays? You forgot the vow to be faithful, and you forgot to take the trash out last Thursday," said Susan. More anger.

"Something tells me you'll never let me forget that."

"I need you to drive me to the airport next Friday. It's before your shift starts and kinda' on your way."

"Now you ask me for a favor? What's with you?"

Susan put the knife down from smearing cream cheese on a bagel and slid the plate across the counter to Andrew. "That's not what I wanted to talk about. Can you do it or not?" She could only take so much at one time.

"I guess so. What time?"

"Before your shift, I told you. I want you to sell your truck and give me fifteen hundred dollars for a deposit on an apartment in Alexandria."

"I'm not doing that," said Andrew, pushing himself away from the counter.

"You told the judge you'd sell your gun collection at auction, split the proceeds with me, and we'd be done with everything. Instead, you stashed them at your mother's house." She'd been saving this one for several minutes. She knew it was painful, but it could be useful, too.

"What's that got to do with the truck?"

"You never drive it. Your truck should have been communal property, and you know it. You put it in your mother's name. Real nice. An honest man would have made it right." Scorn. That was a big one. The only thing left in Susan's emotion bank was pity and sadness. She needed to end the conversation before that came to the surface.

"No."

"I'll take the fifteen hundred bucks, and then we don't ever have to see each other anymore. I'm always hearin' you snore. And I hate it when you come in here so late, stinkin' like cheap wine and cigarettes." Susan could see Andrew's face change. She could feel the tension in her own voice, though.

"Settle down."

"We both wanted outta' this apartment months ago. But somehow, your cohabitation won't let it go. You've got the Chrysler for work, so put an ad in the paper this week. Or find some other way to get me the fifteen hundred." Susan finished spreading the cream cheese and put the knife in the sink. "Just do it." She slid the coffee mug closer to Andrew.

***

Andrew could push perps around with the best of them, beat downs that didn't leave a mark. Chokeholds that got confessions. But he could never win an argument with Susan. Plus, she still looked great. He could see the outline of her B-cup breasts under that vee-neck blue sweater. *When was the last time I pulled it up over her head?*

***

Susan walked barefoot across the apartment, quietly closed the door, and hit the play button on the hi-fi stereo. Journey wailed into the room. She wiped a tear from her cheek and sat down on the bed. She wanted to discuss it more at length, but being in such proximity to Andrew, she could feel the flush of emotions coming on and the tug of heartache in her voice. So, she had to end the conversation quickly. "Asshole" was as good as she could muster on a Sunday morning. The confusion she felt approaching her ex-husband had quickly accelerated to anger and sorrow. And she wasn't comfortable talking with anyone about the nuances and complexities of their shared abode and noxious relationship.

Chapter 5

William: Santa Fe, NM, August 1870

The North Branch of the Spanish Trail was a network of game trails, old Indian hunting trails, and only more recently, a wagon trail. While William pondered his place and carefully planned his personal ambitions, railroads were being built westward by the Union Pacific in Wyoming and by the Central Pacific Eastward in California. But that was fifteen hundred miles away, and rails didn't exist to the north. Santa Fe was the end of the line, a literal dead end for the Atchison, Topeka & Santa Fe railroad. The railroad was a luxury for most and impractical for carrying horses or livestock.

The wagon train was still the safest way to travel, going to places the railroad would never reach. Wagon trains ranged from ten to two hundred souls, or more, the group providing safety for the individual.

Although William had been along the Spanish trail to California twice before, he'd never traversed the North Branch. He had already decided to make the fertile valleys of Vernal in the Deseret Territory his ultimate destination. With the proceeds from granting safe passage to a dozen or more passengers to Grand Junction and from the sale of some of his tradable goods, he would have enough money to carve out a homestead, a home for him and his wife, and finally, a settled life.

William stood once again to look back at the tented saloon and then began the walk back to the stables. *Beef stew from that old Sonoran widow-woman will make a good supper. Not much home-cookin' on the trail.*

William had married when he was thirty-three while on two-month leave from the war in September 1864. Sarah Ann Griggs, aged twenty-four, was still dedicated to life at home on the farm. So she stayed and waited for William to return home. While letters from Sarah were exceedingly rare, William had plans for a homestead and a family. When letters did arrive, usually months old, Sarah talked of family matters from home. And her father's concern for his daughter seemed to grow with each passing month he was gone.

The meandering lifestyle William learned in the Union Army in Tennessee, in Carolina, and in Georgia transitioned naturally to life in Texas and the West. He expected that when her father passed, Sarah would follow no matter what William's circumstances might be. And so, he wrote her letters often.

After the hearty bowl of stew, William returned to the stables and sat down to write to his wife.

***

Susan: Washington, DC, August 1982

Susan received a neatly folded set of papers from Mr. Steggeman the following week and made more notes about the correspondence. Keeping a record of specific interactions was customary, even for the meager documents contained inside—photocopies of three letters from 1870. Susan waited until lunchtime when the office of shared cubicles was quiet and she could focus. The script was metered and elegant, browned from age, and marred with squiggly lines from a poor-quality copier. She admired the page and read silently to herself:

August 19, 1870

Dearest Sarah Ann,

I hope this letter finds you in good health and abundant spirits. I'm writing to you today, a hot and dry Tuesday, to advise you of my plans, and thereby, I hope, our plans. Within the next day or so, my team of six horses and eight mules will embark upon the journey north and northwest to the Uintah. As you are aware, the Uintah is a land of verdant valleys. Upon arrival, I will send for you. This should make clear your best path.

The journey into the Uintah should take forty days. Await news of my arrival, and be prepared to make a journey unto yourself in the coming months. Due to circumstances I'm unable to explain, I cannot return to my previous life.

Recently I was considering our plans. Our years of marriage and our abiding faithfulness. Please make note of the provisions at my disposal which should make for a bountiful homestead. Consider this my offering, not a bribe to your father, but a slight persuasion, of my ability to provide for the both of you. This offering includes the assurance that his daughter will be well cared for and that I am more than capable to provide for a family. This pledge of guardianship includes the accounting of my current possessions: two bales of spun cotton, combed and certified of the highest quality, twenty sacks of sugar, packaged tightly and wrapped in muslin, forty pounds of dried buffalo with red raspberries, enough for the arduous journey ahead. For trading at the most opportune moment, four cases of newly forged rifles, with twelve cases of cartridges. These items should capture a handsome price that will set us up with many acres of land and satisfy your father's demands. My savings include two hundred and sixty dollars which is sufficient to purchase a homestead and sustain us through the winter, which are milder and less oppressive than on the farm.

Give your father my regards and warmest wishes to your mother and siblings. I pray the harvest has been bountiful. Take care, and continue keeping our love in your heart.

Until we meet again.

Yours,

William Mitchell

Susan found herself transported back in time, imagined the circumstances that might keep a married couple apart, and thought back to all she knew about the Civil War. Brother against brother. Families torn asunder. A generation of men scarred, maimed, or killed.

***

William: Santa Fe, NM, August 1870

William addressed the envelope and directed the bank office to include it with the outgoing mail. The 19th of August turned into the 20th of August, and the first cold snap had reached Cochetopa Pass, the first of many passes on the route to Vernal. Autumn snow was threatening in the mountains. But in Santa Fe, the next day was hot and windless.

When William returned to the stables, he gathered his most recent acquisition, a chestnut colt. He saddled the colt, mounted, and wandered back through the streets of Santa Fe, already afoul with saloons, outlaws, drunken men, gambling halls, and prostitution. William rode East towards the Atchison, Topeka & Santa Fe railroad office, the terminus still two miles out of town.

He checked the time. The train was late again, but the telegraph was reliable. He could see the operator inside, clacking away at dots and dashes, keeping tabs on the train's progress.

William wanted to be familiar with the scene. Tomorrow was the day his shipment was scheduled to arrive. And the following week was earmarked for departure towards Grand Junction. A few days to secure his shipment, pay his guide for the journey and sell a few more passes on his wagon train to the Grand Junction. This latest venture would put his settling down in motion and secure his future. The success of this trip hung in the balance, and he was determined to see it through. Determined to succeed and determined to rid himself of the pains of war. Determined to be reunited with his wife.

Back at the stable, Villanueva didn't seem to have time for a conversation. So William waited outside, back behind the corrals, where he could sit and watch his ponies. The twelve horses were a motley bunch, mostly chestnut colored with white stars, but also a few paints.

Lost in thought, William contemplated the journey. *Those paints aren't as willing to work as a team, but I could look at those splotches of color bucking in the brush all day.* He pondered the difficult journey that lay before him. The paints were better for riding than pulling, particularly over uneven terrain, as they were so sure-footed. The paints had a wilder spirit, maybe because many of them started out as Indian ponies, living free upon the plains much as the Indians had. His personal favorite was a bronze colt with black eyes and powerful haunches. The two-year-old colt was named Lusian, a reference to the Andalusian horses sometimes brought from Mexico. Strong and agile, Lusian was also the natural leader of the pack of horses in the corral.

William was still thinking about the horses when a voice called out, "How much is it to go on the wagon train to California?"

"This wagon train only goes as far as Grand Junction," William replied. He was still admiring his horses.

"Where is Grand Junction then?"

He turned and saw a young man of eighteen or twenty years old. "Four hundred fifty miles north, northwest of here. And that much closer to California."

"How much is that, then?"

"Six dollars per man."

"I only have four dollars, but aim to have another three or four dollars when I sell this watch."

"The price is six dollars, paid in advance of the journey," said William.

"I just said I'd have it soon, mister."

"Just the same."

"Then maybe I'll find a cheaper wagon train to California."

"You'll have a difficult time finding another leaving anytime soon, son."

"We'll see about that." The young man turned and walked back between the warehouse and the livery stable. William didn't need to babysit an adolescent for the next forty days.

***

Early the next morning, William got reacquainted with his guide and hunter, reaffirming their arrangement.

"Good morning, Mr. Ford."

"Just call me Ford," came the reply from a man older than William remembered.

Ford wore spectacles, unusual for anyone on the frontier, but other than that, he looked the part of a true mountain-man. He was average height and had a gray beard, almost entirely white, with a particularly handsome mustache that extended beyond the corners of his mouth and curled round at the ends to make a neat loop. Above his spectacles, his eyebrows were the same color as his mustache, a speckled gray, and curled up in a mosaic of trimmings about his face. He wore a buckskin frock coat, a felted cowboy hat with a narrow band, and a dark brown turkey feather.

"Fine. Ford, then. Let's take a look at the wagons first, and then we'll eye the livestock." William led the slower man to the warehouses next door.

"That there wagon is stout but heavy," said Ford, stating the obvious as William nodded.

"I wanted somethin' could withstand the mountains."

"Should do the job." Ford circled round the front rigging and spied the smaller wagon.

"This one here is just a regular prairie schooner that I've refitted with water barrels." William was proud of his wagons and didn't mind that Ford saw his bedroll on the floor. Each of them had spent more time sleeping under the stars than either was willing to admit.

The two men circled the second wagon then proceeded outside to the corral. The morning sun cast long shadows and promised another scorched earth day. Elongated silhouettes pranced on hooves farther afield. They spoke at length about the route, about supplies, and about the towns and settlements along the way. But William had one more concern.

"Are you sure you're up to the task, Ford? Think you'll be able to provide for the group as we make our way through the mountains?" William asked, having delayed the question for as long as possible.

"Rest easy, *patron*. I've killed every kind of animal there is in the mountains, and I aim to kill a few more before I join their number. Deer is still plentiful among the ponderosa pines along the streams below Cochetopa Pass. Beyond that, the terrain is more rugged, and we'll have to rely more on rabbits and such. If we should happen across an elk, that'll take more time to butcher, but the meat is tastier than venison and makes an excellent jerky. But making jerky is a three or four-day process. We may not have the time for that, so we'll try to stick to the deer. Unless we run into some." Ford's voice was calm and steady, but his eyes had a nervousness to them. Some might even say crazy-eyed. Perhaps it was from too many days alone in the mountains, stalking rabbits and deer. And bears. Maybe it was from staring down the sight of a rifle for too long. Most likely, it was from walking the razor's edge of the frontier. Dangers lurked everywhere and nowhere at the same time. The welcome sight of a spring stream for the horses could also mean a dangerous crossing. And the riches promised in the high mountains also meant fierce winters and incomprehensible snows.

"I'm up for the task and then some," came the reply. He was ready for the challenge.

Chapter 6

Jack and Tom: Golden, CO, August 1982

Tom Sullivan finished the morning shift at Gart's Sporting Goods in Golden, a suburb of Denver. He walked across the street and past his usual barber shop, Del's Tonsorial Parlor. Where that name came from, he didn't know. The owner was Charlie, and he'd owned it for forty years. It was full of relics from men's hairstyling from the fifties. Cans of Dapper Dan and combs soaking in blue-green Barbasol tonics. The next storefront was dark except for the diamond-shaped window in the top half of the door, the Ace-High Tavern. A dive bar for a quick beer after work, but the bar wasn't full and he was headed elsewhere. He could hear the jukebox playing *I Don't Know a Thing About Love.* He walked past, the country music fading out as he turned the corner and saw his car. He brushed his thick hair back as he settled into the low-slung bucket seats of his 1979 Monte Carlo. A classic. Just the sight of those smooth, slightly curved lines and the shine of the chrome in the warmth of the sun filled him with pride. The undulating shoulders and hips of the bodywork transitioned perfectly to the powerfully square headlights and hulking grill. Chrome and speed. Alluring and powerful. He cranked it up and continued humming along to the Ronnie Milsap song.

***

Jack Elmore casually waited in line at the bank with his salesman-of-the-month bonus check. He was a closer like no other. He had a confidence that people admired. The lunchtime tellers seemed to dally with their customers so they could avoid the older lady with her change purse and help Jack with whatever he needed that day. The line stalled. Jack made the deposit, smiled politely at the slower but more motivated teller, and arrived home to find Tom waiting in the driveway.

"Come on in," said Jack, in an unwinding and relaxed tone of voice, as he opened the overhead garage door. People just couldn't help being drawn into his bravado, even as they signed the seven-year contract for printer supplies.

"Thanks," Tom said as he opened a worn and creased magazine. *Field & Stream.* Tom Sullivan was a mustachioed and handsome man. He was never one to argue or disagree. Sometimes quiet, he was the most affable guy in a crowd. He never swore, and the ladies seemed to pick up on his quiet charm. He had an easy-going personality that fit with his dedicated work ethic.

Jack motioned with his hand for his regular afternoon guest to sit. He had a calm yet commanding voice, seemingly controlling the room with conversation. Today, all that was needed was a hand gesture. Tom sat in the lawn chair nearest the garage door.

"What've you got for me today?" asked Jack.

Tom turned a few pages to show Jack a single page article about trout lures. In all, only six pages were dedicated to fishing, the rest to hunting, the requisite ads, a handful of cartoons and the standard politics article. Tom never read the political stuff, preferring to daydream about the fishing possibilities, and the fantasy safaris to faraway places. Jack let Tom talk, rare as it was for Tom to say more than a few words. They'd been friends for a few years now, having met at the barbershop, of all places. Jack took the opportunity to light a cigar, something his wife disapproved of, but which he ignored. Tom didn't necessarily care for the smoke but he felt comfortable and welcomed in the man's garage.

Jack had more than a few years on Tom, but it didn't seem to matter to either of them. It gave Jack a reason to stay in the garage and it gave Tom an outlet from the work-a-day life he seemed destined for. They spent the rest of the afternoon talking about fishing and hunting and sipping a few beers. Before dusk, Tom folded the magazine in half and tucked it in his back pocket. He flipped the lawn chair up and headed for the door.

"See you tomorrow, then," said Tom. It had become a habit of sorts for the two men, spending an hour together on Tom's way home from work. He drove home, a short ten-minute drive.

It was an ordinary interaction between two seemingly ordinary men. But they both got something out of it. After finishing school, it had been hard for Tom to make friends. And the same could be said of Jack after leaving the military. The time they spent together solidified their friendship. After this much time together, they'd moved beyond mere acquaintances. They were friends.

***

On Sunday, Jack got up early and did some minor rearranging in the garage. Some people say that men cleaning up a garage is just an outlet for not being in control of other aspects of their life. But Jack was always in control. It just needed a sprucing up after a snowy spring and a busy summer. Jack lumbered about, puttering here and there until 2:45 when Tom came walking up the driveway.

"Whatcha workin' on?" Tom was in his typically positive, friendly mood.

"Just tinkerin'," said Jack. "Thanks for stopping by, now I can quit. Want a cigar?"

"You know I don't smoke," said Tom as agreeably as he could.

"My wife don't like me smokin', but some habits die hard. I try to be a good husband by not lighting it up, but I end up carryin' it around in the corner of my mouth all day. Know what I mean?"

"And you know I'm not married," replied Tom.

"Yeah, well, don't rush into it, if you know what I mean. I love my wife and I wouldn't trade her for anything, but I can't always do the things I really want to do."

"Maybe she's good for you then," said Tom.

"Very true, my handsome friend. Very true." Jack sat back in the lawn chair and struck a kitchen match, cupped his hands to let the flame travel, then breathed in and pulled on the little cigarillo. An orange glow grew and a sweet-smelling aroma wafted over his hands and into the air.

"I suppose that's one of the things that makes a good husband, or even a good man, right? Some people might call it self-discipline, but like I said, I love my wife, and I wouldn't trade her for anything. But respecting her wishes, even when they contradict my own, sometimes that's hard, you know."

"Yeah," said Tom, wiping at his mustache and trying to avoid the growing smoke cloud.

"Just remember that if you ever get married. And I'm sure it's in your future, you handsome devil," remarked Jack, a little awkwardly. "Want some whiskey? I've been sipping on this little mug for an hour."

Tom joined Jack in the awkward phase of getting drunk on a Sunday afternoon. Jack and Tom spent the afternoon talking, swapping stories.

"...and he just left me there alone to finish the guy's shift and close up for the night. I couldn't believe it," continued Tom. He talked about how much he enjoyed working in general and how much he'd learned from working in particular at the sporting goods store.

"You're gonna look back on this time in twenty years and realize how great you had it back then. You know?"

"Maybe."

"That's a fact. I don't know anybody that looks back ten or twenty years without a feeling of nostalgia. Even if it was hard. Or even if it was difficult. Or even if it was Vietnam. I know the Vietnam War wasn't popular, and it isn't what we talk about at cocktail parties, but the time that's passed has healed some of those wounds. And when you get a couple of vets together, whether they served together or not, it's that common experience that bonds them. The common experience of getting drafted, getting their heads shaved, that kind of thing. That mutual experience turns into a mutual respect. That's what lasting friendships are based on."

"You're right."

"That's what we're doing now, creating a common bond that we can look back on. A mutual respect experience that will connect us long after the moment is over."

Tom smiled cautiously at Jack, twelve years his senior. The two men continued talking, Jack puffing on the cigarillo and Tom thinking about his place in the world.

Tom returned home and felt better for having spent an hour with Jack.

***

Susan: Fredericksburg, VA, August 1982

Andrew sat in silence with Susan for forty-five minutes until the sign for *Terminal B–Eastern Airlines* appeared in yellow, blocked letters.

"Where are you headed, anyway?" asked Andrew as politely as he could stand.

"Cincinnati."

"For work?" he asked.

"Yes."

"I haven't sold the truck, but I'll have time this weekend to get the ad going." Andrew fidgeted in his seat and leaned forward to see other passengers waiting in line to check luggage curbside.

"Alright."

"What's in Cincinnati?"

"Like you care," said Susan.

"C'mon babe, 'gimme a break." He could sense the end of their time together. Their divorce had started him on a downward spiral he couldn't seem to escape. A black mark on his career. Nearly every member of the task force was married with kids. After the rumors and complications with J. Edgar Hoover, straight, married men were the unspoken rule, even late into the 80s, ten years after Hoover's death. A divorced man meant trouble at home. Someone who couldn't necessarily be trusted. Marriage provided cover for personality faults.

"A small museum uncovered some letters from the 1870s. Supposedly mentions a wagon train on the Old Spanish Trail. I'm going there to verify the provenance and start the cataloging process."

"They want to keep 'em? Or trade 'em for something?"

"So far, they just want to donate them, assuming they're authentic, but I'm not holding my breath. The curator's kind of old-fashioned."

"I'm sure you can handle him just fine."

Susan took a deep breath and sighed. She hoped the frustration wasn't coming through. "I mean it about the fifteen hundred and the new apartment."

"I know."

It sounded like a canned response to Susan. She took a deep breath and repeated what she'd said dozens if not hundreds of times. "Let's get this finished already. We've been divorced for three years."

"It's been thirty-two months," said Andrew.

"Right," she said. It's like the words just bounced off him. She rummaged through her purse for her boarding pass. "And thank you."

"Yeah, whatever."

"I meant '*thank you*' for the ride." She was past the frustration. Now he was just getting in the way. She didn't need his help, she just wanted what he'd promised months ago. Susan touched the corner of her eye with the back of her hand. A bit of moisture, but nothing the hot wind outside wouldn't dry. She doubled the straps of her purse over her arm and stepped outside into the pulsing crowd and honking taxis of Terminal B, still within the confines of the concrete jungle of Washington Dulles Airport.

***

The air in Cincinnati was hot and humid. Susan stepped off the rolling stair truck of the taxiway and walked into the wind towards the baggage claim and inside the 1970s-style consortium of air-travel-themed buildings, a maze of hallways, expansive terminals, and rental car counters. Her one-and-a-half-inch heels click-clacked on the polished terrazzo tile. She took a bus to Columbus, then hailed a taxi for the forty-five-minute ride into Cambridge and the small county museum. She walked inside and found the curator's office door open to the hallway.

"Hello? Mr. Steggeman?"

"Call me Alfred."

"Is there someplace we can review the rest of the documents, Mr. Steggeman? The first three letters you sent are of some interest." Susan was all business today. The flight was bumpy, and she was already tired but she was on a schedule. And she was not about to be hassled with pleasantries or any misunderstandings.

"Let's go in my office." Mr. Steggeman was in his mid-fifties and wore the same suit every Monday. Dark maroon slacks with a brown jacket. His second wife had picked out the paisley tie. He tied a Windsor knot in 1979 and then put it on over his head every Monday since.

Susan had formulated a plan to deal with the Mr. Steggemans of the world. "My time is very limited. Shall we begin?" she began.

"I wasn't..."

"The Smithsonian certainly appreciates your partnership in this matter. Do you have the letters, please?"

"I thought I could give you a tour." He stood, adjusted the paisley tie, and continued.

"Mr. Steggeman? No."

He wilted back into his chair and slid open the top left-hand drawer of his desk. He handed Susan a manila envelope. She retrieved her specimen gloves and placed the envelope aside, and poured the contents onto the desk.

"Mr. Steggeman, these are photocopies. You have the originals?"

"I'm sorry, but Mrs. Kowalski wanted to send the originals to her great-nephew, Tom Sullivan, in Denver."

"The copies are of no importance. I need the originals."

"I just thought..." Mr. Steggeman turned white and sat forward in his chair. "Mrs. Kowalski said she dropped them off at FedEx yesterday. Perhaps we could call her and..."

"I don't think so, Mr. Steggeman. Historical artifacts can be lost forever with these kinds of misunderstandings. Perhaps next time, you should consider asking for direction or researching the correct protocol. I don't have to tell you the repercussions. Thank you for your time." Susan rose to leave. She could see the fear and astonished look on his face. She confidently walked toward the exit and heard, "Ms. Kingsley." She continued walking at a measured pace, waiting patiently for the second "Ms. Kingsley" before pausing. She turned and smiled and said, "Time, Mr. Steggeman. Time and tide wait for no man. Did Mrs. Kowalski provide her great nephew's address?"

Mr. Steggeman stopped and adjusted his paisley tie. His embarrassment was palpable. "Yes, yes, let me find it."

Susan was used to being underestimated. She steeled her gaze, fought the urge to argue, and calmly accepted his retreat.

"Thank you. Do you have a private office where I can make some notes? The provenance of these historical documents needs to be established. The care and dedication of our respective disciplines are of utmost importance, wouldn't you agree?"

Mr. Steggeman only nodded.

"Of course, we'll need the envelopes, if they're available, for authentication and provenance."

"Of course, I'll explain to Mrs. Kowalski that..."

"When you have confirmation that they've arrived, I would like the nephew's contact information."

Mr. Steggeman gave her the address and invited Susan to the

Apple Cider Festival again. He bumbled over an apology for the misunderstanding and continued calling her Ms. Kingsley.

She hated being called *Ms.* She turned and made sure Mr. Steggeman could hear her heels click-clacking away. She remembered a phrase she'd always wanted to use when someone was wasting her time. *Time and tide wait for no man.* She always kept that boldness bottled up. *Time and tide wait for no woman.* She just didn't have the courage. Yet.

Chapter 7

Susan: Smithsonian, July 1982

At her desk on Monday morning, Susan had to remind herself that Ohio was in the same time zone as Washington. The trip to Cambridge had been very promising at first but then turned into a slightly wasted trip. Mrs. Kowalski was a dead-end, so she was forced to deal with Mr. Steggeman directly. *This chasing history is exhausting.* And her friends always seemed so disinterested.

Susan skimmed the photocopied letters at her desk. *Was I too hard on Mr. Steggeman?* She might have to return and might need further cooperation. The long-hand cursive letters were impressive on the surface. *Dearest Sarah Ann.* Each letter was written to an as-of-yet, mostly anonymous addressee. Susan could only assume it was Mrs. Kowalski's cousin's great-grandmother. The family tree was complicated but provided a direct link to the great-nephew in Denver.

Each of the twenty-four letters was written in the same script, dated at the top 1869 or 1870, and signed at the bottom with a clear, concise signature of the author, William Mitchell, the same as the first three she'd already read. It brought back memories of her own courtship and marriage. Memories she'd rather forget. Emotions welling up inside, she set the letters aside and busied herself with other projects the rest of the day.

Susan had to prepare herself again to call Mr. Steggeman the following day. But this time, she had to be more polite and slightly apologetic. After reading a few of the letters, she realized they held some genuine appeal as a set. The letters mentioned real places by name, with specific events, as well as a possible tie to Native American cultures. They were not historically significant enough to be purchased by the Smithsonian, but she knew they could be curated elsewhere in an affiliate museum. If they could be tied to a famous historical figure, or a geographic place on the stage of history, that might be different. You just couldn't tell about these sorts of artifacts, whether they held any significance other than their age. For Susan, it was the language, the journey, the fluidity, and the unadulterated emotion they showed. For her, this was their appeal. She wanted them. She wanted them all. And there might be more to the history, what she yearned for.

Ambition was something she grew into after a college professor commended her on her research and encouraged her to demand respect from herself. She checked her schedule and made some notes: *Mondays, maroon slacks, and a dark brown jacket.* Cambridge, Ohio, and Mr. Steggeman were already overmatched.

The first few minutes of the conversation with Mr. Steggeman were predictable. Susan was kind but she had responsibilities to the museum and expectations from her supervisor. In a subtle tone, she responded politely. If she wanted the promotion, she'd have to swallow her pride. Short-term travails in exchange for a larger reward in the long term were the requirement.

Mr. Steggeman allowed Susan some give and take and alerted her to Mrs. Kowaski's dialysis treatments three times a week.

In the end, Susan agreed to write Mrs. Kowalski a thank-you note, inviting her to visit the Smithsonian at her convenience. She had obtained the great-nephew's address and his mother's phone number in Denver, along with an abbreviated family tree and a copy of the cousin's last will and testament. Tom, the great-nephew, should have received the originals by now, along with the envelopes. At the end of the conversation, Susan asked about the cider festival in Cambridge–where it could be found bottled, and if any other historic sites might be interested in contributing to Mrs. Kowalski's cousin's story. Ambition disguised as kindness.

In return, Mr. Steggeman apologized for bending her ear back and made a point of recognizing his mistake in assuming her boss, a man, was in charge when in fact, she was the final word on these matters. He stumbled over the delicate parts, but Susan was satisfied with her victory. Mr. Steggeman agreed to contact Mrs. Kowalski and reminded Susan that on Thursdays, he wore his newest suit, a smart navy blue ensemble, just like the boys at IBM wore. Susan resisted the urge to roll her eyes and instead steeled her nerves and sharpened her focus on the task at hand. She made another notation. *Thursdays. Navy blue suit, IBM.*

Chapter 8

Andrew: Fredericksburg, VA, August 1982

Andrew merged onto the interstate in a Potomac fog. The vinyl seats of his Chrysler were cold and hard, but his ambitions burned. After a few hours of driving, he stopped to gas up. He needed another coffee. He winked at the cashier and slowly stroked the outside of his thermos up and down. She replied by showing her teeth, stained with coffee and cigarettes. Andrew contemplated the temptation, then thought better of it.

His ultimate destination was Washington Park, a suburb of St. Louis, on the Illinois side of the river. It was a diverse but working-class town of fifty thousand residents and was the closest town to the big enamel factories and paint manufacturing centers of Granite City. In 1981, the first enamelware processing facility in Granite City closed and moved operations overseas. After that, it was a bloodbath. Jobs lost, homes foreclosed, businesses bankrupt. The so-called American dream became a nightmare. Drugs were cheap and plentiful.

Andrew checked in with the city police department to get acquainted. And within moments of arriving at the third largest municipal building in Wash-park, he could sense which way the cultural and political winds were blowing. A wave of excitement hung in the air at having a federal agent in the building.

"Welcome to Wash-Park." Wash-Park had just one Black officer within a force of fifteen. "I'm Officer Davis."

During a routine traffic stop, he'd arrested a cocaine runner from

Dallas. Facing fifteen years, the cocaine runner was willing to wear a wire in a sting operation to avoid prison. The local police department needed a SWAT presence and assistance from the feds to coordinate with adjacent jurisdictions. Federal busts meant a big-time budget. This was the idea behind Andrew's experimental assignment–to lend a hand to small police agencies to combat the drug trade. It was a solo job, one that Andrew hoped would lead to a promotion to the Task Force Commander's desk.

The bust was set for any Wednesday when the biggest cocaine shipment would be present. Darkness would provide cover to the SWAT team. By the following Wednesday, Andrew had already spoken with a few of the local police who had aspirations of federal work, and he made sure to play the part. He even spent a few minutes with the snitch coke runner to ascertain the names of the target subjects and the location and layout of the scene.

The local police looked on, making mental notes of his suit, his posture, the brand of his coffee, and the size of his balls. Special Agent Andrew Harrison continued to play the part. Returning to his desk, he snubbed them all by leaving for lunch early and alone to the Pelican Hotel a few miles away.

"We've got the bust all set for this evening, sir. Should net two kilos at least, probably some cash and at least five arrests, sir," said Andrew into the telephone in his hotel room.

"Just make sure you get it right, numb-nuts," came the reply from Lieutenant James Gilroy.

"I'll make it stick this time, sir, you can count on..."

"Make sure you dot the i's on this one, Harrison." Lieutenant Gilroy was angry on the phone. He barely even held the receiver to his ear, mostly shouting into the mouthpiece. He continued the tirade and ended the phone call with this: "Finish that arrest and seizure and get wrapped up before the weekend. I've got another call for assistance in Chicago that might be a good fit for you, Harrison. It's an underground fag-bar that's dealing dime-bags for dick-licks. Be there on Monday. Sergeant Paxton in the ninth downtown district will fill you in on the details. Don't screw this up." Bang-ring! The phone slam was half the effect of Lieutenant Gilroy's pep talk.

Andrew couldn't wait until his old-school, backwoods bigot lieutenant retired. He fumed quietly at his boss, hung up the phone, and collected his thoughts. *Bust tonight. Up until at least midnight. Adrenaline'll keep me up later, so I'll need a bit of a release.*

Andrew returned to police headquarters at 5:15 and watched the administrative secretaries and meter maids leave without much interest in his direction. Then he saw a shapely woman. A new auburn-haired duty log officer was starting her shift. Only a skeleton crew of law enforcement remained. Quietly, he turned his attention to Davis and asked about local bars that single women liked.

"There's the Sidewinder over in Collinsville. It's a regular crowd with country line-dancing." Davis was being cautious.

"What else you got?" Andrew said coolly.

"The Ten-Pin, at the bowling alley, is where most of the cops...."

"I don't think so, Davis."

"Well, there's a jazz club down south-a-ways, that I go to on Saturdays when I'm not working. Not sure if that's your thing, though." Davis was on duty until seven and not part of the bust team.

*****

An uncomfortable suspicion came over Davis. He could feel the sweat in his armpits build and roll down his torso. Fear and suspicion seemed like a natural response from the G-man in a black suit. Davis could smell the history of beatdowns emanating from this white cop.

***

"White women go there?" Andrew split his attention between the auburn-haired woman across the room and Davis at his side.

"Oh, yes-sir, seems the place is full most Saturdays but not quite so busy during the week," said Davis, in a quieter voice, out of earshot of his coworkers.

"Meet me at the Pelican Inn on Highway eighty-four, Davis. Ten-thirty. If I'm not there, just wait around a few minutes, not sure how long the bust cleanup will take tonight."

"Uh, ok."

"Don't worry, Davis, it's not a date, and I'm not going to try to fondle your piece. Just need a little backup, know what I mean?" Andrew sat back in his chair and wadded up a piece of paper from the edge of his desk.

"That's a chain of custody form, sir," remarked Davis.

"So," said Andrew, sitting up. He reached back and threw the paper wad towards the auburn-haired woman on duty log assignment.

Gaining her attention, Andrew stood and said, "Hey, punch me and Davis in til 2 am tonight, but fill the duty log in with inventory management."

"That's not a dedicated duty response log, sir," said Auburn-hair.

"Make it vehicle maintenance, then, cutie."

"Patrol officers aren't authorized..."

"Authorized, my ass," was the reply from the black-suit.

"...for overtime, sir, oh, uh...." Auburn-hair flushed and turned her full attention to Andrew.

"I'm authorized, sweetie, know what I mean," Andrew said, grabbing his crotch. "Just put us down for administrative duties or whatever. On the clock, but not active radio response. I don't have time for this small-town song and dance." Andrew turned back to Davis, hitched his belt, adjusted his black tie, and whispered, "Davis, ten-thirty, got it?"

Davis nodded and left. As he did, Andrew just caught a glimpse of the attractive woman eyeing his muscular build. He walked up close and spoke into her ear. "This is a federally-assisted liaison bust tonight, got it? Lots of overtime to go around. You like a little dirty overtime, don't you?" Andrew felt the urge in his crotch swell. But his advances were ignored. With that, Andrew began focusing on the bust at hand. *Somebody's gonna get a beating tonight.*

***

Ford: Wyoming Territory, October, 1869

The year before being hired as William's guide, Benjamin Ford, aged sixty-seven or so, he couldn't remember exactly, had killed three bears. The last was a grizzly, north of the Colorado Territory. It was a cold, yet clear October afternoon, and Ford had trailed the grizzly for nearly a week. Opportunities for killing a grizzly bear were rare. Most were killed when an elk hunter happened upon one. But Ford had been intentionally stalking this bear for a week.

The beginnings of a snowstorm brought a westerly wind. Ford found himself above a streambed, concealed by the cliff face and within shot of the bear, cruising the water's edge. The bruin was grazing on moss and grubs–feeding on frogs and sedge grass, and anything else uncovered. The bear was methodically turning over rocks, tumbling logs, and filling his belly for the fast-approaching winter. Each step brought a mouthful of sustenance. Life thrived along the muddy stream and each step brought him closer to his winter sleep. Ford carefully took aim, resting his elbow in the crook of a splintered granite boulder. It had been split by an ice dam, nature's chisel and hammer. The stone was otherwise unbroken. Ford's face was grizzled and worn. Wrinkles around his eyes traced the seasons, the years, and the miles. A scar above his eyebrow recorded the struggle between an ax and a particularly stubborn hickory stump.

Ford watched the bear for five minutes or more, gathering his focus, then put a bullet through the massive animal. The bear didn't even flinch. It took two more steps, sniffing and scouring the ground, then raised its head. Ford waited. The bullet had struck the bear, a double lung shot. The bear remained, then with eyes squinting behind his spectacles, Ford saw a stream of blood drip from the bear's nose. The bear looked down at the blood, then looked away, never acknowledging its fate, then fell onto its side, dead.

***

William: Santa Fe, NM, September 1870

"Hey, there, mister, I've got the four dollars we talked about." The young man stood in the doorway of the warehouse.

"Who's that sneakin' around?" William said, startled.

"Boy?" said Ford, unaccustomed to being surprised. "Get yer-self shot, that way…"

"It's me, Clarence Henderson. We spoke yesterday, 'member?"

"Yes, I remember. The trip is six dollars," said William. He'd had plenty of people try to haggle him down on the price. While the journey was to begin soon, he didn't want to risk it with passengers with little to lose.

"Take this here four dollars and I'll git you the other two in the mornin'."

William glanced at Ford and said, "Yeah. You got a mount, Mr. Henderson?"

"I got an old mule, and a used saddle at my camp."

"This'll do for now, but I'm trustin' you to have the other two dollars by trip's end," said William. He preferred the full amount, but compromises could be made for a young man.

"If you make it that far," murmured Ford. It was evident to all he was trying to size up the kid.

Chapter 9

Andrew: St Louis, MO, August 1982

The borrowed SWAT team was a model of efficiency. Flash-bangs were tossed in three windows. The blast was immediate. It was the official "GO" signal. An officer in black fatigues and a bulletproof vest hoisted the battering ram, then *BAM*, the door swung open. A troop of six officers from neighboring St. Louis stormed in.

"Police! Don't move!" The abandoned enamel processing facility was filled with smoke and confused suspects. "Police!" Then, in less than one minute. "All clear, all clear!"

As part of the secondary search team, Andrew entered through the side door with a Kevlar vest, gun holstered, and hair slicked back. This was his twenty-fourth knockdown drug bust in twenty-one weeks. And by now, he was a pro. He quickly surveyed the situation. His heart rate was steady. *What's in that sofa cushion? How many kilos could someone fit in that backpack? Did anyone check the freezer for cash? How many cops were watching now?*

After the primary SWAT team was done, they regrouped back on the street and let the secondary team clean up the mess. The secondary team of local police, inexperienced with the process, began the inventory. The suspects were cuffed and photographed. As each was led outside, their pockets were checked and inventoried, a tedious process. Andrew silently kept himself apprised of the situation. The baggies of cut and counted crack, but also the unsearched locations and the tiny mountains of white powder in the back room.

Andrew had experience. "You, punk, with the stupid look on your face, where's the dope? Don't make me ask twice." Andrew pulled the punk up onto his feet.

"I don't know, man. I just got here, man." He marched him around the warehouse, through the kiln rooms, and past the conveyor lines frozen in time. Andrew continued scanning the rooms, searching for the big cache. He watched the rest of the suspects for eye movement. *Did you just glance up at that freezer? Why are you staring at the filing cabinet? Why was no one else in the back room except the one guy in the green shirt? Why is he not complaining about being arrested? Does he know more than...?* Andrew escorted the young punk towards the door and handed him over but remained inside.

Overall, the bust netted eight arrests. The real score was the pink Barbie suitcase under the desk in the back office. Police recovered five unopened kilos of cocaine, blue plastic wrapped tight. Each package was marked in black ink with various numbers and letters in crooked writing. He made a big show of cataloging the evidence. He ordered the prosecutor's representative in and out of rooms. He instructed how the evidence should be collected.

None of it was FBI protocol. But Andrew loved breaking the rules. He arranged dozens of plastic evidence boxes on the floor, then rearranged them based on priority. He opened five-gallon property bags and distributed them in alternating patterns. Confusion and crime-related evidence. The local police were stupefied. Officers started congratulating each other as soon as the dust settled and the perps were being loaded into the patty wagon. Andrew held his calm and refused to let the situation get out of control. Overtly, he shouted orders, and led officers around the facility, pointing out locations and dispersing evidence tags. Nothing was to be touched unless Andrew gave the ok.

The crime scene investigator was overwhelmed–it was such a huge place. It was the largest arrest operation in the department's history. For Andrew, it was a Wednesday. Everything was going according to plan.

He was a one-man show. *Calm. Bust won't take too long to clean up. No injuries and no shots fired. No paramedics. Same with the still-in-the-closet firemen. Always playin' with their helmets and hoses.*

Andrew continued barking orders, playing the part, and maintaining control of the room. The operation was complete. *Just enough time.*

At nine-fifteen, the sting operation liaison, rid of the Kevlar vest and back in black, terminated operations and sent everyone back to the station. At nine-twenty-five, Andrew drove around to the back of the post office, a secure location, and got busy with the real work. He pulled out two neatly packaged bricks of marijuana from a garbage bag in the backseat. Each was over a pound of weed, secured around a one-pound block of concrete. The blue plastic wrap was an exact match, and the weight was close enough, two-point-two pounds. One Kilogram. The marijuana was worth about twelve-hundred bucks, a small investment considering the return. Andrew pulled out two of the cocaine bricks. He placed the seized kilos of cocaine in his briefcase. He put the investment of blue plastic-wrapped marijuana back where the cocaine had been, replaced the zip-tie evidence tag, and drove back to the police station. As far as the local police were concerned, nothing would be amiss.

The station was alive with activity. A few extra sheriff's deputies were even called over to help with transport to the tri-county jail. And, of course, they took the opportunity to take a few photos and admire the haul. Once they were back at the station, Andrew was only too welcome to have all the police officers handle and photograph the drugs–never even a suggestion of any impropriety. Nearly every on-duty officer handled the drugs, admired the ease with which Andrew handled a kilo, and tried to make smart-sounding comments to the G-man. For most of the local officers, it was their first SWAT takedown.

Andrew finished up some paperwork, then promised to return

the next afternoon to meet the county prosecutor. *A real team effort.* Many of the local police officers felt like they'd just witnessed Al Capone unearth Jimmy Hoffa. It was just another day at the office for Andrew. One step closer to the promotion he really wanted. Plus, he scored a little coke right under their pig noses in their small-town pig uniforms.

Andrew retired to the locker room, washed and dried his pits, applied a heavy spray of deodorant, and retrieved a new gleaming white button-down shirt. He dressed, knocked a wrinkle out of his pants, wiped a spot of mud from his patent leather shoes, and adjusted his coat and tie. He pumped some hair gel into his hand, then brushed it into his hair, slicking down any unruly cowlicks. Andrew checked his teeth, washed his hands, and returned to the station conference room to claim his reward.

Andrew heard a smattering of claps upon his return, mostly for his clean looks and slick smile, he assumed. He casually picked up his keys and strode toward the door as blood started to flow into his member. Auburn hair was sitting up straight at the duty desk.

Andrew leaned in close and whispered. "Care to sample the evidence with me when you're done here? I promise to pull your hair while you're riding my cock."

Auburn's eyes widened, then slammed to the side. "As if," she said.

"Suit yourself, honey. On duty till two a.m., remember? Don't forget."

***

Andrew returned to the Pelican Inn, showered and shaved, and put on his khaki pants with what some would call a conservative Hawaiian shirt. It was blue and had a plaid sort of pattern with pale-yellow palm trees. He did a bump and checked his watch. Ten-thirty on the dot.

He could see Davis waiting in the parking lot. Andrew waved casually and nodded, and walked over to the trunk of the Chrysler. He opened the kilo and broke out a golf ball-sized chunk with his keys. He scooped it into a little baggie and stuck it in his front pants pocket. The trunk lid slammed shut just as Davis backed into the empty space next to the Chrysler.

"Ready?" asked Davis.

Chapter 10

Tom: Golden, CO, August 1982

Tom answered the phone from a deep sleep. He exchanged pleasantries with his great-aunt, Linda Kowalski. Despite her age and the regular dialysis treatments, she was lively and engaging on the phone.

"Such a shame about Margaret. We've been cleaning out your cousin's house, donating the clothes, and whatnot. She left the mobile home to your Great-Uncle, Jimmy, 'cause he's here in Cambridge. But she wanted everything else to go to the next male heir. That's you."

"Ok." Tom recalled a Christmas in Cincinnati from who knows how many years ago. He must have been fourteen or fifteen then.

"Well, I was going through some boxes of papers and found these letters she had."

"I don't know any Uncle Jimmy."

"He's in the nursing home here in Cambridge, and we're selling the mobile home. But these letters, see, are from the old west–a wagon train, and they mention all these places out west. Some near where you live, I think. And I thought *you* might like to have them."

"That's cool." Tom remembered the Waldorf salad she'd made. It was a strange conversation up to this point, much like the Waldorf.

"I've made copies, but the local museum didn't know what to do with them, so if you want, I can mail them to you."

"Yeah, that'd be great."

"They're part of your ancestry, and there's only me and Uncle Jimmy left here, and he can't see too good anyway. Can I mail them to you and trust you'll take care of them?"

"Sure I will. How can..."

"They're pretty old, like from 1869, some of them. And the paper is all yellowed, and the ink is faded, but you can read it real easy in good light. They talk about your great-great Granny, Sarah Ann."

"Oh, ok."

"I'll put some notes down about your mama's side of the family here in Ohio. A simple family tree. There's not too many grandkids. Just a couple of great-nephews and one great-niece down in Florida, but she's a looney, ya know."

"Yeah, I know."

"Anyway, take care of yourself and look for my package. I'll put it all in a padded envelope with '*Fragile/Do Not Bend*' stamped on it and tape it up real good."

"Ok."

Mrs. Kowalski exchanged addresses with Tom and invited him to stop by for Sunday dinner if he was ever in the Cambridge area. Tom was nodding and talking louder than usual into the phone to make sure she understood him but limited himself to answers in the affirmative.

"Alrighty then, love you bunches, bye-bye."

Tom was slightly surprised by "the love you bunches" from a woman he only vaguely remembered. Shyly, he replied, "Love you, too." and hung up the phone. He brushed his fingers over his mustache and settled back into the recliner. The midwestern attitude was easy to like, but it was sometimes just too much.

Chapter 11

Susan: Washington DC, August 1982

Susan trudged through the Thursday workday and poured over the acquisitions planned for the next month. But the weekend brought a welcome relief. The annual Museum Curator's Symposium would give her a chance to catch up with two girlfriends from college and a history professor they all loved to swoon over, even if he was approaching sixty. It was a chance for Susan to be herself, free from the drive that consumed her career during the commute and at the office. And it was satisfying knowing that the Smithsonian picked up the tab for a nicer than normal downtown hotel. Most years, after the day's events, she and her girlfriends would stay up late, drinking, laughing, and swapping tales with unabashed innuendo. The symposium wasn't just an excuse to get together, though. Susan wanted to hear new speakers, to learn new acquisition techniques, and take in the informational seminars and technological advances.

This year, the symposium was held at the Philadelphia Museum of Art. Despite all the men who dominated the conferences, lectures, and brief exhibits, a few top-notch women history collectors from renowned museums made their presence felt. She only had two nights booked at the

Four Seasons, but she still looked forward to the escape. Plus, the hotel would have a bar.

Susan returned to her upstairs apartment after picking up the dry-cleaning for the trip to Philadelphia. Andrew was away in St. Louis, a welcome respite. There was a flashing '2' on the answering machine. She changed into her comfiest pajamas, poured a glass of chardonnay, and pressed *play*.

"Hi, sweetie, it's your mom. Just wanted to let you know that your uncle Joe passed away last night. Remember, he's the one who drove that white Oldsmobile and parked in the handicapped space at church? Anyway, call me when you have a minute. I want to tell you about the funeral arrangements and what your cousin said about your father. Hope everything is good with you and Andrew... and at work too, sweetie. Call me."

Susan rolled her eyes, took a sip of wine, and hit the advance button on the answering machine.

"Suze, its Miriam. Sorry, it's so early there, you're probably at work by now though. Listen, I'm not gonna be able to make it this weekend. I'm so sorry, but ... uh ... Jane next door is having a baby, and they asked me to watch their four-year-old. I can't say no, and they just asked me this morning. We'll catch up soon. Call me."

Susan pressed the erase button and walked over to the sofa. She took another drink and set the glass on the end table, no coaster. *That means it'll be just me an' Liz this year. Wonder if she's got anything to discuss except* Dynasty? *That stupid show doesn't come on until ten. Why would I watch that anyway? I've got enough drama going on in my own life.* Susan got up off the sofa, annoyed at herself for caring, and returned to the kitchen. She downed the last gulp of wine and pulled the vodka bottle off the refrigerator.

An' I don't care how your darling Tiffany still drags her R's when she says 'Mommy, I want anothew storwy, pwease' at bedtime. Argghh, kids.

Susan picked up the cordless, tried to forget about little Tiffany, and threw herself into the corner cushion of the sofa.

"Hi, Mom, it's me," she said, trying to sound cheerful.

"Oh, hi, sweetie, how are things? Did you get that apartment?"

"Not yet, I've been busy at work. How's Dad?"

"That Andrew needs to help you with that, doesn't he? That Andrew was so sweet that time he helped me trim back the azalea bush. Have you asked him to help you?"

"No, Mom. How's Dad?" Susan worried that her mom could hear some slurred words.

"He's fine, sweetie. He was just asking if you remember going to the summer camp. He loves that picture of you on horseback, your little pigtails. *Honey, do you need help with that?*"

"Mom, talk to *me*, please."

She continued on, shouting into the background. *"... it's on the counter, by the sink. Don't make a mess....* Are you coming to your Uncle Joe's funeral? Remember, the Oldsmobile?"

"No Mom, I have the symposium in Philadelphia this weekend." The relaxed vibe of the alcohol was not as effective now. She wished she had more. Or had none.

"What should I say to your cousins? They're going to ask."

"That I'm at an important museum symposium, Mom." The frustration was rising again. When would her mother take her seriously? Susan grabbed a coffee cup bearing an Amish farmer carrying a maple syrup bucket she got in Vermont last year. She poured a healthy dose of vodka, then a splash more.

"Alright sweetie, I'll try and pass it off as important. I'll give them your condolences and say it was compulsory to your job."

"OK, Mom."

"Sweetie, are you coming home for Thanksgiving? Your father wants to go to the Volunteer's alumni rally in Knoxville on the Friday after. Will you be here then?"

"I don't think so, Mom. I've got work, and I went to Northwestern, remember?" Susan tried to sound positive. A longing came through in her voice. Somehow, her mother couldn't hear it.

"I know sweetie. Do they have football there?"

"Yes, Mom, they have frickin' football," said Susan, as the vodka started to remove the filter in her vocabulary.

"Oh, are they going to a bowl game this year? Your father thinks the Vols have a shot at the national championship."

"Tell Dad 'hugs', I've got to go, Mom."

"Oh, sweetie. Don't go, yet."

"I'll call next week, after the symposium."

"Don't you want to talk to your father?"

"Got to go, Mom, love you."

"Oh, sweetie, love...."

"Bye."

Susan hung up the phone just as a tear started to well up in the corner of her eye. She sniffed, wiped her eye behind her glasses, and swallowed hard. "Stupid fuckin' football." Although she said it aloud, no one heard. The sound of her own voice was enough to push the tears out.

She took another sip from her cup, wiped another tear, and pursed her lips. For a moment, she thought a cry was inevitable, but she forced it down, stood up, and returned to the refrigerator.

"Not tonight, mother. Not tonight. And not you either, Andrew," she said as she noticed a photo of Andrew. It was his FBI graduation day. She'd asked Andrew for a divorce the following day. It was a move up for him, but she couldn't tolerate the lies anymore. She replaced the vodka bottle atop the refrigerator and got ready for bed.

***

Susan was glad to leave the house Friday morning to concentrate on some reading during the commute. At work, she got a phone message from Mrs. Kowalski. She had sent the letters to Tom, talked to him on the phone only once, and didn't know where the letters were exactly. And it was clear she didn't understand the importance of the provenance. It was a hassle Susan would have to deal with later. Tracking down their origin and linking them to a specific person was paramount after finding the letters. Susan decided to review the letters again. She picked up a photocopy containing the shortest letter and read it again.

August 30, 1870

My Darling Sarah Ann,

The wagons are fully assembled and we are departing for Deseret tomorrow. Although there are only a few paying travelers, I'm confident we will arrive with a healthy bounty and stock. The thought of seeing you soon has increased my momentum. Love and ambition will carry us through. Audentes fortuna iuvat.

I pray your family is well.
I will write again.
Farewell, my wife, from your faithful spouse.
William Mitchell

Susan set down the page and looked away from her desk and into the parking lot. Families and couples stepped between the rows of cars and reunited at the curb near the entrance to the museum. Parting and reuniting. She thought of Andrew. She tried to imagine William. *Who was this man?* It was a remarkably short letter, yet such powerful language. *Fortune favors the bold.* These were words she'd never heard from Andrew. *Faithful?* Not anymore. Susan's hands trembled and her heart swelled in her chest.

Susan circled the phone number for Mrs. Kowalski again. She might need more help with the family tree. In her mind, linking these letters to a verifiable past brought the old language to life.

Susan left on time from the Smithsonian complex and walked to her usual train, and sat in her regular seat in the second car. She was able to continue reading without having to speak to anyone, a bonus. It was an academic paper from a research fellow in California about politics in the Deseret Territory prior to statehood. She blocked out the sounds from the train, blocked out the insurance salesman in the opposite seat blowing his nose, and blocked out the pain her mother ushered in last night. Blocking out Andrew wasn't necessary. She wanted so badly to move on. But the pain was still there.

Blocking in place, she turned her focus to the extra ninety minutes to read about the Deseret Territory. She gained some new background in the story.

The term Deseret was taken from the Book of Mormon, first published by Joseph Smith in 1830, and was said to be written by prophets of the Church of Latter Day Saints living on the American continent between 600 BC and 421 AD. Modern academics had dismissed the ancient prophet's writing as fictional, but Mormons adhered to Joseph Smith's original text with unquestioning steadfastness.

Susan dismissed it all but absorbed the knowledge. She kept reading. Some complex ideas can only be revealed in four hundred pages.

The Mormons were descendants who fled from the Tower of Babel and built barges that propelled them to North America. In 1849, Brigham Young organized his followers, inspired by the word Deseret, or honeybee, to resettle in the "promised land" on the shores of the Great Salt Lake and apply for territory status.

Susan adjusted the heavy book in her hands and turned the page, focusing on the words.

The proposed state would have extended from Western Colorado to South of present-day Phoenix, Westward to present-day Los Angeles, all of Nevada, and Northward to the Silvies River Valley in central Oregon and Fort Bridger in Wyoming. In all, it would have included parts of nine current US states.

Susan looked up when the insurance man blew his nose again but then continued reading.

Before statehood was considered, bands of Mormon militias had lived in a constant state of agitation, if not outright war, with the Utes and Shoshones, native peoples they called Lamanites. The Mormons treated them as a tool, as a means to an end, and regarded them as a lesser species.

Susan could feel the powerful forces shaping history in her hands. The letters were gaining momentum in her mind. She tried to relate the lessons to her own life. Events of the past failed to make a connection. She just wasn't there yet.

She checked her watch and thought about the history of her own life. What would be significant? It was after five, and the train station in Philadelphia would be busy with commuters. She put the thoughts away and got ready for the sweaty crowds and hurried commuters of another East Coast metropolis.

Susan didn't mind that Miriam couldn't make it to the Four Seasons or to the symposium. She was looking forward to some relaxation and wanted to leave her cares at the train station. Even if she had to listen to Liz talk about Tiffany's preschool and *Dynasty* all weekend. Maybe Liz would have something else to offer.

Chapter 12

Jack and Tom: Golden, CO August 1982

Tom sat on the back porch chair and cracked open a beer. The foam oozed and stuck on his mustache as he sucked in the cold snack. He licked his lips and looked up at a cloudless sky. Tom clicked on the stereo and belched as the first country song of the day warmed to his ears.

Conway Twitty started in: *So don't call him a Cowboy, Until you've seen him ride.*

Tom wiped his mustache and tapped along when he noticed Jack walking up the drive.

"Come on. Pull up a chair."

"I've been thinkin' about a fishin' trip," said Jack, unfolding a lawn chair.

"I might have a place in mind."

"Where's that?"

"Oh, this place my dad took me when I was young. Something I just read reminded me. Want a cold one?" Tom went back in the house and returned with a remnant of a ring of cans. Coors Light. The sun was high in the sky, but Tom was seated up close to the house on the south side, just out of the reach of the radiation. He put the beers away on ice.

"Where's this place you're thinkin' about?"

"Oh, it was way up past Dinosaur on the Green River. They was just puttin' the finishing touches on the campgrounds and the picnic tables back then. I don't remember too much about it other than that. I was probably eleven or twelve." Tom took another swig from his beer and leaned in closer to Jack.

"I been readin' about this place the last few years in *Field & Stream*. You know where I'm talkin' about?"

"Where's Dinosaur? Did you just make that up?" Jack pulled a cigar from a pouch and stuck it in his mouth, not lighting it.

"I've got time on my hands sometimes at the store. I've read every *Field & Stream* cover-to-cover for the past two years. It's way up the northwest part of the state, Dinosaur is anyway. This reservoir is across the border, though. It's mostly in Wyoming, but we didn't go that far."

"What's it called?" asked Jack.

"Granite Springs," said Tom. "There's supposed to be lake-trout and even some kokanee salmon in there. They were introduced twenty-plus years ago as a kind of experiment.

"What's a kokanee?"

"Well the Department of Wildlife stocked these salmon from the Pacific Northwest in there and they've started swimming upstream into the little creeks all around to spawn in the fall. Only trouble is, none of those creeks go anywhere. It's mostly desert canyon country out there, so after three or maybe four miles, they just peter out into a box canyon.

"Gotcha," replied Jack.

"But anyway, the kokanee love it. They've been reproducing like crazy and filling the reservoir with tons of little kokanee fry. Perfect meals for big lake-trout."

"Ok, so?"

"So that means there's tons of catchable kokanee and tons of growing lake-trout, just feasting on kokanee fry in September."

It was August, it was hot, and all was right with the world, from Tom's back porch. "Anyway, I've been wantin' to go back up there, retrace some of the times I had with my Dad. Maybe catch a kokanee and some lunker trout." Tom let it linger.

"Your Dad lived around here, right?" asked Jack.

"He lived in Stapleton, right by the airport. But he passed four years ago."

"Oh... uh..."

"I know. I think the same thing sometimes. Why didn't I suggest we go back, spend some time together before he got sick?" said Tom. "The longer he's been gone and the older I get, I realize we should have spent more time together as adults. It's hard though, you know?"

"Yeah, I hardly ever talk to my pops. Usually about the cattle business. He always thought I was wasting my time." Jack sat back in the lawn chair.

Tom took his time and responded in kind. "I didn't realize it when I was younger. We always spent the summers together, pallin' around, campin', fishin'. My mom would put me on the train from Baltimore the day after school let out to visit my Dad for the summer. I never knew what it took for him to earn all those vacation days just to spend them with his eleven-year-old son." Tom paused, took the last gulp of his beer, and looked directly into Jack's eyes. "You don't realize when you're a kid, how great it is to have a grown man on your side until he's gone." It was the most emotion Tom had ever shown to his friend. And possibly the most he'd ever said at one time.

Jack looked down and tried to see inside the aluminum can. "Yeah. My wife is always telling me to call my pops. But he's no conversationalist, you know. I'd rather just drive by and see if he's sittin' in the garage, waitin' for the mailman."

"Yeah, I get it," said Tom. He wanted to say more but didn't know where to start so he changed the subject. "Let's do that trip to Granite Springs at the end of August, it'll be a blast."

"Just gotta ask for the time off at work. Shouldn't be a big deal," said Jack.

"Don't worry, just a couple days over the long weekend for Labor Day," said Tom, relieved at the transition.

"Ya know, my buddy Frank will want to go too. He's cranky but loves the outdoors."

"No problem. All settled then. Labor Day weekend. Campin' and fishin' and no trouble," responded Tom with a jovial smile and a pat on the shoulder. Tom had an affable look on his face that just wouldn't go away. And he felt better by revealing some personal details to his friend.

***

William: Santa Fe, NM, August 1870

With Clarence Henderson added to the list of passengers on the wagon train, that brought the total number of travelers and customers to eight. It was short of the dozen William desired but it was a manageable number.

Just after noon, William drove the big wagon to the train station with Ford seated beside him. The train was on time and just arriving, steam rising from the boiler and coal smoke spewing into the New Mexico sky like a signal. Progress could be seen in the sky for ten miles in any direction, the smoke dissipating in the air high overhead. It was a signal to all. People and goods were on the move, like a prophet on wheels, baptizing the sinners, scouring the land, looking for converts.

William handed the reins to Ford and walked to the stationmaster's post. His shipment had arrived. He had a telegram waiting for him. He read it quickly, stuck it in his pocket, and signed for the cargo. At the adjacent warehouse, William spoke with one of the hired railroad hands and pointed at Ford.

Ford may have been a man of few words, but he wasted none. He was seasoned in the ways of trade on the frontier. He was Irish by birth, English by force, spoke Spanish of necessity, and knew enough Algonac and Arapahoe to differentiate himself from the other fur trappers. After a brief discussion and a check of the manifest, Ford nodded, released the hand brake, and drove the wagon to the loading platform. William eagerly walked along the tracks, showed the receipt to a railroad man, and followed Ford two more cars back.

After a hasty melee of shouted instructions over the noise of the scene, Ford and William loaded the freight into the belly of the wagon, obtained the stamp from the stationmaster, and drove back to the warehouse, arriving just after three in the afternoon. Inside the warehouse and away from the prying eyes of strangers, William inspected his freight. He couldn't wait to show Ford his prized articles.

William revealed five wooden crates, sealed on the ends with wax, surrounded by cardboard packing on the inside. Each crate was filled with young pine shavings, which had an intoxicating smell. Each crate contained a dozen Henry repeating rifles, forty-four caliber.

"These here are the finest rifles money can buy. Henry repeaters."

Each rifle was etched on the underside of the receiver, just ahead of the tumbler, with the year of their manufacture, 1869, along with a two-letter and four-digit serial number. The serial numbers were also stapled to the underside of the crate lids along with the address of the New Haven Repeating Arms manufacturing plant in New Haven, Connecticut. Each of the five crates was identical except for the serial numbers affixed to the underside of the lid. The crates were stenciled on the outside with "CERTIFIED PARCEL POST" in black block letters along with a smaller "Guaranteed by the Postmaster General, Washington, Federal District of Columbia."

Ford admired the long gun and took a rifle from William. "I've used my old Ferguson for going on twelve years now, Mr. Mitchell. Some of those Federal Cavalry boys used to carry Henrys like these, back when Texas was joining the States."

Among the other crates were boxes of ammunition, barrels of salt, sugar, a twenty-pound box of sixteen penny nails, a dozen brass hinges, and other sundries.

William and Ford spent the rest of the afternoon checking receipts, reviewing the list of travelers, and packing the wagons for the journey. Each item was carefully wrapped, labeled, and packed to endure the arduous journey ahead of them. At the end of the evening, William retired to the bunkhouse and took pen to paper in the amber glow of an oil lamp. His silhouette cast a hazy, inky apparition on the far wall.

***

Jack and Tom: *Golden, CO, August 1982*

Jack and Tom continued making plans for the camping trip when Tom announced, "By the way, let me show you one of these letters my great-aunt sent me." Tom retired into the darkened house and returned a moment later with a single folded letter, faded yellow and barely legible. In the sunlight at the edge of the patio, the words were revealed. Tom read aloud to Jack:

August 25, 1870

My darling Sarah Ann,

How anxious I am to complete the journey ahead of me and make arrangements to meet you and see your smiling countenance. Sadly, the journey north and west to the Uintah has been delayed again. The blacksmith and stable master in the town, Abeyta, who takes care of my horses, fell ill with a fever and died within a fortnight. His surviving two sons then argued with me about the bill which was already paid but which they insisted was not. They refused to allow me to take back possession of my two best mules and I have been forced to suffer an additional payment unfairly. In the time since, many fine trackers, guides, and Indian agents have already been employed for journeys westward. But I have since gained the employ of a man named Benjamin Ford, who can supply us with game and show us the way across the Cochetopa. He is a different sort of man, a mountain man, and difficult to know. And I have employed a fine horseman, Villanueva, to drive the second wagon and care for the horses. He appears more honest and forthright than the previous stable master. I pray this last delay shall be but a moment and arriving to the Uintah will not be much longer. Ready yourself for the train journey west in the next month. It is my sincerest wish that we see each other soon.

Warmest regards to you and your family. I hope to hear from you soon.

Yours,

William Mitchell

Tom looked up from the page as Jack puffed on the cigar. They looked at each other, then out at the mountains surrounding Golden.

"Wow," said Jack. That's really cool. That's written to your great-aunt?"

"It's to my great-aunt's cousin's great-grandmother. The family tree is complicated, but it's part of my family, alright. There's probably twenty more of these in a package from Ohio I got the other day. Some are hard to read."

"Those are to be cherished, my friend. Not many people get to see into the past like that. Real history there," replied Jack, waving a cloud of smoke away.

Chapter 13

William: Santa Fe, NM, August 1870

With the wagon train fully assembled, William gave the order to move out. He had sent Ford on ahead to scout the trail, return if he encountered any obstacles, bandits in waiting, or treacherous river crossings, and meet in four days at a camp north of Santa Fe where the Embudo River flows into the Rio Grande. The first wagon, driven by William, was pulled by a hitch of four horses. Nicholas Florette, Nickie to most, was employed to make camp, do the cooking, and serve as a backup to Ford.

Nickie was in the saloon when William gave his little sales pitch. He still carried a single-shot musket and sang songs in his native French. He had agreed to tend the fires and make biscuits each morning, accompanied by whatever Ford supplied.

Next in line was Villanueva. Born Francisco Robles de Saltillo Villanueva, he had decided to leave the employ of the blacksmith shop after his employer's death. Villanueva joined with brothers Eduardo and Jose Flores-Martinez, which made three Mexicans heading to California. Also among the paying customers was Dupree, a black man, heading north, and Clarence, the youngest, on the journey. Together, the eight men headed out northward, walking or riding, just after ten-thirty in the morning.

It had taken William more than two hours to rein in the horses and bring each out, in turn, to be harnessed and yoked to the wagon and secured to the rigging. The big wagon was heavy, and the cargo was at capacity, with only a narrow aisle where one could stand or rearrange the crates and bales. The big wagon, pulled by the four-team hitch, had a canvas tarp pulled taut on the sides. A long pair of ropes weaved between the buckles on the wagon and the stitch-reinforced grommets of the tarp. The mules followed behind, coupled with lead ropes.

"It's a beautiful day for a long walk, sir," Dupree declared, a big smile forming on his face.

"It is indeed," replied William, not taking his eyes off the road.

"I certainly appreciate the opportunity to join this here outfit, sir. I won't let you down, sir. I don't know horses and wagons too good, but I's a reliable deckhand and a fair right sail hauler, sir, a right good son of a gun," Dupree said. William kept his eyes forward and his pace even. He didn't want to be caught up with any distractions within sight of their origination. And certainly not from a black man.

"You're no son of a gun, Dupree, not if you stay in line, keep the pace, and not be the cause of any trouble," he said.

"I am so, a son of a gun, sir. I was born into this world under the gun carriage of the privateer Jean Lafitte aboard *The Pride*, sir. She had twenty-four twelve-inch cannons plus sixty more eight-pounders with grapeshot aboard."

William knew the conflict that men faced during the Civil War. He would just as soon forget the lot of it, but this man didn't seem to carry any scars from it. William resented the four years of his life it stole and the circumstances that meant being apart from his wife. He didn't care about the man, one way or the other.

"There was gunpowder on my first teet, sir. I've been sailin' a'most of ma life. But my bones is old, and I can't get no acres in Loosiaan. So I'm headed west."

"Then you're headed the right direction," William said, still eyeing the road ahead. Ultimately, William's wife would be at the other end of the same road.

"Yes, sir." Dupree was smiling and looking up the road.

A tandem team of two horses pulled the second wagon, rigged with most of the daily supplies, cooking implements, and water barrels. Nickie drove it with Villanueva seated beside him. The Flores-Martinez brothers walked with the leads of their mules behind. And last in line was Clarence with his mule. The group was more than eighty feet long. It took twenty seconds to complete an entire circuit of its length. On open ground, with a good trail and few constraints, the second wagon team could trot at a faster pace. But the big wagon with the four-horse hitch was not as maneuverable. It was difficult to control at an increased speed. So William kept everyone at a walking pace. It was four hundred fifty miles to Grand Junction. William kept every detail accounted for, knowing his dreams hung in the balance.

***

Susan: Philadelphia, PA, August 1982

Susan already had her entry badge to the symposium. The title under her name felt like a stepping stone. *Collections and Acquisitions Assistant, American History, Smithsonian.* She wore it with pride. Her latest research text was shrouded in her stylish portfolio. She carried a smart, over-the-shoulder Jackie-O purse and was sporting her favorite Ferragamos. She pulled a tidy overnight roller behind her. She had been to Philadelphia several times before, but she was unsure of the location of the Four Seasons. It was on the same street as the train station, JFK, Jr.

Boulevard, and across the Schuylkill River, but she didn't know if it was three blocks or thirteen. The evening sky turned orange, and traffic was heavy, but Susan felt good walking. She crossed at the crosswalk but spied the neon sign of a liquor store down the side street to her left. *Dynasty might be more interesting with something to drink.* She paused to avoid a small mud puddle outside a construction site, then ducked into a temporary plywood pedestrian tunnel shielding her from the future Chase Bank building. Her heels echoed on the plywood floor as she walked, reaching the other end a hundred feet from the liquor store.

As she exited the last step of the plywood, a man grabbed her. He grabbed her by the elbow and wrestled her roller suitcase away. She stumbled and hit the ground.

"Gimme the bag, lady," shouted a burly black man in a green T-shirt and jeans.

"What... oh... wait... no...."

"And gimme that watch too. Hurry up, lady."

She struggled on the ground, arms tangled in the straps of her purse and leather portfolio. The man pulled her up by one handle of the portfolio. He raised back, swung, and struck her face. She collapsed, face down, dazed from the blow. Stunned, she tried to steady herself on her palms. The man grabbed her wrist and pulled the watch free, then ripped the portfolio clear, tearing the nail from her pinky finger and bruising her hand.

"Don't... Wait... No...."

Words were useless as the man faded into the alley's dark recesses. The last image Susan saw was her burgundy roller being pulled by a bodiless pair of white Adidas, hopping up and down, fading into the abyss of the city. The three reflective stripes hustled into the shadows and disappeared. She wiped a finger to her temple, smearing mud into a tiny cut above her eyebrow. She attempted to stand but fell to a knee. The heel on her left Ferragamo was broken.

She stood, empty-handed, and returned the way she came. She avoided the pedestrian tunnel. Her feet made a sloppy, uneven sound in the gravelly puddles along the dirty street. Tears streamed down her face, but she wasn't crying. A fierce scowl appeared across her forehead, and the corners of her mouth twisted in a rage. Her eyes were bloodshot and teary, yet focused.

Chapter 14

Susan: Fredericksburg, VA, August 1982

Susan returned home from Philadelphia exhausted. But she was also more determined than ever. After the mugging, she hadn't slept well. The symposium was a blur. She wasn't having nightmares, but she always had the urge to check the door lock, double-check the bathroom window, then look behind the door and under the bed, a daily routine for most women living in a big city. Not that it made her feel any safer. Just enough paranoia to prevent a good night's sleep.

At the apartment, Andrew was gone, yet she wasn't exactly relieved. She locked the door behind her and poured herself a vodka. Her apartment was just as she had left it, the comforter had the same smell, and her bathroom countertop was littered with makeup disks, lipstick tubes, lotions, and perfumes. She had been looking forward to connecting with colleagues in Philadelphia. Looking forward to the archaeology seminars and the newest museum exhibit lectures. Spending time with friends. But now, a violent, vivid episode she'd just as soon forget stood in its place. She hadn't bothered contacting the police. She just wanted to get back into the routine of work. The commute, the research, and the work.

***

"Good morning," said Susan.

"Morning," said Andrew, his head still foggy from the night before. He had driven all night and got home from St. Louis just after four in the morning.

"I can make breakfast if you want," said Susan, feeling restless yet wanting a calm start to the day. A reassurance but distanced. An ex-husband, yet law enforcement. Alone yet roommates. She couldn't place her emotions. She brushed her hair gingerly, touched on some powder, and checked her eyebrow in the dresser mirror. A small cut was visible and a slight greenish bruise remained.

"Sure," came the reply. "I'm getting in the shower now."

Susan pushed past the bagels and cream cheese and came up with some white bread, three eggs, and a slice of Velveeta. She popped two slices of bread in the toaster, pushed the button, and grabbed the coffee pot in one motion. She poured two cups of coffee, and walked into the bathroom of Andrew's bedroom, where the shower was already running.

"I set your coffee on the sink. You working today?"

"Not until five, why?" said Andrew.

"I just hadn't seen you in anything except that uniform in months. Was thinking you might be going for a run. Anything besides that uniform on your way into the office."

"No, I'm going in late after I drop a card in the mail to Mom. You know her birthday is next Sunday," said Andrew.

Susan paused, tried not to rush, and said, "You're so intimidating in that uniform." It had the intended effect.

Andrew was taken aback, started to beam, hesitated then continued, "I know, it's just part of the culture at the FBI. If I want to make Task Force Commander, I have to look the part, you know."

"Ok, it's almost ready." Susan retreated to the kitchen, cracked the eggs into the non-stick, peeled the cheese wrapper, and put it on the toasted bread. She sipped her coffee and considered her approach. Susan shuffled some of her work papers on the kitchen table out of the way and flipped the eggs. The nail on her pinky would grow back eventually. As Andrew walked into the kitchen, he wore his usual black pants, but only an undershirt on top.

"That's better," she said. "Want mayonnaise on your egg sandwich?"

Andrew pushed some papers aside and asked, "What's this you're working on?" He could be charming when he wanted.

"Letters from the 1870s. Want more coffee?" asked Susan.

"Why are you being so nice? I swear you wanted to stab me in the neck last week. Should I be worried about eating this egg sandwich?"

"Don't be silly, just want us to be civil until we can, you know…" Susan attempted a smile and sat down next to Andrew. Ordinarily, she would have sat across from him, closer to the kitchen and closer to the telephone. From this slightly different position, her eyebrow was hidden. She could see some age on his face and a stress wrinkle on his forehead, the hairline ever receding, even for a young man like Andrew.

"They're letters from a wagon train that started in New Mexico. They traveled north along the Spanish Trail to someplace in present-day Utah." Susan paused to gauge Andrew's interest and was surprised to see him still perusing the photocopies. So she continued. "Each letter is addressed to a woman he was married to. It's not clear why they're apart. I've only read about half of the letters, so I'm curious to see how the story turns out."

"What's this part about U-in-tah, is that a spelling error?"

"Uintah is a Native American tribe. After they were expelled from the land, the colonizing white settlers continued calling the area Uintah. It's partly the base for the name of the State of Utah. Before that, it was the Deseret Territory."

"Where was?" asked Andrew, focusing on the quality of the penmanship and the uniformity of the letters.

"Deseret," repeated Susan. "Before Utah became a state, the Mormon Church ...that's the Church of Latter-day Saints you sometimes see commercials for on TV, tried to start their own country."

"That can't be true. I've never heard of this," Andrew said, looking up.

"Politics always took a backseat to religious zeal. The Mormons had been driven out of Illinois and then forced out of Missouri. It made them distrustful of outsiders." Susan displayed the knowledge she learned of the related history, part of her job description at the Smithsonian, and she just couldn't help talking about it.

"Their own country, huh? Must not've worked out," said Andrew. He was losing interest, but faking it for now. He took a big bite of the egg sandwich and picked up the sports section of *The Washington Post*.

Susan recognized the change in Andrew's attention but charged ahead with what she had read. Repeating it aloud, even to an ill-equipped listener, it helped her categorize her thoughts and commit it to memory.

"The Mormons had, what they called, an Indian problem. We say Native American now, by the way. They were occupying the Promised Land that Joseph Smith had prophesied. 'This is the place,' he said, or something like that. The Mormons were systematically exterminating the Utes, the Uintans, and the Shoshones, but they were also wary of the United States and wary of outsiders. There are stories, mostly unproven, that the Mormons, with the backing of the church, would disguise themselves as Native Americans, attack wagon trains of settlers on their way to California, and wait for the settlers to retaliate against whatever tribe was locally available. There's speculation based on third-hand accounts that the Mormons were arming the settlers to attack the Native Americans. And vice-versa too–arming the natives to attack the wagon trains emigrating through Deseret. The church has always denied it, but there's not much proof of such baiting."

"Huh?"

Susan eyed the coffee pot and glanced back at Andrew. He was still reading the sports page, a sure sign that Andrew cared not for Susan or her thorough research. She returned her thoughts to the letters. Although this was not a famous or historical figure, William's everyday life events made the letters genuine. *Devoted to Sarah Ann.* The letters transformed the words into something more personal to Susan.

"Want more coffee?" she said shyly. She made sure Andrew couldn't see that part of her face.

"Sure."

"The religious aspect of society is their identity. They're Mormons first, Utahns second, and Americans a very distant third. If the moral authenticity or religious zeal of any member is questioned, it's a problem. If any citizen was found to have any degree of variance with the church's stance on prayer, work ethic, clothing, lifestyle, anything really, they could be excommunicated. Banished, shamed, and forced to leave the Promised Land. Friends, family, land, and home, all gone. That sort of dogma dominated their culture at the time. It probably still does." Susan was beginning to sound like a supervisor already, the breadth of her knowledge showing.

"Uh-huh," said Andrew. He flipped the paper back and turned it to page five.

Susan returned the coffee pot, stood in the kitchen, and prepared to make her case again for her and Andrew to end their relationship permanently. They'd been divorced for so long, and it was exceedingly difficult to explain her situation to her family.

"Listen," she began.

"Don't even start. Breakfast was great. Thanks. But I'm sick of hearing about your work. Your commute. The lack of women in supervisory roles. I don't want to hear it anymore."

"What? I wasn't..."

"And I don't care about these letters or who they're from," barked Andrew.

"They're from a faithful husband and a good man, but you wouldn't know anything about that." Susan was right, but she regretted the remark.

"You're no doting and obedient wife, either, you know."

It was these kinds of remarks that cut the deepest. She loved Andrew once, but she could see the career trajectory he was on would lead to more nights away from home. And the temptations would only get worse. "Let's not get into it right now," Susan said, holding her gaze. She wasn't willing to waste any more time on someone she couldn't trust. She took a deep breath and tried again. "I'm taking that apartment three train stops closer, in Woodbridge, next month. I want what you promised the judge. Fifteen hundred dollars and this'll be done. No more delaying the inevitable." Susan felt her cheeks turning pink and had the urge to touch her eyebrow. She sat stoic. She hoped the common sense approach would appeal to him.

"You think you're gonna have success as a career woman? I don't think so. Half those broads are sleeping with their bosses just to keep a paycheck. I don't get it," snarked Andrew.

"That's not–"

Andrew interrupted her and continued his tirade. "I'm not giving you anything. I'm gonna get a bonus this year, and Lieutenant Gilroy says I'm gonna make GS-12 before the year is up. That's only one level from Task Force Commander. And if you think you're gonna get in my way, you're sadly mistaken." Andrew pushed the plate away, strode through the kitchen, and threw the remaining coffee in the sink, splashing most of it out on the counter.

"Damnit. Wait," Susan said, stepping back. "What's the matter with you? Don't you see we can't keep doing this? I'm taking that apartment and if I have to, I'll go…"

Andrew spun, and stomped to the bedroom, apparently to change into his uniform for work. He slammed the door just as she finished the sentence, "… back to the judge."

Andrew returned in his uniform, almost standing at attention, clip-on tie on the starched white shirt. He glared at Susan. Badge in place on the pocket of his jacket. The nine-millimeter Beretta was tucked tightly in the brown leather, three-quarter holster. Susan instantly felt the cycle repeating. It wasn't worth discussing anymore after he put on his uniform. He was intimidating, to be sure. But it was like he'd put a mask on too. There was no getting through to him now.

"I'm flying to Kansas City tomorrow for a week-long project but Gilroy already said I'll be gone three weeks. More and more of these small towns are warming up to the idea of cooperation with SWAT guys if it means a payday. And it's all overseen by a CRAWL liaison."

"So." Susan couldn't help being defensive, then combative. "I'm going to Denver next week."

"We'll be one state apart. Want to fight and make up, west of the Mississippi?" Andrew was smirking as he hitched up his pants and tightened his belt.

Susan stayed in the kitchen, wiping the counter, washing dishes. She averted her eyes to avoid the knife she used to butter the toast. ... *refuse to shed one more tear for that asshole*, she thought to herself.

***

The train commute felt like an old friend on Monday. She sat in her usual third row of the second car, with the morning sun at her back, so she could see well enough to read. Susan nodded to a steward she recognized as she quickly turned away to find her seat. She had a new volume from the library, *The White River Ute War Colorado, 1879: The Ute War: A History of the White River Massacre*, by Thomas F. Dawson, E.V. Sumner, and Thomas Sturgis. Susan was hopeful the textbook was more scholarly than the title was concise. Despite its lengthy title, the book was engrossing enough that Susan only glanced up from the text twice to check her surroundings. Once to check the halfway point with a backup Timex and a second to look for the school bus picking up kids at the stop before hers. It was a routine. It was comforting. And it was stupid. Sometimes the bus was early, and her train passed it on the highway. Sometimes the bus was late, kids tumbling on with coats, backpacks and bundles. But either way, the sight of it confirmed her East Coast routine, and Susan consumed the words on each page like it was her last meal.

By the time the train arrived at her stop, a little before nine, she had a firmer grasp on the history of northwestern Colorado and northeastern Utah. There had been volleys of attacks back and forth between white settlers and native tribes for decades. These areas of the American West still held considerable populations of Utes, Shoshones, Arapahoes, Paiutes and Crow.

White settlers, Mormons, and California-bound miners in the area perceived almost no difference among the tribes, assuming that one was just like another. Meanwhile, the Native Americans held the credence that all land was communal. And the cattle that lived on it were semi-communal. The theft of stock animals was considered a rite of passage, not a hanging offense. It certainly wasn't expected to be met with the kind of brutality that white ranchers doled out. Retaliations by the whites were often carried out against a completely different people, who were unaware of the transgression their counterparts were angry about. Those attacks were often one-sided, but just as often led to counterattacks on nearby settlers. It was a story Susan saw retold often in her research at Northwestern. And the victors always wrote the history.

***

Susan arrived at her desk armed with more knowledge than she started the day with. The White River Massacre. Brigham Young. She turned her attention to finding and contacting the nephew of Mrs. Kowalski. She called 411 and got a handful of phone numbers, addresses, and a contact at Metro State, a local college in Denver, where Tom was taking classes at night. She left a message for Tom at his mother's house. She got no answer at the phone number Mrs. Kowalski had given her for Tom's duplex in Golden. She then decided to call the college.

After being put on hold, transferred, put on hold again and then given a different number, she finally reached a graduate assistant in the arts and sciences building. Hearing the commonality of an aspiring academic, Susan explained how she wanted to contact Tom as soon as possible and wanted to meet with him in person. It was necessary to preserve the historical documents and arrange for their transfer back to the Smithsonian. Susan learned that the graduate assistant, Cindy, an anthropology major, was working on a thesis about the Sand Creek Massacre of 1864, near Lamar, a couple hundred miles from Denver. Arapaho women, children, and elders were gunned down in a dawn raid. More commonality and connectedness with the letters.

Susan began to put together some ideas and coolly offered a little more background on the letters she was trying to obtain. She shared how she didn't want Tom folding them or stuffing them into a box with tape on them, or using a highlighter on them. These were all things Susan had seen and wanted to avoid.

"I understand, Mrs. Kingsley. My graduate thesis defense was difficult. " Cindy was immediately more helpful. Then in a quieter voice, "You know, I've met Tom a couple times. He works at Woody's, and I don't think that's the right phone number."

Susan could sense that another field trip might be in her future. "Is he reliable?" asked Susan.

"I'm not sure."

Susan continued making some notes while wrapping up with the graduate assistant. Just out of her periphery, she noticed the light change in her office and on her paper. She looked up and was surprised to see her husband standing in the doorway. Her ex-husband.

Her nerves instantly put a scowl on her face. But she carefully glanced down at her notes, put a bookmark into Dawson-Sumner's *White River Ute War*, and closed the hardcover text. Underneath was a well-worn paperback, *Hearts Aflame* by Joanna Lindsey, complete with a shirtless and muscular Viking clutching at a voluptuous maiden in a revealing peasant-top dress.

"Hard at work, I see," said Andrew, still in his uniform and clip-on tie.

Susan began to formulate a tirade of insults based on Andrew's inadequacies. But Viking Lord Royce's devotion and robust passion was fresh in her mind. She waited, keeping that to herself. She decided to wait until the time was right.

When the graduate assistant returned Susan said, "Let me call you back later, please. Thank you, goodbye." Susan ended the call rather curtly but circled the anthropology graduate assistant's name and number and looked up.

"What do you need? I'm working."

"Just need a minute. Don't look so angry, it puts wrinkles around your eyes," said Andrew, cutting his eyes back to the notes on her desk.

"What do you want? I'm really busy."

"I just wanted to tell you that the Kansas City case got canceled. I got a new case in Fort Collins, Colorado, some college kids making bank dealing methamphetamine to the cowboys in Wyoming," said Andrew.

"Yeah, so?" Susan was so ready to be rid of this creep. And he was invading her career space, a space she considered off-limits.

"Well, this will be my forty-second request-response from the bureau, and the other CRAWL Liaison had forty-eight when he was named to the Task Force Command desk." Andrew was gloating.

"You get a set of steak knives with that?" Susan sat stoically behind her desk and continued putting older projects away and stacking them neatly, but still within reach, and out of Andrew's prying eyes. She could sense a change in Andrew. And she felt a bead of sweat forming on her forehead and now he made her nervous.

"Just thought you'd like to know I'm weeks away from getting the promotion, and then I won't need the apartment anymore. I've talked to a realtor about a townhouse in Georgetown. Earnest money is already in escrow," Andrew said confidently.

"Goody for you. Think that neighborhood will like having a grease-ball middle-management goon moving in?" Susan was ready to follow up with more vitriol but hoped Andrew would just turn and leave. Susan still had hole cards Andrew didn't know anything about, and she wasn't about to let him take the upper hand, despite his false bravado. She intended to safeguard her workspace.

"Don't expect any help from me when you're moving out either. You can go find your own place, maybe somewhere with that big-titted babe on the cover of that book you're always reading. Oh wait, she doesn't have any flat-chested friends." Andrew never missed an opportunity to twist the knife and continued scanning Susan's desk.

Susan sighed and sat back in her chair. "Is that what you came here to tell me? I really do need to get back to work." Susan refused to let the hurtful jabs show on her face or in her voice.

"Museum hostess emergency, huh?"

"I have important responsibilities you wouldn't know anything about. And I'm not a hostess," replied Susan, regaining her composure. "Do I need to call security?"

"I know it says assistant on your door, there. Isn't that just filing and answering the phone?"

"I'm in line for a supervisor job if you must know. But keep your voice down. There's still a lot of politics, and I'd rather not discuss it now," said Susan. She regretted letting that juicy tidbit slip out. She was working hard to land the promotion, and she didn't need Andrew's complications ruining her chances.

"What's in Golden? Woody's?" Andrew asked.

Susan stood to block Andrew's prying eyes from her desk and took a step to the side as he continued his verbal abuse. "Don't expect any help from me, like I said. The sooner we part ways, the sooner I can move out and crack the Task Force Commander's desk."

"Fine," replied Susan, looking past Andrew into the hallway, where a few bystanders were trying to hear the G-man in a black-on-black suit. She was ashamed of Andrew, but more, she was embarrassed. He no longer fit within the culture of the museum or the sophistication in which she tried to carry herself. She steadied herself, attempting to escort Andrew out.

"See you in Colorado, then, sweet-cheeks." Andrew attempted a grab at her backside but didn't give it much effort. Susan turned, rejecting his advances. Andrew took a last look at Susan's notes and the *Ute Wars* textbook, then turned and walked back through the door and down the hall. Fuming on the inside, she was pained by his embarrassing demeanor. But on the outside, she displayed a veneer as strong and defiant as any woman. Susan cut a hole in the back of his head with her eyes.

"Not so bad yourself," Andrew said as he walked past Karen, a museum educator in a long dress and sweater, eyeing her up, then down, and then back up again. The sight of him talking to her co-workers burned in Susan's stomach.

Andrew was clearly up to something, and Susan didn't want to be anywhere near him when it happened. His crisis had started as soon as she had asked for a divorce. And he'd never gotten over the shock of it. She got back to work by closing her office door, opening the textbook, and picking up the phone again. She left the romance novel on her desk for now. She would read a dozen pages at lunch, and besides, she had already read it five or six times.

"Focus on the task at hand," she said under her breath. "Don't get ahead of yourself."

Susan called the graduate assistant back, apologized for her curtness earlier, and tried to make small talk once she got the information she needed.

***

After lunch in the Smithsonian cafeteria, Susan had a meeting with some visiting affiliate museum representatives about an upcoming special display, then a federal appropriations committee report from the budget office that would take up most of the rest of the afternoon. The meetings continued until nearly five.

"Late train again," Susan said to herself as she returned to her office. She glanced at the clock, checked her notes, and decided to try Tom at his mother's house again.

"Hello?"

"Hi, Mrs. Sullivan. This is Susan from the Smithsonian Museum. I'm trying to get hold of Tom."

The conversation lasted more than fifteen minutes as Susan patiently listened to Tom's mother talk about his job at Woody's, his second job at Gart's, and the night classes he was taking. She revealed how his father had passed, how he had always thought golf was superior to every other sport, and a girlfriend Tom brought over last July 4th but never mentioned anymore. The conversation finally turned back toward his schedule.

"Is there a good time and place I might be able to meet him?" Susan asked. The conversation was friendly, and it reminded Susan she hadn't called her own mother this week.

"He's usually working or sleeping these days. He's got a roommate at his duplex, but I can't remember his name."

Susan ended the call, stuffed the romance novel into her purse, and headed downstairs. She took the late train home, quickly showered, and called a cab to take her to the airport.

Susan boarded the DC-9 bound for Denver with a new roller

suitcase. She was wearing chenille business pants with a micro-striped blouse. Her new Miranda leather pumps gave her a firmer attitude among strangers. While some preferred to travel in comfort, Susan felt more comfortable in work attire. She sat down in row 17, chose an aisle seat, smiled at the woman in a flower print dress by the window, and pulled out the thickest research paper in her new portfolio. The memory from Philadelphia was still fresh in her mind, but the bruise had faded. She never mentioned the attack to Andrew, partly ashamed, partly afraid of his reaction, and partly to avoid giving him any ammunition.

She arrived in Denver well after midnight and took the circuitous walk across the street to the stair-stepped Hilton. The cab rides and the stylish hotel were all expensable. The air was thin, and the mountains were looming.

Chapter 15

Andrew: Washington, DC, August 1982

Andrew left the way he had arrived, through the side entrance closest to the underground parking garage at the Smithsonian. He climbed back into his Chrysler, started it, and pulled a notebook and pen from his pocket.

Andrew reviewed the notes he'd made from Susan's office, as he started putting the pieces together. *If she thinks she's gonna one-up me in the career department... all I have to do is shake down the nephew into giving up the letters, and her whole trip will be wasted. I can still make the sting operation in Fort Collins by the end of the week.* Andrew tempered his rage. *I'll get my promotion, and she'll be stuck as a museum hostess forever. Maybe then she'll realize what she let get away.* Blindsided by Susan's demand for a divorce, he had never mentioned it at work. And after three years, he couldn't reveal the web of fiction he'd spun for himself.

He circled the name 'Tom Sullivan' in his notebook and underlined 'Woody's' the same way Susan had. He put the car in reverse and adjusted the rearview mirror to see if his white-toothed smile still matched his strong hairline. It did.

Smiling, and sure of his cause, he pumped the Chrysler back and spun into the lane, tires squealing, and crashed into a tan Chevrolet sedan parked in the row behind him.

Slightly irritated, he sprung out of the Chrysler and kicked the side door of the Chevy, leaving a footprint-sized dent. He reached up, then brought his elbow down, breaking the side mirror off. He returned to his own car, turned it off, and used the keys to open the trunk.

Among the tools of his trade was a small, but very effective door breach plus various handguns, a gas mask, a bean-bag shotgun, pry bar, spike strips, bolt cutters, and signal flares. And a kilo of cocaine in a backpack. Andrew brought the door breach up to shoulder height, then smashed the front window of the car. He continued around, breaking the headlights, the taillights, and the front grill. Then each of the passenger windows got the same treatment. Back on the driver's side, he smashed the window, repeating the motion until the glass was broken into fragmented shards. Andrew scraped the bottom side of the window smooth, flinging glass in and out of the opening. Placing the door breach on the roof, he calmly looked over the tan interior carpeting and Naugahyde, while he unzipped his pants.

With a casual glance down at his penis, he sprayed the inside with urine, shaking it off among the ragged, wretched shards of glass at his feet. He zipped up and returned the tool to his trunk. After the violent episode, he felt more at ease almost immediately.

A man and woman with two small girls appeared from behind a concrete column of the underground garage. "What are you doing?" the man shouted.

"Official government business," came the reply as Andrew slid back behind the steering wheel and put the car in gear. He gently gave the car some gas and pulled away as the front bumper of the Chevrolet pulled off its mount and banged onto the ground.

For Andrew, the use of force calmed his mind and made the tunnel vision of envy fade. His career ambitions returned, cleansed and focused. The covetous nature of his devious thoughts were only slightly muted. Determined, Andrew drove through the remaining lanes of the parking garage without incident. A middle-aged woman took his validated parking stub at the gated exit to the parking garage, punched his ticket, and opened the gate arm. Andrew took a look at her badge. *Debbie.* He smiled and winked and sped away.

***

Andrew continued on to his office and took another tongue-lashing from Lieutenant Gilroy as soon as he arrived. He forgot to mention the damage to his vehicle. But Andrew dutifully collected the files and the contact information, completed a few forms for his flight, submitted his timecard, and posted another request for overtime. Lieutenant Gilroy knew he had an ambitious man. But he questioned him aggressively about his timecard, his expense report, and why the arrests only netted two kilos of cocaine when the local sheriff's office intelligence suggested three. Andrew had all the answers. He was calm, cool, and collected. He looked the part of the FBI agent, and he felt like this was just another token "bust in the chops" from Gilroy.

He looked straight ahead, took the abuse, and even made a few remarks in his pocket notebook on how he could improve. An air of confidence made Andrew taller somehow, and when he stood at attention, he looked as though bullets might just bounce off his chest, rebounding off the black suit. His black-on-black uniform, creaseless and stiff.

"Make sure you've got the evidence to make the case before you get the arrests, Harrison, or you'll be punching parking tickets back in Bethesda."

"Yes, sir, Lieutenant." Andrew tucked his assignments under his arm and returned to his desk. *Someday I'd like to punch that guy in the mouth.* The other agents were hesitant to take on this new role when it was announced. But Andrew had taken a chance. A chance to work independently. *CRAWL Liaison.* Set himself apart.

He made arrangements to meet with the deputy police chief in Fort Collins, an hour's drive from Golden.

***

Andrew got home later than he intended, after nine. He rummaged through the kitchen, chewed up a couple tums tablets and sat down at the dining room table. On the little bowl where they kept the keys and pens and matchbooks and such, was a handwritten note from Susan.

Andrew,

I've let the landlord know we won't be renewing our lease. I'll be in Denver until the 28th. Let's try not to leave any mess and we'll get the full deposit back.

Susan.

In a swelling mood, he went to the bedroom, packed his regular suitcase, showered, brushed his teeth, and put on a clean set of clothes. Returning to the Chrysler, he opened the trunk and reached for the backpack. He found some loose powder and a tiny plastic coke spoon. He snorted two quick spoonfuls, put the rest of the kilo in his suitcase, and slammed the trunk lid closed.

Washington Dulles Airport was only an hour away, compared to Susan's flight from Richmond, Virginia, at almost two. And Andrew was sure he could get a direct flight to Denver, ahead of Susan's, which stopped in Atlanta-Hartsfield. It would give him a head start and put him in the driver's seat.

"Speaking of head start," Andrew whispered to himself. He pulled out the coke spoon and took another bump.

Chapter 16

Andrew: Denver, CO, August 1982

Andrew arrived in Denver on time. He had a detective from Fort Collins waiting for him. It took about an hour and a half to make the trip northward. He took the opportunity to attempt a little shut-eye.

As soon as he arrived at the station house, he could sense all eyes on him, eyeing his suit, his stance, and of course, the size of his balls. It was a trait that Andrew could sense among the macho men in the room, and he used it to his advantage. He carried himself with confidence and chose his words carefully but also asked tough questions from those he sensed weakness. It was almost an arrogance, yet also a skill. A skill he wielded with authority from "the bureau" and from Washington, DC. That skill would make him Task Force Commander one day.

Inside, overhead ceiling fans twirled and rattled above a puke-green tile floor from the height of the disco era. Andrew was given introductions to some key staff, shook hands with some small-town punks turned police bullies, and nodded some how-ya-doings across the desks.

Andrew bided his time, did his duty as a guest of the jurisdiction, then was escorted outside, across the parking lot to the annex building, away from the law enforcers, to a set of three conference rooms surrounding a central staging area. Behind one half-wall was the evidence room and firearms cage. One uniformed officer signed in evidence and checked out weapons, while a second cataloged the evidence into storage and operated the keyed gun cabinet.

This was a tightly run operation. Any deceptive acts wouldn't be possible here without a major distraction. A car explosion outside might do it, but Andrew wasn't worried. He had enough blow to last, and the operation he was requested for had been delayed a week because their snitch had been arrested in Wyoming on an unrelated charge. That would give Andrew plenty of time to find Tom, take his great-aunt's letters, and give his ex-wife the finger one last time. And maybe he could talk her into giving him more than a finger. That thought, and the satisfaction from seeing her struggle at work, maybe even being demoted, gave Andrew a hard-on.

But first, he'd need some wheels, something he could get around in without being noticed, something he could put some miles on. By the end of the twelve-hour day shift, Andrew rolled into the Peakview Motor Lodge in a brand-new Dodge police cruiser. It was on loan from the motor pool, as a guest of the department. Despite his conspicuous vehicle, it did get him free breakfast at the RoadKing diner just down the block.

Andrew checked his notes again. Susan should have arrived late last night. She wasn't necessarily a great flier, so she may have slept in. She'd hit the museum or the library at the college first, so that meant finding Tom before noon, two o'clock at the latest. After a breakfast of eggs, bacon, and the toughest bagel Andrew had in a year, he radioed the station complaining of a travel stomach bug. He said he'd be back in before the shift change, to meet a few more of the SWAT guys.

Chapter 17

Susan: Denver, CO, August 1982

It was still early in Knoxville, but Susan was certain her mother was up. Her mother was always busy. She usually wore an apron but had never worked outside the home. Susan hadn't missed a day of work in almost six months. It was this disconnect that drove an invisible wedge between them. Susan wanted more from her mother, more from their relationship. To have deep conversations about the intimacies in their lives. To have someone to share secrets with and to comfort each other in troubled times. Their current relationship had fallen short. Susan was disappointed that she had gotten divorced. But Susan's mother was devastated by the divorce.

The yearning in Susan's voice was evident right away. "Hi, Mom. It's not too early, is it?"

"Heavens no, dear. I was up before your father and got started on the invitations for the gardening club's Tour of Roses. Is everything ok? How's Andrew? Did he get that promotion yet?"

"Everything's fine. But why do you always ask about him? We're divorced, remember?" Susan was looking for something. A confidante?

"Oh, I know, sweetie. I just thought since you're still living together, you might get back together. FBI agent sounds like such a good job. And exciting too!"

"I'm gonna get my own place, Mom."

"Oh, dear. He was so handsome, and his folks seemed so nice. Remember, they saved seats for us at the restaurant after the rehearsal dinner just so we could talk."

Susan tried changing the subject to anything other than her ex-husband. "I'm traveling for work this week, Mom. I'm in Denver right now."

"Oh. Is everything ok?"

"Yes, mom. I travel for work quite often. It's an important position." Susan felt like she was talking to a child.

"I just don't understand why they can't find someone there to do whatever it is you're doing. Oh, these invitations aren't right. I'll have to call the printers and see what can be done. Who's doing your job back in Washington? Oh, these are all wrong."

"How's Dad?" Susan tried changing the subject again. Maybe something would click and they could have a moment of adult conversation between them. It didn't happen.

"Oh, you know your father. Putting in long hours. He was invited to be an usher at church. Can you imagine? He'd have to greet each person by their name and make small talk with everyone. I just don't see how he'll manage. Patty Gibson picked the printer, and I told her. But she doesn't listen."

"Why don't you support me at my job? Why does it always have to be your way?" Susan dramatically changed the subject but regretted the last remark. She didn't let her voice crack. Anger and disappointment were clearly audible, but Susan wasn't even sure who it was directed towards.

"Oh, sweetie. I love that you work in that museum."

"That's exactly what I'm talking about. You don't even know

the name," said Susan.

"It's the Smithsonian, right? I just worry about you being so far from home, dear."

"Washington, DC *is* my home. Why can't you just support me for who I am? And why can't we talk like adults? Why can't..." Susan kept the emotion bottled up below her voice, but the last sentence wouldn't come out.

"Oh, my, there, there."

"You haven't even asked why I'm in Denver or how the symposium went. That's more important to me than anything else right now. Why can't you..."

"Oh, of course, dear. I'm sure I wanted to ask about it. Were there any eligible men attending? There must have been. Oh, sweetie, I just want what's best for you. You know that."

Susan could sense the conversation going nowhere, fast.

"No, Mom. No men. It was fine, and I'll be in Denver through the weekend. Tell Dad hugs and kisses."

"Ok, sweetie, and.... "

"I've got to go now. Talk soon. Love you."

"Love you too, sweetie."

"Bye." Susan hung up the phone and threw her journal across the room. *I don't even know why I bother calling.*

Susan sighed and walked over to where it landed, leaning against the wall, under the pale green curtains facing the runway. It lay splayed open, upside down, and open to a random page from two months ago. She picked it up, opened it to a random page, saw an entry about Andrew and turned a few more pages forward. Another entry about Andrew. *What's wrong with me?*

Susan could feel some powerful emotions welling up inside but couldn't let them out. *Why can't I turn these feelings into the right words? I can't.*

In the back of the journal was a three-year calendar. She opened it, reviewed the months and dates, and checked for last month's date circled in red.

Shit.

PART 2

Chapter 18

Clarence: *San Acacio, Colorado Territory, September 1870*

Clarence woke to the crackle of cured ham frying in the skillet and tugged at his swollen groin. He pulled on his cotton pants, hiding his member from sight, and threw off the buffalo blanket. His feet hurt and he was anxious to tell somebody about it. He re-strapped his suspenders and pulled a wool blanket over his shoulders, then pulled it down below his waist to hide his protruding manhood. He put his shoes on, feeling every worn angle and exposed crease on his sore feet. The holes were pea-sized at the start of this journey but were growing daily. "I should have spent my last two dollars on those boots the washerwoman had," he said, talking over his shoulder towards Nickie, and scratching at his groin. "How much farther to a town?"

Nickie, the camp cook, responded with a grunt, "Three days, four at the most."

"I can't wait to get to a town."

"Another town, another way to spend money," Nickie said, glancing up from his cookware. Nickie had one job, to prepare the meals, which really meant keeping the fire going, especially early in the morning. Or rather, if anything remained from last night's dinner, he'd fry it up with some grease. Buffalo fat, pork fat, or butter if any could be traded for, along the trail. Breakfast usually consisted of salted ham, fried in a skillet, with a biscuit. His biscuits were just flour and water, smashed into oval disks, resembling the inside of Nickie's palm. The smashed dough was laid directly on the edge of the fire, right down on the coals, and baked for ten minutes with ash, dirt, and bits of whatever the wind blew around and the fire did not consume. With little care, they would last two days in a pocket. He was proud of his biscuits.

"Don't you know how to make anything else except these biscuits?"

"Don't you know it's disrespectful to complain about the food with your johnson pointing at me?" Nickie continued turning the biscuits, some blacker and more ashen than others, and tending the fire.

Clarence turned away, cheeks flushing, stammering about the cold, the biscuits, and Nickie's comment, none of it making much sense. He hobbled over the rough ground, seeking a private tree to relieve himself and calm his fire.

Clarence was just nineteen years old, still young, even in this frontier country. His mother had died of a fever three days before his seventh birthday. After that, he and his father tried to make a go of a hog and cotton farm in East Texas. But without a wife for his father or a mother to Clarence, they bickered, argued, and came to blows when he was sixteen. He stopped working on the farm and his father stopped caring for him. When a band of Apaches was captured near his home, he volunteered with the local posse to help march them back to Lubbock. Eventually, they were sent to a reservation in Oklahoma.

He had no intention of returning to the farm. It seemed like an obvious choice to depart the only home he had known. He stole three dollars from his father and an owl broach sewn into a lace collar from what was left of his mother's things. Despite a rough upbringing, Clarence found himself at home eeking out a living in the open country, camping under the stars, stealing chickens from nearby settlers, and hoping for a small reward when he reached Lubbock. That was his new life and he would never return to the old.

The young man strode up to the back of the wagon, reached down, and picked up a biscuit. He searched around for a fork or a knife to stab a piece of ham but found none. He tried reaching into the pan with his fingers but instead found Nickie holding a big wooden spoon and smacking the skillet with a wap, wap, wap.

"*Maitenant*, you just wait a minute there, son," Nickie said. "Have you paid up the two dollars you owe Mr. Mitchell yet?"

"Uh, no, but we talked about it and I'm still trying to sell the watch and this revolver here." He paused, then continued. "I'm no good with a gun anyway."

"Not too good with your fingers, either, I reckon."

Nickie passed him a tin cup, took the ashed biscuit from his hand, and dropped it sideways into the cup. "Hold still," he said, more forcefully this time. He reached for the skillet with a brown mitten, held it up above the cup, and spooned a few bites of ham and some leftover beans into the cup along with the rich grease.

"*S'il vous plait*, let it cool and soak up some of the grease before you eat it," Nickie said, the spoon at his side like a medieval weapon.

"Thanks," said Clarence, looking away.

"*Merci.*" Nickie continued tending the fire and turning the biscuits, ignoring the young man's injured pride. Nickie suddenly remembered the last time he was with a woman, nearly three years ago, at a brothel in Juarez. A biscuit caught fire and burned on one side as Nickie was lost in thought.

The rest of the group came and went, sopping up the grease with ashen biscuits and dirty fingers, and returned to tend the livestock, water the horses, and get ready for the day's climb. Having left Embudo two days ago, they would be entering more mountainous terrain. They were still following the eastern plain of the Rio Grande. The first river crossing proceeded as planned, with no problems. The Utes in the area sometimes camped near the downstream side. When the water ran high, especially during spring runoff, the chances of a wagon overturning or belongings being washed downstream were high. They would gather the belongings from downstream, keep them for themselves, or offer them back as a sort of ransom for crossing the river. But this late in the year, the water was low and no danger lurked about. They camped for the evening just beyond a small Ute village. Nickie had taken the opportunity to trade with the locals for some corn sweetened with honey and a small pouch of tobacco.

The next two days on the trail were unremarkable with one exception, their speed. This alternate route of the Spanish Trail made its way north and northwesterly. The trail had only recently been used as a wagon route, with some difficult stream crossings and fewer settlement stops. The pass was rumored to be easier than the traditional route and more direct to William's final destination. Gaining elevation as they approached the Colorado Territory, the wagon road was even and not heavily rutted. Nickie took the lead for the group and brought the tandem wagon to a trot for a few miles then slowed to a walk. He was a little surprised to see William and Dupree riding the big wagon at a trot. Even the Mexicans had made the transition, trotting their mules. Clarence was walking his mule at an even clip but couldn't get the animal to trot.

"Damn this animal," the young man shouted, after catching up in the afternoon. The sun was high and the air stagnated.

"Give him a rest and make sure he's had plenty of water," Nickie replied as Clarence and his mule walked into the shade of a cottonwood. A nearby stream flowed into a pool and continued its search for lower ground. The air was dry and no clouds were visible except to the far north. Toward the west, pyramid-shaped mountains rose from a seemingly barren plain, in almost perfect sequence. This was the first of the Spanish Peaks, named for the Conquistadors who rode this plain on horseback three hundred years before.

"My feet hurt and my hips are sore from riding this stupid, shit-for-brains animal," said Clarence, tired of the mercilessly slow pace.

The cool water of the stream had started high up in the Spanish Peaks as a single drop of snowmelt, then combined with two more drops to create a flow among pebbles. Over the next fourteen hours, the flow merged with others and became a narrow creek winding through the conifers. It slowed, then sped up, seeking the gradient, until it merged with another minuscule creek, a tiny canyon really, until it found the slope, constantly seeking the easiest downhill route. Continuing across the plain, the creek received another coulee of water, the entire watershed forming a stream. The stream grew tired at the base of the cottonwoods and resigned to ebbing across the plain at less than walking speed.

"What is the name of your mule?" asked Villanueva.

"Git-up-go," Clarence snapped. "It doesn't matter."

"You are correct, Señor Henderson, it does not matter to him. But what is the name of the animal you purchased? He looks like a ten-year-old mule, no?"

Clarence wiped his brow, the scorch of the sun already

reddening his forehead. "I don't know, I found him by, uh, he was just wandering around in the tall grass by the Aztec Springs, away from the railroad office."

"Senor Henderson, esto mula es mas elegante que tu, jovenes soldado," Villanueva commented to his fellow compatriots.

"Easy now," Ford said, interjecting. "Have you introduced yourself to this mule? They don't like being told what to do without proper introductions."

Clarence looked around and saw most faces relaxed and bodies at ease in the shade. It was another five miles to San Pedro Springs and the end of the day's ride.

"I don't know 'mister villa-novo', but he don't run when I kick him." Clarence spat the words out.

"Let me take him down to the water," Ford said, calmly taking the old mule by the halter. Villanueva only watched as Clarence sat in the shade and rubbed his back. Ford guided the animal to the stream, pushed its head away from the closest riffle, and loosened the halter under the animal's chin.

"Easy there, Padron, easy does it... all the way from Santa Fe, without a proper pause to check your hooves, check your saddle blanket, and advise you of our plans." In the background, and under the shade, Villanueva offered the brothers a drink from his canteen.

Clarence hesitated, then challenged Villanueva about his mount. "What do you know about it, Hombre Villa?" he said. No one spoke until Ford returned with the mule.

"His name is Picante and he had a burr under this blanket you've been squatting on the past day and a half. There's a small stone in his left front hoof. You can't ride an animal like that." Ford waited for a moment until Clarence was about to argue the point again. "Take this blanket off and rinse it in the spring tonight before sundown. Make sure you, and not anyone else, lead him to the fresh water above the marsh. Don't hobble him until the campfire has died down. Lead him back to the freshwater with a long lead tomorrow morning."

Clarence shook his head and said, "He don't follow, I'll beat him again."

Ford glanced at Villanueva and said, "You do that again to that mule and you won't make it across the pass. There's another seventy miles of open trail. And you'll need a steady mount to trot you across. Without him, you'll be walking the whole way."

Clarence squeezed his lips together, refused to argue another word with the old man, and looked for a spot to rest farther away from Ford.

Chapter 19

Ford: Colorado Territory, September 1870

Ford had been hired as a guide, having traveled the Cochetopa Pass many times in the past year. But he was also expected to be the hunter, the provisioner, to provide fresh meat for the rest of the traveling party. That meant riding ahead one or two days, hunting, and preparing the meat in advance. Anything that was left over could be dried and stored for the winter or traded in towns for other essentials. Ford had hunted buffalo but lost the inclination after seeing huge herds gunned down for sport, their tongues outstretched, rotting in the sun. During the slaughter, only a handful of hides were taken, a difficult task. The rest were left on the plain for the coyotes and the wolves. *No way to treat an adversary.*

Ford unfurled his bedroll, poked at the fire, and drifted off to sleep before the rest of the men had even settled down. The air was cold, and a biting wind whispered in his gray, curled mustache. Stars were plentiful in the clear sky. He slept easy but chilled, like a soul on the wings of a prayer.

Ford woke with a start. That is, he simply opened his eyes and outstretched his legs. In a span of ten or twelve seconds, he apprised the situation. Still dark. Sunrise was still an hour away.

"Up and at 'em," he said to himself. Throwing aside the buffalo blanket and slipping from under the whitish-gray wool cover, he scratched rusted parts and rubbed aching joints.

"Gettin' healthier every day," Ford thought, joints refusing to cooperate on such a chilly morning. Rolling away from the cold, black, fireless coals, he reached for his canteen, took a few steps into the darkness, and quenched his thirst. Ford relieved himself and stretched his back, vertebrae cracking, the first sound that escaped beyond his personal space.

Re-dressing in the cool predawn air, he added a vest, then his field coat, a fine buckskin layer that fell below his hips. He grabbed a reddish-yellow strip of wool for a scarf for his ears and neck and slipped into his calf-length leather boots. The boots were stiff around the top and ankles but bottomed with a softer material. They were lined with calfskin and tied on with a half-yard of hemp crisscrossed front and back.

Ford immediately noticed a change in his demeanor, sensing the hunt ahead as he slipped on his hunting boots. The calf skin boots made him eerily quiet and somehow attached him to the earth he tread upon, silent as a bobcat on the hunt. He checked his pocket watch and headed north-northwest. His calf-skin boots reminded him of when he was a boy back in Iowa, stalking rabbits in his Lakota moccasins through the tall grass. Stepping light on his feet, barely a sound escaped from the ground when he walked. He walked downhill along the stream to the first side canyon of any count, paused, and noted the direction of the wind. Turning perpendicular to the wind, he walked along for half a mile, avoiding the clumps of grass and cracking sticks from the nearby wood line. He slowed to a walk and hugged the treeline, holding close to the shoulder-high brush for just a moment, watching for any sign of movement. He deliberately placed each foot in front of the other, cautiously avoiding any noise or rustle of grass. His soft buckskin field coat folded and returned its shape in a silent dance.

Pausing at each step, he crouched, waited, and watched. On the far side of the open valley, a wider section of flat land extended towards a stream and revealed a bright green sea of summer grass. Ford waited for nearly ten minutes, watching the woodline beyond for any movement. Dawn was approaching, and a few birds and grasshoppers sang their respective songs. A particularly proud canyon jay squawked, casting an echo of sound across the open land. Ford took two more steps, expecting to move on another hundred yards or so before seeing any game. Behind the next clump of rabbitbrush, he paused again, listened to the jay, and for just a split second, thought he saw a stalk of Apache Plume twitch opposite the natural flow of the wind.

He waited and watched, looked up at the separating cloud cover, and felt for his rifle. Another two minutes passed, and the jay flew up the canyon, squawking about the oncoming winter. Ford waited and saw again the Indian ricegrass slide silently against the grain of the adjacent vegetation. Ford pulled his rifle off his shoulder and carefully set his canteen behind him. The sun was just beginning to shine on the walls of the canyon across from him. He was still in the shadows, frost tipping each blade of grass and each exposed fallen leaf. Across the meadow, the first peaks of the sun melted the frost in nearly an instant, returning a drop of water to the roots of the stoic grass. Carefully, he added another half-step forward and watched. Silence overtook the canyon, the clouds still covering more than half the sky. He adjusted his crouch and clicked the safety off. With that sound, barely audible, a head stuck up above the grass and ears turned.

Ford slowed his breathing and waited. A spike-horned buck, barely two years old, held his ears pricked, scanned the tree line, and then relaxed his shoulders. With no sound and no smells, the deer returned to munching at the grasses between the fallen leaves. Ford waited, his heart speeding up again, and took account of the situation his senses absorbed.

Half-clouded sky, a slight breeze coming steadily from the northwest, almost directly towards the rising sun. Behind him, dense woods rose above the brush. In front of him, clumps of grass grew from between the rocks, mostly sandstone, red and ancient.

Ford raised the rifle to his shoulder and tried to relax his crouch. The spiked buck, still hidden behind a tall mound of rabbitbrush, carefully inspected each bit of green grass, lips quivering and nose damp with moisture. Another half step from behind the brush and Ford could see the leading edge of the buck's ears. Wait. Pause. He tried to imagine the movements of the deer, anticipating each step, each breath, becoming the animal. The deer weighed a hundred and twenty pounds, perfect for two days of fresh meat and a week's worth of dried pemmican. The deer was young and mottled, a small size, but its hide would be suitable for boots and satchels. Ford waited, relaxed and confident. He looked toward the rising sun and saw just a hint of mist or clouds evaporating before his eyes as he pulled the scarf delicately down below his shoulders. The wind was still coming from the northwest, rustling the grass and attempting to turn over the leaves but without success. The smell of sagebrush lingered in the air and a hint of campfire smoke escaped from his wool shirt. The rest was quiet.

The buck took another step, twitched a may-fly from near the delicate hairs in his ear, and munched on another clump of grass. Ford brushed an imaginary insect away, shouldered the rifle, and estimated the distance at about a hundred or a hundred twenty yards. His time working with the General Land Office gave him an advantage in estimating distances. The distance he could walk in half an hour, the distance his packed horse could trot in a half hour. The distance his stripped-lean horse could gallop in fifteen minutes. These were all known quantities. Ford had walked only thirty minutes before beginning his search, barely a mile and a half from camp. And he was less than a minute's walk from the deer's graze.

He flipped open the sight, adjusted the cross-hair up two clicks, then rechecked the wind and added a third click. Even a slight crosswind could slow the bullet. Ford exhaled lightly and tried to imagine the breathing of the deer, the cautious movements. Another step and three light breaths. A twitch of muscle from above the deer's shoulder blades down to the legs. Another half step. Ford was one with the animal. *The wet nose brushes against the clumps of grass. Hairs in the ear bristle and relax.* Ford steadied his elbow against his knee and aimed just above the thickest part of the deer. He took another breath, held it, and squeezed the trigger.

A click, a snap, then the powder flashed, and the recoil jumped back. Ford was temporarily blinded by the smoke but was confident the deer was hit. Only the briefest of glimpses were still in his mind's eye of the deer recoiling upward, struck by the lead bullet, then shocked by the slower soundwave. Ford remained still but advanced another round into the breech and watched.

The deer, struck in the shoulder, lurched and leaped, undecided about what direction the danger came from and undecided about which direction to run. Three hind-quarter kicks and his fight-or-flight response was already failing. Ford had witnessed these moments many times. The deer's lungs filled with blood even as the heart began to pump harder. A leap up the ledge behind failed and he landed on his haunches, kicking in the air amid unstable footing. With limited strength left he galloped across the sagebrush bowl and collapsed in a heap just short of another ledge of rock. Blood spurted from his nose and mouth, a gaping wound under his side. The beastly kicks slowed, and darkness closed on his eyes.

Ford watched, knowing that a running deer could put half a mile between it and you in just over a minute. Watching the direction of flight is the most important matter at the moment. *A noble beast.*

Ford waited. *Rather not hike half a mile looking for this scrawny deer. Rather walk up and see a blood trail.* Following a blood trail could take hours and sometimes the prey was not recovered.

Watching from his still-concealed nest below the trees, he saw the deer disappear into the grass. There was no sign of him closer to the clearing and no sign of him galloping higher up in the trees. Ford folded the sight, rose to both knees and looked up and down the clearing for any movement. Seeing no other souls, he lifted the canteen and slid it over his head. He winced at the pain in his joints, the cold air still biting. He headed up the wash, crossed a gravel bar, and walked to where the deer had stood, rifle still in hand.

He cautiously looked for the deer and saw the blood splatter in the grass. A few more steps and he spied the deer, angled awkwardly against a juniper growing out of a stone. He poked the deer with the rifle and circled around to its head. The deer was dead, a clean kill. Ford decided to clean and gut the deer on the spot, but first, he put his rifle, canteen, and headscarf aside, below the stone ledge. He pulled his skinning knife and began at the hind knees of the still-warm deer. Slicing under the skin, he pulled part of the hide down and away from the meat.

Satisfied with the start, Ford tied the hind legs to the juniper and pulled the carcass over to the ledge. He secured the rope end to the now bloodied juniper, and pushed the deer over the edge. The deer hung upside down from the ledge, blood still leaking from its mouth and nose. Ford checked for movement around the little clearing, then climbed down under the ledge. He opened the deer's belly with the knife and pulled the insides free, away from his work area. He continued with the skinning, easily reaching up the ledge and pulling the hide down from the hind legs. He sliced through the sinew, along the spine, and down the neck, careful to keep the hide intact.

After twenty minutes, the deer was ready for butchering. He cut away each hind quarter, preserving the loins separately. The remainder he cut or sawed into packable pieces. He wrapped them in a cotton sheet and folded it shut. The once-white sheet was stained with blood and dirt from outdoor use, much like Ford himself. His now white beard and mustache were once a proud chestnut. His hands were spotted and scarred. His shoulders stooped more than they once did. As a man of nearly seventy, his physical stamina was less than that of a younger man, but his experience and quiet confidence gave him an edge that wasn't teachable.

He packed the meat and tied it into bundles and carefully folded the deerskin inside out, and rolled it neatly into a canvas bag. Together, sixty, perhaps seventy pounds of meat filled the bundles, more than enough to feed the group of riders. Ford began the now slower walk back towards the camp he had left earlier that morning. His feet glided over the grasses, still treading quietly among the waking forests, canyons, and meadows. His calfskin boots were damp on the bottom, but his feet were warm and dry.

Chapter 20

William: North Branch of the Spanish Trail, September 1870

The sun angled higher in the morning sky, and William readied himself for the day's ride when Benjamin Ford returned to camp. The Mexicans had already loaded the smaller of the wagons and had put a half mile behind them. The sun had evaporated the frost from the grass and the open ground. Stones along the creek that were shaded from the rays were already creeping toward a long winter, frozen with their comrades in a season of time.

"Gettin' an early start, I see," said Ford.

"They're always on the road before the rest of us. But they tend to fall behind after a noon meal, not sure what that's about," replied William.

"Where's the kid?"

"Relievin' himself, I think."

"His bedroll is in the way of my wagon, and we're already gonna be a long time catchin' up if we want to finish butcherin' this deer."

"I'm comin', old man."

"Watch your mouth there, son." Ford stood his ground.

"What?" Clarence strode up with an air of arrogance about him. Even Dupree stopped his loading of the wagon and paused to gaze at the kid.

Clarence continued on, stammering, "Get outta my way, I said, old man."

"Move your bedroll out from under the wagon, we can all get moving while we're still young."

"You wanna make me? Go on and mind your own business, you old sonnova bitch."

William took another step toward his mount but kept an eye on the kid. He knew Ford could handle himself, but he didn't know if the kid knew. It was the first dust-up of the journey, and William had been expecting something of the sort, but maybe from one of the Mexicans, not the kid. He was just so young.

Ford seemed surprised at the young man's tone but then responded the way William knew he would. "Move your stuff and be quick about it or just get out of the way."

"What are you gonna do about it, old man? Sonnova bitch."

William watched, then looked over at Dupree, who took off his hat and looked at the ground, taking exception to Clarence's tone.

Ford responded in kind. "I'm gonna bend you over my knee and give you a whippin' like you deserved from the time you was still shittin' in yo' drawers, young man. Do you want me to show you or are you gonna get movin'?"

"Get out of my way." Clarence took two steps toward Ford, then veered away to the wagon but made the effort to give the old mountain man a shove on the arm. Ford pushed him off. Clarence stumbled, went to one knee, and noticed that the black man saw him fall. The kid jumped to his feet, cursed at Dupree, who outweighed him by a hundred pounds and kicked dirt in Ford's direction. Ford kicked the dirt back, took half a step back, and dropped his canteen to his side. For a split second, time stood still. William imagined the blood pumping in Ford's ears, his anger rising.

Clarence took it as an act of aggression and moved to kick the canteen away and tried to shove him aside. Ford stumbled slightly, cursed under his breath, and then stood straight, a calm but determined demeanor on his wrinkled face. The kid made a punching lunge toward the older man. As Ford dodged his thrust, he widened his stance and caught the kid in motion. The two tumbled to the ground and rolled down towards the creek in a hostile embrace. Clarence got to a knee first and struck Ford in the top of the head with his fist. Ford pulled himself up and forced the kid onto his side in one motion. The two stood, but Clarence was half a beat slower. Ford punched the kid square in his nose and followed it up with a gut punch that took Clarence's breath away. With that, the older man went to work.

He snatched Clarence up by the neck and began his address: "My name is Benjamin Ford, and I'm old enough to be your grandpappy. When your elder tells you to get movin', you don't give lip, boy." Ford punched the kid in the gut again and spun him around. He grabbed him from behind, clenching him up under the chin, delivering a medium-strength rabbit punch to his kidney. Blood flowed from the kid's nose, and his heated breath steamed upward, obscenities spewing into the cold air. All William could do was watch. Clarence's eyes turned red and watery. Ford continued with a series of alternating punches between his kidney and his reddening cheek.

The kid fell to the ground, and Ford followed him down. He gripped the kid's bedroll and smacked his face with it.

"When I tell you to get movin', that means now, you snot-nosed cachorro." Ford grabbed him by the wrist and spun him across the slope, moving stealthily in his knee-high calfskin boots. He latched onto the kid by the ear and spoke into his face again.

"Take your shit and get in line. Everyone else in this pack's pullin' their own weight. You're the only one nobody gives a shit about. Take a lesson from this and mind your elders." Ford picked up his canteen, slung it up over his head, and adjusted the shoulder strap. He grabbed the staggering Clarence by the elbow but the kid cowed away. Ford reacted and clutched the kid by the throat, pulling his chin up to his eye level. He wiped his mouth and spoke to Clarence eye to eye. All within earshot recognized the forceful nature of Ford's delivery. "Next time Mr. Mitchell calls you out to gather water or take the horses out to pasture. Or next time I see you eyein' Villanueva's pistols. Or next time you're slow bringin' firewood, I'll take you out again. Next time I see you bad mouthin' that sonnova gun Dupree I'll crawl your hump and leave your sorry ass in the bone orchard, savvy?"

Clarence could only grunt and avert his eyes from Ford's face.

"A dirt nap. Comprende?" Ford picked up the remainder of the kid's things and flung them at his feet. "Show you my skinnin' knife."

Clarence wiped his nose and picked up the nearest items strewn about the camp. A tense minute passed as William and Dupree cautiously adjusted packed items and steadied the horses.

"And don't take it out on that mule, or you'll never make it over the pass," said Ford, firmly. "Send you home in a box, toes up."

Clarence only nodded and wiped the blood-snot from his nose. He looked away when Dupree's gaze met his. Ford watched his movements but continued adjusting his pack, tightening the cinches on his own mule.

William saw the young man wander off muttering to himself, hiding the tears that streamed off his beaten and bruised face. William looked away. After Clarence's humiliation of the public defeat, William recognized the kid's sides would hurt from the body punches but he was not physically injured. And William was amazed at Ford's strength and quickness.

William waited as Clarence slowly gathered his possessions and packed his mule. He took the opportunity of the calm to speak to the mountain man in a measured voice but one that Dupree could overhear. "Ford, you were a little hard on the kid."

"You sayin' he didn't deserve it?"

"We don't want that kid gettin' sour and slippin' up on you the final night of our journey and slittin' your throat."

"I don't want that either. Might get in the way of my social agenda if you know what I mean. He just don't listen too good, Mr. Mitchell."

Ford saddled his horse but remained standing. "Funny. My eldest wanted to read books all the time as a young'un and I scolded him regular for it. *'Wastin' your time'* and *'only lazy folks take up readin' like that.'* He fought me tooth and nail about school versus ranch duties an' huntin' obligations. I thought I had won. He just finished lawyerin' school in Pennsylvania. He's workin' in Washington DC now."

"You don't say?"

"I never mention it much 'cause I was wrong about the schoolin' and readin'."

"Men make mistakes all the time. Makes you just like the rest of us," said William.

"I always wanted him to be better than me, ya know, but all I could teach him was what I already knew. How's a man supposed to make his son better if you only teach 'em what you already know?"

"I understand."

"Was so hard on him. But I'm so proud of him now," said Ford.

"I get it."

"But bein' proud and talkin' to him is two different things. Somehow, my pride is just a pebble compared to the mountain of regret I have for tryin' to get in the way. You should see him in his lawyerin' suit with his stack of law books."

"That's only bein' a mortal man, Ford." William took another step forward and spoke in a softer voice. "Take some of that regret and show that kid a little kindness. Find out what he might be good at. Lord knows he's no good at fighting."

Ford grinned and clutched his shoulder. "I'm sorry, Mr. Mitchell. Fightin' and whatnot is no way to behave as the wagon train guide. Don't expect that from me again, sir."

"Was just defendin' your position, no harm in that."

"And somethin' tells me I ain't as young as I used to be. My shoulder's awful sore and you wouldn't want to see an old man get beat down. It's not respectable."

"As respectable as your poker game?" asked William, turning the conversation a bit more cheerful.

Ford grinned again and let out a little chuckle.

William continued, "Teach that kid to use better judgment, before he picks a fight with another mountain man that ain't as gentle as you."

Ford grinned wider, then relaxed his face into a slight grimace and handed William his canteen.

William continued, "Thank you, Ford. Maybe all that ranch work and huntin' duties made your son a stronger law candidate. Molded him into who he is without you even knowing."

"I ain't no saint, Mr. Mitchell."

"Just keep us in fresh game and I'll keep prayin' for your soul. The flank of that spike horn buck's gonna taste great tonight."

Ford continued harnessing the horses, attaching the lead to the hackamores and pulling the slack of the reins, and tying it to the hand brake. The horses whinnied and nickered, anxious to get moving.

"Thirty miles or so of open ground till we hit the first of them mountain creeks, sir. Two days up to the Cochetopa Pass and then a week of ridin' down to the Gunnison."

"Let's get movin'. Days are gettin' shorter and you ain't gettin' any younger," said William.

Ford grinned again but then returned to a scowl when Dupree looked his way. Dupree responded with an easy smile. William climbed aboard the big wagon, released the hand brake, and gently touched the haunches of the horse team. The horses responded with a start and a tug, the wheels of the wagon creaking in a skid and then rolling to an easy pace. Ford mounted his horse, turned a wide circle to lead the mule in behind, and walked his team up to the rutted trail. Dupree followed close behind.

"I've got three boys myself, Mr. Ford." These were some of the first words Dupree had spoken to Ford since the journey began. Ford's scowl turned into a grimace. But William saw an understanding between them, a shared connection, both fathers, a knowing of what compassion looks like.

Dupree headed up the trail. He looked as though he wanted to say something more. But a black man in this part of the world was considered a second-class citizen, especially among white men with guns in a lawless frontier land. And William didn't want any more trouble.

Ford walked his team to an open area off the trail, nodded and let Dupree pass, and looked back at the kid. Clarence was hopping in circles, attempting to hoist a foot into a stirrup as his mule sidestepped, his eyes darting nervously.

"Calm yourself and rub his shoulder as you talk into his ear, son," called Ford. Whisper in his ear what you're gonna do and how long the ride will be. Tell him about the grain in your pack, and the next waterin' hole. Then try it again."

Clarence did as he was told, pulled the mule close, and spoke directly into his ear. The mule swiveled his ears, listening, and looked down at the ground. His eyes steadied and a shiver swept down its withers. Clarence grabbed the horn of the saddle, put a foot into the stirrup, and slung his leg over in one motion. His mule took a single sidestep and then eyed Ford's team waiting ahead. Clarence clicked his tongue in his cheek "Tsk-tsk-tsk," and touched his heel to the flank. The mule walked easily up the bank and onto the trail following in line with Ford's team.

***

To navigate up to Cochetopa Pass, Ford had to show the way. Following the river was the idea, but at the first fork, it wasn't clear which was the right way without a guide who knew the route. The same thing happened at the next fork. And the next, and the next. Over the course of five days, the wagons churned slower. Each stream-crossing was a gamble with gravity, tempting the fates to overturn the precious cargo. Broken spokes or damaged felloes could create costly delays. Injuries to the horses were always a concern, but navigation was paramount. One wrong turn could lead the men into an unknown, hostile environment with few chances to turn around. Keeping Ford within a quarter-mile of the lead horses became the routine. The branches of the creeks got smaller as they ascended.

On the sixth day, the creek disappeared completely and Ford announced that it was six miles to the pass and then another nine to the first watering hole, a series of beaver ponds on the other side. From there, following the creeks and the remnants of the trail became easier, mimicking the water's course downhill until it reached the mighty Gunnison River.

Chapter 21

Jack and Tom: Golden, CO, August 1982

Tom called and got Jack on the third ring. "Let's do that campin' trip…"

"I'm in. When do we leave?" Jack bellowed. "Don't mean to get ahead of myself. Yeah, I love camping."

"Want to do a little fishin' then?" asked Tom.

"Does a bear shit in the woods?"

"Uh–"

"If you prick us, do we not bleed? If you tickle us… " said Jack.

"I'm not sure."

"Do we not laugh? If you poison us, do we not die?" Jack continued in his best stage voice. "And if you wrong us, shall we not seek revenge?" Jack may have hit the "revenge" too hard, but he didn't care. "When do we leave?"

"I was thinking in two weeks, just the Thursday and Friday before the Labor Day weekend," said Tom in a slightly hurried tone.

"Count me in. I'll get started putting gear together this afternoon."

"OK. Lets–"

"I've mentioned my poker buddy? He's a hoot," said Jack.

"What about–"

"Perfect. Stop by Friday at five for a cold one. My wife's got bingo. We'll sort out all the details."

"What's this about the bleeding revenge?" asked Tom nervously.

"Shakespeare, my handsome friend. *The Merchant of Venice*. It's a comedy, but there's a reckoning at the end. I'll explain it all to you on Friday," stated Jack.

The next few weeks dragged on for Tom with the anticipation of camping and fishing in the remote and isolated parts of Northwestern Colorado, Northeastern Utah, and Southern Wyoming. He replayed in his mind what he knew from *Field & Stream* and what he could remember as a kid. Granite Springs reservoir was created when the Green River was dammed just above Dutch John, Utah. The impoundment back upriver snakes its way more than ninety miles through red rock canyon country to within eight miles of Green River, Wyoming along Interstate 80. The Uintah Mountains rise up from the Southern and Western edges of the reservoir in the Ashley National Forest. The east-west oriented mountain peaks reach an elevation of over thirteen thousand feet and cover a contiguous area above tree-line, only matched by the San Juans in Southwestern Colorado. This wild and treeless area is the second largest in the lower forty-eight. In all, the Unitah mountain peaks span almost a hundred miles, all above tree-line.

***

The following Friday, Tom sped off in his Monte Carlo and tried singing along to "*Come On Eileen*" for a few blocks. "What has happened to rock-n-roll?" he said to himself as he punched the second preset button and heard Eddie Raven belting out, "*Who needs you, I've got Mexico.*"

The rest of the ride to Jack's house was easy rollin'. "*Eatin' right and I'm livin' good…*" sang Tom. When he got to Jack's house, the garage door was up, and Jack was smoking a cigarillo. They exchanged pleasantries as Jack admired Tom's Monte Carlo.

They made plans for the camping trip to Granite Springs by way of Dinosaur National Monument, taking Jack's four-wheel drive Chevy three-quarter-ton van. It was rusty in spots, brown in spots, and had the remnants of a wide, tan horizontal stripe down the sides. It was suitable for towing Tom's dory. If Jack's poker buddy joined them, he'd bring his Jeep. They'd meet at a Diner in the town of Dinosaur, about twenty miles from the Utah border, and continue up Harpers Corner Road to the turnoff to Echo Park Campground, at the confluence of the Green and Yampa Rivers.

The plan was to spend two nights there, then drive on up through Wyoming, back into Utah, and along the west side of Granite Springs reservoir. They'd meet at the dirt road turnoff, twenty-seven miles past the marina near Sheep Creek, where a finger of the reservoir was only a mile or so across, and find a remote area to make their camp for the next four nights. Then back home Monday night, ready to resume their busy lives. Tom's fourteen-foot dory came complete with a set of long oars, a pair of casting platforms, front and back, and a little twenty-horsepower Johnson motor on a tilting transom mount.

Tom and Jack bonded over a pint of whiskey and a cloud of cigar smoke. Tom talked, and Jack listened as Tom recalled times he spent with his dad in Baltimore before they moved to Colorado.

"We used to stop at The Crab Shack on the way home. A little seafood joint. The food was good, and Dad always enjoyed having a beer.

This was one of the few places you could still get a National Bohemian Beer on tap. You know, it was the official beer of Memorial Stadium, where the Orioles played. We spent so many summer afternoons at that place. Dad would drink a cold Natty-Bo. I'd lean in close to listen to Jon Miller call the Orioles. WFBR AM 1590."

Tom felt like a teenager again. Jack savored his cigar and listened carefully.

Tom continued, a little quieter. "But then my dad had a heart attack four years ago, which surprised everyone. He was only sixty-eight then and in decent health, or so everyone thought. Doctors performed an emergency double bypass, but a blood clot broke loose, and he had a stroke on the operating table." Tom looked up at Jack to make sure he'd heard, then continued. "Doctors did what they could, but he died the next day, September 3rd."

Tom waited a beat. "That night, the Orioles were swept by the Yankees and eliminated from the American League Eastern Division pennant race."

Jack ashed his cigar, waiting to make sure Tom was finished. "Fuck the Yankees," said Jack. It was the only thing to say.

A darkness lived in Tom. It wasn't depression, and it wasn't anger. It was more of a longing. Like he was missing something. He had his first panic attack the day his father died. And a second the day before the funeral. After that, they subsided but remained a part of his life, with one or two occurrences every year.

Chapter 22

Susan: Denver, CO, August 1982

Susan drove to Tom's mother's house. They had a very brief conversation in which Susan learned that Tom worked at Gart's weekdays, Woody's Pizza on the weekends and dabbled with night classes at Metro State.

Susan then drove to Tom's house in Golden, a bedroom community in the Clear Creek Valley, on the outskirts of the big-city metropolis but a world away. Surrounded by mountains, Golden felt like an old frontier city. She kept missing street signs and other landmarks as she watched in awe as the plains suddenly gave way to the mountains. She stopped twice to check directions but was able to find the duplex, the second from the corner, with the Florida Gator mailbox. She stepped up to the door, rang the doorbell, quietly knocked three times, and cleared her throat.

A burly man in his early forties came to the door. He wore shorts and a sloppy t-shirt but he also had rubber boots on, the kind you might milk cows or muck horse stalls in. Or the kind you mow the grass in because you don't want your tennies to turn green.

"Yes."

"Is Tom here?"

"No, he must be at work, I guess."

"Oh, uh... "

"Can I help you with something?"

"No, I called and talked to him last week. I just came from his mother's house."

"Is it an emergency?" The burly man in the muckin' boots seemed genuine and looked Susan in the eye.

"Oh, no. I just haven't been able to reach him."

"He rents the basement from me. If you'd like, I can relay a message, or you can leave him a note or something," said Muckin' Boots.

"No, thank you. Is there a time I could come back?"

"Oh, sure. Tomorrow. Tom's usually up by eight or so. Is that convenient?"

"That might work."

"Or, I can give you his work address? Do you know where Woody's Pizza is?"

"I don't think so."

"Let me see if I have a menu. The address and a little map are on the back."

The burly man retreated into the house, still wearing the dirty, well-worn rubber boots with grass clumps stuck to the soles. He returned a moment later with the paper menu and an electric bill in an envelope he happened upon. He used it as a pointing device.

"Here's the menu with the map. Golden's downtown is pretty small and Woody's is right by the Howdy Folks arch. Know where that is?"

"I'm afraid not."

The burly man stepped outside and extended his hand to Susan.

"By the way, my name's Harley, like the bike. Harley Myerson."

Susan shook the man's hand, felt the strength in his palm, and noticed rough, callused areas.

"Pleased to meet you, sir. Thank you for the information and maybe I'll catch up with Tom this afternoon or in the morning."

"Glad I could help, Tom's a good kid." He seemed comfortable in shorts and rubber boots.

"I'll mention how helpful you were. Thanks again."

The burly man shuffled his feet, commented on his lawn, and pointed again with the envelope, repeating the directions. With that, Susan turned, checked the street for cars, and crossed over to her Ford Taurus. She got in and paused for a moment to take in the view behind Harley's house. A mountain rose up from the checkerboard of lots in town, with a vertical cliff face at the top. She turned the car around and checked the mountain again. It was still the same shade of burnt orange in the afternoon sun. A dry wind blew in the window and Susan felt an urge to get outside. Maybe take a walk in town.

She'd find Tom this afternoon at Woody's Pizza and make a firm appointment to pick up the letters. If she could stop staring at the mountains. She'd traveled to many places, but somehow, these mountains were alive. Alive and perhaps whispering her name. And she couldn't look away.

***

Andrew: Denver, CO, August 1982

Andrew felt a little out of place in his black uniform coat and tie sitting inside the new police cruiser. He'd never driven anything as nice during his time with the FBI or the Baltimore Police Department and wondered how Fort Collins could afford vehicles as nice as these. It had all the bells and whistles a small-town cop would want.

He eased onto Humboldt Street and parked behind the fence of the adjacent apartment complex. He opened the glove box, retrieved the binoculars, got out, and found a suitable spot at the end of the fence, yet largely hidden by a cluster of lilac bushes. He adjusted the focus, steadied himself, and found his target. Susan was just crossing the street and knocked on the door of the second house from the corner. She spent a few minutes talking to a burly man in shorts and blue rubber boots. At the end of the conversation, he handed her a document.

Am I too late? Andrew was alone. *I can't let that bitch beat me.* He seethed and snarled into the bushes, then quickly retreated when he saw Susan heading back to her car. He returned to the patrol car, checked his hair in the mirror and drove around to the far side of the complex, further concealing his car, and walked up to the second house.

"You just missed her," a man wearing rubber muckin' boots said. In his best Mid-western tone, he continued, explaining that Susan needed directions to Woody's. He repeated the directions, failing to mention Tom's work schedule, the package he received, or his lawn.

Andrew spun around without saying another word and walked back across the street, down the sidewalk. He slithered between the fences and back through the lilac bushes. Muckin' Boots followed the black suit's actionable movements and watched as he rounded the corner of the apartments and disappeared from sight.

***

Tom clocked out at Woody's at three-fifteen, grabbed a leftover slice from the warming counter, and walked out the back door. He drove his Monte Carlo back through downtown Golden's main drag,

Washington Street, under the Howdy Folks arch and through some residential neighborhoods to the highway. After a near miss with a rock-hauler truck returning with a full load from the mines farther up the canyon, he turned onto his street at three-forty, parked in the driveway, and walked up to the front door.

"You're a popular guy today," said Harley. He had changed out of his rubber boots and had taken a cold shower to knock the sweat and grass off and get a revitalized afternoon going.

"Yeah?"

"Some lady stopped by earlier looking for you. Real nice. I was certain she'd catch you at work, so she didn't leave a message or anything, but it seemed important. You in trouble or anything?"

"Not that I'm aware."

"I sent her down to Woody's. Guess she missed you, huh."

"I guess so."

"Well, I told her you'd be up tomorrow morning by eight. So you can talk to her about whatever it is she's after. Seemed like a nice lady, well dressed, and sort of important. Sure you're not in any trouble?"

"No, probably trying to sell me something. Besides, I'm gonna be gone. I'm goin' camping with Jack and his buddy."

"Here's the weird part. So this lady leaves. Then, less than a minute later, a cop of some kind came by. Flashed a badge and was asking all about the lady, where she was going, and if you'd gotten any packages. Kinda strange I thought, so I didn't tell him about that package from Ohio you got last week."

"A cop?"

"I'm not sure. He wore a black suit and was just walking up the street," said Harley.

"No trouble I'm aware of. Just sort of looking forward to the camping. You know, get away for a while."

"Good for you, Tom."

Tom reclined on his bed in the basement, then thought better of it and started packing a few items. He wasn't concerned about the lady who had stopped by or the other guy right behind her. *Probably an election canvasser. I never should've filled out that petition to save Heritage Square.* He thought about camping and was excited about taking the dory out on the water. Tom continued packing, arranged the fishing gear, then rearranged it, and inspected his trailered boat. *An early start's a good idea.*

Chapter 23

William: Creed, Colorado Territory, September 1870

William Mitchell and Napoleon Bonapart Dupree were an unusual sight, a white man and a black man, seated next to each other as they approached the town of Creede, Colorado. It wasn't really a town, more like a set of mining camps with a central storehouse, a saloon, and eight or ten stick-built structures. The central bank building, the center of activity and the only stone building was where gold could be changed to hard currency, mining claims could be bought and sold, and debts could be accrued. The hotel, a boarding house with a restaurant on the upwind side from the row of outhouses behind, sat perched on the hillside. The stockyards were across the downhill road, all bordered by an accumulation of mine tailings and waste barricades. A dozen or so burros, some blind, some near death, and all overworked in the mines, stood sentinel over the proceedings.

This was the hardscrabble reality that William had already seen too many times in his travels from Colorado to California. The men he crossed paths with in this high-elevation locale were not much better off than the burros. Some had given up, begging for coins outside the saloon, while some walked past with disfigured limbs and haunted faces from mishandled dynamite or the scars of a rolling ore cart. The smell coming from the row of outhouses was overwhelming. Recent summer thunderstorms had flooded every low-lying pothole and muck-filled path between the buildings. Desperate men and readily available firearms made towns like these dangerous places.

But despite the stench and the eye-sore of the cluster of civilization and amidst the mountains of the Colorado Territory, men survived and even thrived in the mines. The value of precious metals outweighed the struggle of fracturing the mountain, breaking rocks, and sifting through the gravel in search of a vein of color, a river of gold. And it could all be measured by the blood of a man's lifeline. Fortunes could be won with the single strike of a hammer and chisel, or lost over two years of fruitless labor. It was the heartbeat of the burgeoning town.

The men found the stables, arranged for three days' worth of good grain for the horses, and set about searching the town for a hot meal and some respite from the last three weeks on the trail. Dupree insisted on walking back toward the camp, a half mile outside of town, where Ford was staying with the still-loaded wagons. William let him be and walked the boardwalk in front of the restaurant and down to the telegraph office. He wrote out a short message explaining his whereabouts and his anticipated arrival in Vernal in a month's time. The cost of sending the message curtailed his eagerness to connect with his wife.

Towards the end of the day, and just as he was about to return to camp outside the town limits, he was drawn toward a small crowd that had gathered beside the stone bank building. A dapper gentleman dressed in a polished three-piece suit with tails was gathering the crowd closer. William wandered over for a better view of the occasion.

The middle-aged gentleman's suit was blue and gray plaid, and the vest was a houndstooth pattern with two outer pockets on each chest and a bright blue satin ascot tied in a simple bow. His tophat was of the curved-brim Wellington style, and the gray wool hat fit him perfectly. His clothes set him apart in the rugged mountains. The gentleman removed a large scarf, bundled about his neck and cheeks, revealing a smooth and clean-shaven face. He called to the crowd and made a show of folding the scarf into fours, then folding it in half again and pressing the fabric smooth, and tightening the edges to a sharp crease. He laid the scarf onto a delicate folding table and retrieved a small stack of cards from his inner coat pocket and placed it on the table as well. From a large trunk behind him, he pulled a shiny blue-green bottle and placed it gently in the center of the table, making a show of turning the bottle so the label faced outward, like a ballerina turning gracefully into her partner's arms.

Calling to the crowd, then asking for, "Quiet. Quiet, please." He returned to the trunk, swung the tails on his overcoat aside and adjusted his ascot up to his neck, and carefully retrieved a second bottle, the same size, and shape as the first. A hushed murmur fell over the crowd. In an elegant, if overly rehearsed, Welsh accent, he began.

"Ladies and Gentlemen, let me introduce myself. My name is Sir Walter Roberts, Medical Doctor, of Her Majesty's Foreign Service and I'm here to demonstrate to you, my honorable citizens of these wonderful United States and frontier territories, a marvelous elixir for bringing health and wellness to the wretched ills of the work-a-day mines. Waring's Tonic Water. Yes, a marvelous elixir combining the sweet syrup of the English maple tree, the eternally effervescent spring waters of the East Indies, and a touch of healing quinine, direct from the Orient, to create a tonic with properties so grand, I can hardly expound upon them. I dare say this spirituous and wonderful fluid gives the user such strength and vigor as to make him rise up from the ashes like the Phoenix in flame. A well-being tonic guaranteed to ameliorate sore muscles and aching joints and certified by Lord Thomas George Waring, the first Earl of Northbrook, as the secret to his vitality and a life-giving tincture. Taken twice daily, it resulted in the family Waring being ascended to the title of

Baron and Baroness over all Northbrook in the Pembrokeshire council area, a mountainous and remote county not dissimilar to this town of Creede, a delightful village of fine citizens at the sharpest edge of the steeled and stately Colorado Territory."

With a quick breath and the air of a showman, he continued.

"Let it be known, fine gentlemen, that the solution to your everyday pains, your relentless suffering can be eased and quieted with this concoction of syrups and medicines and healing herbs. Waring's Tonic Water. This delicious elixir provides days of relief and pounds of strength to your stamina. Each emerald bottle contains enough sustaining liquid to dispense a year or more's worth of robust vivacity and a confidence in limitless force. A single drop before the day begins creates a euphoric energy in the bones and a single drop in the evening before retiring will bring a sense of peace and calm."

The gentleman continued on, twirling the bottle, and proclaiming the end of aches and pains in a masterfully sultry and dignified voice. The crowd began to disperse, even as his oration ascended. A small cluster of men, giddy with the intoxicating words, stepped forward for a taste of the future and a changed life. William was intrigued by the pitch and even offered to buy a bottle from the gentlemen in exchange for a few moments of his time.

"I was wondering, sir, if you could tell me if you have come from the north recently. Any news of the Grand River crossing?"

"I cannot say, sir."

William purchased a bottle of the elixir and returned to camp.

On the last day in town, on his way to retrieve the horses from the stable, he encountered Sir Walter Roberts, again. This time he was perched in a wooden folding chair, legs crossed, reading a hardbound book, *On Liberty*, and casually taking in the afternoon air. After a brief discussion, William was invited to join Sir Walter Roberts for a "proper cocktail" as he put it. The two retired to the saloon, a stick-built building with an unusual name emblazoned across the entrance: *The Holy Moses.* Roberts took the lead, ordered a pair of gin shots, and began to hawk his tonic water on a much smaller scale. They sat at a teetering tabletop, held up by the stump of an elm as Roberts retrieved a folding, stag-handled horseman's knife from his inside pocket. The outer pocket of his coat contained a plum. He inspected it closely, winked at William, and sliced the plum into segments, removing the pit.

"Step one, place a bit of crushed ice in a glass, preferably clean. Step two, add any London dry gin, preferably Hodges' Old Style, but any clear grain liquor will do. Step three, top with Lord Waring's tonic water. Step four, garnish with a lemon and enjoy." Roberts placed a segment of the plum into the glass, admired his handiwork, and raised a glass. "To your health, and to the success of your journey. May you reach your destination on time and in good spirits."

William was taken aback by the formality of the toast, but held Roberts' gaze as he said, "To bein' fore-handed." They gently touched glasses, sipped their gin and tonics, and spoke about the finer things in life in the darkest corner of the grimiest saloon in Creede, a lawless domain of the Colorado Territory.

***

The wagon train continued, following the North Branch of the Spanish Trail along the Gunnison River. It was more than a hundred miles to Fort Uncompahgre where old Antoine Robidoux used to trade, and the Gunnison River crossing. The wagons rumbled on, northwesterly, following the old trail blazed by Atanasio Dominguez and Sylvestre Velez de Escalante in 1776. Around five in the afternoon, they turned off the trail at a side stream that Ford knew, to camp for the night.

***

Susan: Golden, CO, August 1982

Washington Avenue wasn't busy this Tuesday. Few people dared to venture out into the heat radiating off the stone facade buildings and bouncing off the concrete sidewalks. With the mountains still calling her name, Susan ambled along the storefronts, past the Gart's sporting goods store, and crossed the street to avoid the Ace-High Tavern. A sparkling array of jewelry, plates, and polished furniture caught her eye. She walked into the antique store and felt the soft wood floor creak and give under her feet. The sparkling front window cast reflective light about the darker interior. Remnants of the past sat in slumber, waiting for the right passerby, keeping time in decades.

Susan admired a quilt, eyed a collection of rusted miner's tools, and checked the price on a handsome armoire. The afternoon sun continued its dawdling and measured arc, as a chorus of chimes struck the two o'clock hour. Susan saw a twinkling blue-green reflection on the wallpaper to her left. She held a hand up, catching the light, and turned to find the source. The front window of the storefront narrowed her vision and drew her in like blinders on a workhorse furrowing the last row of the day. Susan caught the blue-green reflection in her palm again and located the origin. She picked up the tiny glass bottle, swaddled in a layer of ultra-fine dust, and read the words machine-pressed onto the side. *Waring's.* The glass of the bottle had air bubbles and inconsistencies throughout, and a chip was evident on the mouth. But the color of the glass was exquisitely unique. She held it in her hands, felt the cool of the glass, thought of the sand that bore it, and rubbed her fingers over the fine letters. She tried imagining those who might have held this bottle last.

Chapter 24

Jack and Tom: Golden, CO, August 1982

When Jack and Tom arrived at Frank's place, the morning still had a chill to it. Jack wanted to pick up the cases of beer his poker buddy had been saving for him. Tom hadn't met Frank yet, so he wandered around outside and checked the tires on the van. They were still there.

Free beer was always a reason to drive across town. Frank had been working at Coors for six years, but it had an added benefit: a case of beer provided with his paycheck every two weeks. After six years, the cases of beer had started to pile up in his kitchen.

Frank had never threatened to quit until the day he did. And he didn't give two weeks' notice or even two minutes' notice when he did. He simply said, "I'm not coming back here tomorrow," and walked out. He was eccentric and never used three words when just one would suffice, but Jack knew his backstory.

Frank was from a small town outside Durango where his family had a dairy farm. He was one of six siblings, somewhere in the middle. Before Vietnam, Frank's whole family took turns milking the Holsteins each morning.

Frank got his first draft notice six months before his eighteenth birthday.

So instead of getting drafted, he volunteered. It gave him a leg up on the draftees, maybe a higher quality enlistment service, something other than infantry. He ended up with radio repairman, in closer contact with the base, closer to where the vehicles, planes, welders, and explosives were kept.

He didn't know it then, but he'd learn to love these things. And by then, Frank had enough of the dairy business. The milk was clean and bright-white and the creamed butter was sweet and delicious, but the farm was dirty and the cows made a mess.

Frank left for Vietnam, via Fort Ord, California, in March 1969. He would never return to milking cows in Cortez. Between the sweet creamed butter and the faceless enemy in black pajamas, a drab-olive-colored divide had developed. But that was years ago.

Jack walked around to the back of Frank's house and found Frank asleep on the sofa under the aluminum patio.

"Frank, it's time, let's go." Jack nudged him awake and looked at his surroundings. Frank's place was littered with car parts, beer cans, and porno magazines. He lived in a house on the outskirts of Golden and didn't seem to miss the job at the Coors plant. *Don't forget to recycle the aluminum.*

Jack pushed Frank's lawn mower out of the way and the carburetor cover fell off blanging off the concrete, the echo rebounding off the aluminum overhead. Frank stirred, farted, and opened his eyes.

"What do you want?"

"It's time to go, my friend. Remember, we're camping, and you said I could have two cases." Jack pushed the lawn mower farther away and the cover slid along the concrete.

"Easy with that, asshole, it's a classic," grumbled Frank. He sat up a little more, farted again, and swung his legs out onto the ground.

"Let's go."

"Sure you got everything?" Jack asked, eyeing the scattered parts and doubting his poker buddy's organizational skills.

"Everything I need's in the Jeep. Anything I don't, ain't." Frank was a man of few words, but he chose them carefully. Despite his gruff demeanor and grumbling voice, he had a soft spot for friends, even Jack, who took fifty-eight dollars off him at last weekend's poker game.

"Three queens with an ace should have beaten your three-five-seven showing. Nobody plays four-six in the hole. I don't care if they were suited," said Frank, pulling off his socks and picking a mismatched pair from the laundry basket in the garage.

Jack learned to play poker in the Navy, and although he was a Vietnam War veteran, the closest he got to live action was the Philippines in 1968. He already had four years in by then and a ticket home. Honestly, he was happy to have avoided it. Jack had an air of confidence that most men lacked. Most people would have pegged him as an officer in a forward area. But his EOS left him a chief petty officer.

"Four-six in the hole. Them's cards I can get behind," he said. Jack was ready to make a run for it without the free beer, but Frank seemed to be going along with the whole camping thing, something Jack hadn't anticipated.

"Sit tight for a minute," said Frank.

Jack felt around in his shirt pocket and found the cigarillos. He pulled one from the pouch, smelling the earthy sweet aroma, and stuck it in his mouth while Frank rummaged around the back patio, made his way into the kitchen, cracked open a beer, and put the rest of the six-pack in a waxed cardboard box.

Jack followed him into the house, noticed a sickly sour smell, and decided to hang back by the still-open sliding glass door. "What's in the boxes, Frank?"

"Work stuff."

"You need four boxes of...uh...55% extra for work? What is this, Frank?"

"You don't want to know." Frank closed the lid on one of the boxes.

"Why is it marked with dates and ... uh, strength-to-weight ratio? What's ANFO? What is this?"

"It's dynamite," said Frank, casually. "But they're only half sticks and 55% extra, so don't worry, they won't have to put you back together with tweezers and forceps for your funeral. It just makes a little bang."

Jack didn't speak and slowly lowered the box back onto the table.

"In case it wasn't clear, I'm gonna follow you up there," said Frank. "I'll meet you at Echo Park a little later."

"OK. If you want," said Jack, chomping on the cigar.

They worked methodically, loading boxes, packing the camping stuff, and stashing away the beer in coolers. Tom was anxious to get back on the road. He turned the van around in the cul-de-sac and left the engine running.

Jack continued to help as best he could and thought about Frank. *This guy's nuts.* Frank hoisted a floor jack into the jeep. *What'd ya need a floor jack for on a camping trip? And dynamite? Who is this guy?*

"I'm ready," said Frank, slamming the tailgate closed. To Jack, Frank had always been a man of few words. Today, he'd said even fewer.

"Ok, finally," mumbled Tom, who paced back and forth near the van. He didn't seem to want to wait an extra five minutes. "Burnin' daylight."

Jack waved at Frank and switched the cigar to the other corner of his mouth. "Ya grumpy asshole," said Jack. Frank somehow sensed the insult and grinned like the cat that ate the canary. Like he'd forced a friend to call him an asshole on purpose. Jack just nodded back.

Tom piled in the van and slammed the door in one motion.

Jack still had the cigar, unlit, in the corner of his mouth. Frank placed another few items into the bed of his Jeep CJ-7 and slammed the half-door which made a crunching sound. The lap belts had been cut out years ago. He took the last big gulp of Coors, tossed the empty can in the front yard and drove up the road following Jack and Tom. They turned onto Old Golden Road and made for the interstate. It was 9:15 in the morning.

***

Ford: Powderhorn, Colorado Territory, October 1870

The sides of Ford's brown canvas tent had seen better days, as they flapped in the breeze. While the tent didn't exactly blend into the background, it didn't stand out either. Beyond the tent, a meandering stream flowed by, lazily searching for a lower elevation. Past the stream, a stand of trees stood watch, maybe in honor of the few dead or dying willows along the stream. Above it all and perhaps fifteen miles further on, an unnamed snow-capped peak anchored the backdrop, unmoving, unchanged, and unrelenting. A few clouds drifted helplessly by, the only signal of the passage of time.

Ford didn't want to look away from the scene to address his employer. And he didn't want his boss to look away from the beautiful sight either. So he held his gaze down the valley as he began to speak.

"There's something about a mountain stream that makes it special. Different from the ocean, certainly, but also different from a lake or even a big river. In a stream you can see life moving right before your eyes—seasons change, insects hatch, fly and reproduce, all in a matter of minutes. The water moves, transforms almost, giving life." Ford was watching downstream, the sun at his back, and enjoyed a moment of peace. The solitude, to the few who paused long enough to see it, gave respite and relief.

In this part of the country, most of the rivers and streams ran generally northwesterly, away from the highest peaks of the Rocky Mountains. This stream was no different than many he'd traversed. Yet somehow it was unique. Maybe it was the miles he'd walked or ridden, never noticing the tranquility all around him. Maybe it was time for him to slow down. The thought of it brought Ford to tears.

***

The horses nickered and whinnied at the smells from somewhere in the darkness. William listened intently to the sounds of the wilderness, just as the men settled in for the evening, each wanting something different. By candlelight, he scratched out a few sentences.

***

Jack and Tom: Georgetown, CO, September 1982

Their destination lay west. West used to mean toward the setting sun in the Atlantic. Then, west meant across the Allegheny Plateau in the frontier regions of Pennsylvania. After, west meant beyond the Mississippi River. Now, west meant across the continental divide. And the nearest way west advanced via the Eisenhower Tunnel.

The Tunnel, part of Interstate 70, was built at an elevation of over eleven thousand feet and crossed under the continental divide at the saddle between Sunbeam Peak and Gander Mountain at an elevation of thirteen thousand feet. The tunnel was two thousand feet underground. At the time of its construction in 1973, it was the longest tunnel in the interstate highway system and the highest vehicular tunnel in the world. During the three-and-a-half minutes it took to drive the tunnel, neither Tom nor Jack spoke.

Exiting the tunnel into a sun-filled valley and continuing on their road trip, Tom and Jack turned northerly onto Highway 9 at the town of Silverthorne. Tom grabbed the Ohio package from the backseat and began perusing the letters. For some unknown reason, a single-page letter caught his eye and he read aloud to Jack, staring into the two-lane.

October 2, 1870

My darling Sarah Ann,

We have just crossed over to the downhill section of our journey. My guide, Ford, has assured me we are on the right route. We have crossed several small streams, the names of which are unknown to me, but have arrived at a place Ford says is called Powderhorn. Tomorrow we will drive our wagons across the Cimarron River, an area upstream of which Ford says is unexplored. Some of our party wish to stop and pan for a day before continuing on, but I have assured them, we will not wait. My journey is only half complete and it is the memory of our time together that urges me on. No amount of gold or silver will keep us apart.

Good night my love and sweet dreams.

Yours,

William Mitchell

***

Jack: Steamboat Springs, CO, September 1982

It was a quarter to noon by the time they drove into town. Frank, Jack and Tom ate hamburgers from the diner and Frank ordered a piece of lemon meringue pie.

"Got a sweet tooth, Frank?" asked Jack.

"Yeah, I guess."

"Let's get back on the road," said Tom. He was anxious to have some more quiet time perusing the letters. The script was fine, elegant even, but difficult to read while bouncing down the road. Tom tried to imagine this man from somewhere in his family's past, sitting down to write a letter. And the dedication and devotion he demonstrated to his wife was something missing in his own life. Tom had had girlfriends, some serious, some not, but he'd never felt like William apparently had. And where was *his* homestead? What it must have felt like to travel cross-country with all your possessions in a covered wagon and wagering it all on a hope, a promise, or an expectation.

Chapter 25

Andrew: Golden, CO, September 1982

Andrew followed Susan into Golden, pausing at each block, hoping to parallel her turns a block back. When she finally got out of the Ford Taurus and walked under the "Howdy Folks" arch, he parked on a side street and got out on foot. He continued quickly up the street, avoiding the few pedestrians and making note of concealment options along the way. Susan casually entered the restaurant, then exited in less than thirty seconds. She walked up the street and stopped at a tiny sandwich shop called 'The Alley'. Andrew took the opportunity and walked right up to her.

***

Susan: Golden, CO, September 1982

While she was seated alone, several other customers sat at outside tables, and occasional people strolled by, window shopping on

Washington Street.

"Taking in the sights, I see."

"Andrew! What are you doing *here*?" Susan's eyes flitted back and forth in an uneasy assessment of the public interruption.

"I told you I'd be in Fort Collins the same time you were here, just checking up on you."

"Are you *following* me?"

"Just keeping tabs on my wife."

"Ex-wife," she said, quieter but still aloud. She sat up in the chair.

"Yeah, well, I can still keep tabs on you. Don't want you getting into trouble."

"Trouble?"

"I talked to Tom just after you. He didn't seem all that helpful and thought he might be sending you to some dive."

"That wasn't Tom, you idiot." Susan regretted escalating the situation. She felt ashamed of Andrew and embarrassed for him making such a scene.

"It wasn't?"

"No, that was his roommate. He does the maintenance and yardwork for the three duplexes. What is it you're doing here?"

"Oh, uh, there was a delay on one of my cases for a week and I thought I would check up on you. What were you doing in that Woody's restaurant?"

The tone in Susan's voice sharpened when she saw the friendly waitress within earshot. "You are following me, creep. What's wrong with you?"

"Listen," said Andrew, raising his voice and using the black uniform to its full effect. "Don't make me call down the big boys from Washington DC on this. I just need to meet your contact to make sure you're safe."

"Stop making a scene," said Susan trying to keep quiet but still sound confident in a crowd of onlookers.

"Where can I find this Tom guy?"

"You were just at his house. And it's none of your business. He's just a history contact, for cryin' out loud. Is that safe enough for you?"

"And where's the letters he supposedly obtained?"

"Why do you care?" Susan could feel Andrew's jealousy. Or jealousy disguised as resentment. He might try to destroy her career with sabotage or false accusations.

"Just curious," said Andrew, sweating from his brow. Most of the restaurant's eyes were upon him.

"I haven't talked to him, so I don't know. I don't understand what you're doing here."

"Can't a husband keep an eye on his wife," asked Andrew.

Susan felt people staring at them. She raised her voice slightly and said, "Now you're really pissing me off. I don't need you snooping on me night and day like some crazed stalker. What I do is none of your business. It's a routine assignment. I already got the go-ahead from the museum to make an offer to buy them if necessary. They've increased my allotment fund to two-fifty." Her voice trailed off at the end as she dug in her purse for a tissue.

"Two hundred fifty dollars, I don't think that's going to sway too many punks with an arrowhead to give up the goods."

Susan calmly wiped the corner of her left eye, sat up straight, and looked Andrew in the eye. "The allotment fund is two hundred fifty thousand. So yeah. And it's not any of your concern."

"Oh, uh, that's great. Let's go shopping!"

"It doesn't work like that, Andrew. Every item has to be properly provenanced, cataloged, and expensed down to the penny from an affiliate museum or private donor. Similar to the chain of custody for evidence."

"I knew I'd be wasting my time here. I'm heading back to Fort Collins. Did you get the letters from him or not?"

"No, not yet. I told you already. And maybe you should get back to what you were sent here for. Your lieutenant is the one should be doing the checking up. Don't you think, dear?"

***

Andrew: Golden, CO August 1982

With that, Andrew's face turned another shade of red and his ears started to burn. "I knew I was wasting my time." He turned, knocked a chair out of the way, and walked angrily up the street toward Woody's and his patrol car. He would make it his mission to finally get to Tom, whoever he was. He wasn't going to let Susan beat him.

Andrew returned to his car, made a U-turn, and stopped at the traffic light. He took out a little glass vial and did a line of coke from off the saddle between his thumb and index finger. He put away his secret and turned back onto Washington Street. Just as he did the radio sounded in the patrol car.

"Collins patrol car forty-five, report your ten-eight and ten-twenty. Agent Harrison, are you available?

Andrew grabbed the mic off the dash and stammered bits and

barks into the airwaves. An air of superiority or arrogance came through in just four syllables. "Yes. What is it?"

"We've had a call from a Lieutenant Gilroy. He'd like a ten-twenty-two. Over."

"Tell him I'll call him from the Golden substation within the hour."

"Uh, ten-four, Harrison, ten-five Gilroy. Over."

Andrew punched the gas, spun some gravel into the wheel well and headed to the local precinct he had seen from the highway.

"Collins forty-five, that's a ten-five to Gilroy. Do you copy? Over."

"Yes, I copy. Ten-four. Now stop bothering me with this penny-ante bullshit. Copy dip-shit? Over and out." Andrew turned the squelch knob up to five and clicked the thumb receiver three times. "Dumbass." Andrew had enough of their small-town antics. He was angry at himself that he had walked into Susan's allotment fund trap and couldn't believe he'd underestimated his wife, er, ex-wife, and made a mistake in assuming the burly man in muckin' boots was Tom. He wasn't about to make any more mistakes.

***

William and Ford: Little Cimarron River, Colorado Territory, October 1870

The men packed up their belongings, enjoying the warming sun, and continued on the last leg of their journey. Ford led the procession with his pack mule with William walking along, just behind. The cross-slope of the trail eased to just noticeable, particularly on the downhill side. The valley opened up before them, dotted with very modest homes, lean-tos, and a smattering of cattle. As they approached, details began to emerge about the beginnings of a town. A group of homesteaders in the Uncompahgre River valley.

In the foreground and nearest to them, a cabin appeared. It was relatively new and of exceptional quality. It was also unusual to see a second story in such a remote location. The house was built of rough-hewn timber with white clay patched in between the logs. The second story was pine planked and clapboarded leaving just enough room for a tall window at the gabled roof line. A bone-bleached sliver of cloth drifted through the glassless window opening. At some point more recently, the western half of the porch had been enclosed. For now, the chimney was still, and no smoke rose from it. The noon-day sun began to warm the men as they strode ahead. Stands of cottonwoods waved, letting go of their leaves, telling the story of the wind. Not a cloud remained, and the horizon was clear. The most distant sights included low cliff-lined mountains with virgin timber on their flanks. The Gunnison River valley. Montrose.

***

Susan: Golden, CO, August 1982

Susan wiped another tear and glared as Andrew walked away. She stuffed the tissue back in her purse. *Not one more...* Before she could get a word out, a waitress stepped up and set a glass of water down. "He's not worth it, whoever he is, dear. You're better off without him, anyway."

Susan glanced up, the sun bright in her eyes, and quickly looked down again. "Uh, thank you, uh ..."

"I've got two ex-husbands, and neither of 'em's worth a damn." The waitress smiled, pulled a red and white peppermint candy from her apron pocket, and set it down. Susan did her best to smile back, but a look of defiance was all she could manage. The waitress tucked a notepad into the front of her apron and slid behind Susan. She pulled a big umbrella stand closer to the table and cranked it open. As she turned to leave, she winked at Susan. "Men," was all she said. The waitress pulled out the notepad again and walked up to the adjacent table. "What else can I get for you?"

***

After lunch, Susan wasn't ready to get back in the car right away. So she opted for a walk along the main street, down to the creek, and then along a side street. At the far end, the street angled away from the creek into a cul-de-sac. A wide sidewalk that wound through leafy green bushes growing in the shade of cottonwood trees ran along the creek. Susan continued walking, taking in the fresh air and listening to the creek crinkle and scrabble along the rocks.

She thought about Andrew, about the mistakes in their marriage, and about how she could avoid seeing him when she inevitably moved out. The move would take several days. She'd need to organize her things, pack up the kitchen and deal with the landlord. The harder she thought about it, the faster she walked. The farther she got, the easier the move seemed to become. What did she really need from the apartment, anyway? And what would another apartment be except a shelter between commutes to work?

She walked and listened to the birds in the trees. Somewhere in the foliage, a black-capped chickadee sang: *mee-ker, mee-ker.* The creek continued, a constant stream of fresh water coming from who knows where, seemingly always from just beyond the next bend. She walked on, listening to the crunch of her shoes in the gravel beneath her feet.

After forty-five minutes, she was two miles away in a residential neighborhood of big, two-acre-sized lots. The homes were all unique, some with barns and wood-rail paddocks. People seemed more at ease than they would have been back home. A woman clipped rose bushes, some kids were playing hide-and-seek, and a teenager was washing his car. Susan then noticed an older man waving a fly rod in the stream. She could only see his silhouette in the sparkling creek. In the background, a mountain rose up, disappeared out of view behind the trees, then reappeared again at an acute angle higher above.

Susan slowed her pace, then stopped when the fly-fisher reappeared in a window framed by cottonwoods. A calm started to ease over her. Susan suddenly thought she heard footsteps. She looked over her shoulder, expecting to see a black suit. Instead, a little cotton-tailed bunny hopped across the trail and froze in place. She let a smile escape and locked eyes with the rabbit. A breeze swayed the branch of a golden currant and caught Susan's eye. When she looked back, the little bunny was gone. She turned back to the window on the stream. The flyfisher picked up his line and began another overhead swing. His cast was like a syrupy, sinuous dance with an unseen partner. Susan continued, slower now, watching the fly fisherman until he disappeared from view. She picked up the pace again and passed the last house that backed up to the trail. As she was walking, the cottonwoods thinned and the blue sky brightened her view. With an entirely different view, she stopped at a clearing of sedge grass. The breeze was bending and swaying the grass in near uniformity, to and fro, in harmony with the last of the cottonwood trees. The path led away from the creek and back into an open space with few houses. She was alone.

Clouds threatened rain, but the mountains continued to dominate her periphery. They were so silent, so large, and so unmoving. How had she never seen this before? And why had she never felt their power, their draw, their energy? Susan heard some leaves shuffle behind her. She turned, fearful for a split second, then stood defiantly, waiting for Andrew to emerge from behind the tree.

"A beautiful day for a walk, isn't it?" A stately woman spoke in a soft yet bold tone.

"Yes, it is," said Susan, a spark of relief on her face.

The woman introduced herself as Katherine Jennings but preferred to be called Kat and commented on Susan's view. Susan eyed her cautiously. The two continued with some idle chit-chat, talking about the mountains, the streamside trail, and about the neighborhood. Susan politely gave way, realizing Kat could tell she was from out of town. She noticed the rather unusual, strappy, buckled boots Kat wore but didn't dare comment on them. The two walked on, talking and taking in the western sky. Their conversation was only occasionally broken by the sound of the crunching gravel under their feet or a chickadee hidden in the foliage overhead.

"Sometimes people see these mountains for the first time and are drawn to tears," said Kat. "I moved here from Kansas when I was nine, and I remember thinking mountains would be fun to play in. Of course, a nine-year-old doesn't understand the rugged nature of the mountains or the dangers."

"It's just so beautiful here," said Susan.

"I can show you some properties if you like."

"What do you mean?"

"I'm a realtor. I was just showing a home to a young couple from Denver. It's a big city, and Golden is really close, but it feels like a world away. The mountains do that, ya know."

"I'm not really in the market right now," said Susan.

"It's alright, I want to show you this gem of a property up by Evergreen. Have you been to Evergreen?"

"I'm afraid not. I'm just here for work for a few days and don't expect to come back."

"Let me show it to you anyway. It might change your mind. I have to go up there to meet the roof inspector."

"Oh, I don't know, I'm supposed to..."

"It's no big deal, Suz. It might inspire you to move to the mountains one day."

Susan hated being called anything other than her full name but felt comfortable talking to Kat. "It's funny you mention that. I swear, I heard something back there by the creek. It was just the wind, but for a moment, I thought the mountain was trying to tell me something. It's weird, I know."

"It's not weird at all. The mountains speak to almost everyone." Kat paused for effect. "But they only speak to people when you're alone, when you feel small, or when you need it the most."

"What?"

"The mountains are alive. Just don't tell anybody else," said Kat.

"I'm not sure I can do that."

"People have been moving here from back East in droves the last few years. I'd hate to see this property go to some yuppy from Philadelphia who doesn't know a horse's ass from a hole in the ground."

With the mention of Philadelphia, Susan recalled the mugging from just a few weeks ago. Her face froze in place, and the allure of the mountains were stripped away.

They continued talking, Kat mostly, with Susan nodding and confirming Kat's observations. The two walked on as the open meadow slowly morphed into a more rugged sort of tumbling hillside with majestic trees she didn't recognize. Susan slowly forgot about the past.

The walk in the fresh mountain air certainly did something for her soul. They walked and talked all the way back past the houses and up to the creek. Susan secretly hoped the fly-fisherman would be there and the near-religious moment would return. Instead, a man and his dog were playing in the water on the far side of the bank.

As they got closer, the dog barked and a little laugh escaped from behind a stand of trees. Again, Susan thought Andrew might suddenly spring up from out of nowhere. Instead, Kat casually said, "Well, this is me." She took three more big steps and untied a dark chestnut horse from the split-rail fence.

"Oh, my god, that's a horse. I didn't know..."

Kat led the giant beast closer as Susan stepped back in awe.

"Is that yours? What are you...."

"Of course she's mine. Holly here is my regular ride to properties in this neighborhood. I live just two miles upstream and the trail gives her a chance to stretch her legs."

"I haven't been on a horse since... How do you..."

"It's ok, Suz..."

The look on Susan's face showed fear, as the horse stammered back, snorted, and pricked her ears. Although this was a residential neighborhood, no one seemed to notice the majestic creature. And despite the row of homes stretching back towards town, few people populated the area, and certainly no one within earshot.

Susan hesitated, then blurted it out. "I wanted to ask you about your boots, but uh...are those horse boots?" Susan realized right away she had no idea what she was asking. *Horse boots?* She thought to herself. *This woman must think I'm an idiot.*

"These are my regular riding boots, yes." Kat let the faux pas fade.

"Where did you learn about horses?"

"In the Westernaires. It's a club for high school girls. You start by mucking stalls, brushing the horses, and hauling hay. Then, you learn to ride, Western-style mostly, and we did parades and little shows. It was great."

"Western-style?" asked Susan, still eyeing Kat's boots.

"Yes, as opposed to English style."

"Oh...," came the reply. "I used to ride horses at summer camp in Tennessee when I was a little girl. I can't remember too much about it though. But I stopped going after..." An uneasy pause bubbled up for a beat as Susan realized she almost revealed a hidden pain she'd kept for too many years. Kat let the moment pass, as Susan tried to think of something intelligent to say. "Those buckles on your boots are part of the horse's um, outfit?" Susan was still in shock.

"No, these are spurs. They're just a little reminder to Holly, here, that I'm in charge. These are what you'd call bump spurs. See? They're just little bumps on the back of the heel. The leather straps buckle over the top of any boot. Bump spurs are common in barrel racing. Horses have tough hides and thick skin. But don't be afraid of Holly, she's a gentle little filly."

Susan was still a little stunned and felt suddenly out of place in her rubber-soled, tasseled, low-heeled, Samantha Worthington wedges. She took another step back and realized she was standing in the grass, on the far side of the trail.

"Filly?" asked Susan.

Kat laughed, smiled, and pushed Holly onto the trail, sidestepping gingerly. She grabbed the saddle horn, tested the cinch strap, and hoisted a boot into the stirrup. "Us fillies have to stick together," she said as she pulled on the horn, and hopped her right boot off the ground. In a single motion, she pulled herself up in the air and slung a leg over the cantle, and adjusted her hips into the seat. "Call me at the office in the morning, we'll check out that property in Evergreen, and we can talk about getting you some boots." Kat extended a red and blue business card toward Susan.

"Ok," said Susan, still trying to gain her composure. With Kat in the saddle, she was so much taller and intimidating. Susan was cautious of the horse and kept her distance as Kat turned the horse around, waved, and touched her heels to the animal. Holly went from a gentle walk to a trot seamlessly and clip-clopped down the trail. Susan didn't realize she was still smiling until she noticed her face hurt. How long had it been since she was up close to a horse? All she could think about was Mister Ed and how she couldn't remember anything about horses. How wild was the West? What else was she unaware of in this part of the world? She tried to remember riding horses at summer camp but she wanted to forget so much from that time. Susan watched as Kat rounded the next bend in the trail and disappeared. She felt relieved and refreshed, somehow. And ready to get back to work.

As Susan watched them go, she turned to take in another mountain view and was surprised to see the fly fisherman from earlier standing in the stream, barely fifty feet away. He was fidgeting with something, then pulled a tool on a zipper from his vest. Susan couldn't see what he was doing but noticed all the jangly clips and snips hanging from his vest. He cautiously replaced a little bottle of something and tossed an invisible fly into the air. He unfurled big armfuls of green fishing line, more apparent than she had seen before, and twisted and curled the rod until the line stretched out behind him. He took another two steps into the stream, now above his knees, and began slinging the rod overhead. The dance began again. The partner appeared to be a large set of boulders just ahead. He tossed the line behind, then forward in a slow, swaying curl, inches off the water, then delicately replaced it in nearly the same spot as a tiny brown insect landed atop the mirrored glass, nary a splash or dimple in the water.

Susan realized she knew nothing about this fly-fishing. But she would learn at the earliest opportunity.

Chapter 26

Andrew: Golden, CO, August 1982

Andrew had taken a risk at Tom's house and he wasn't going to let another opportunity slip through his fingers. His post at Fort Collins was delayed one more day and he wanted to know for sure what his wife was up to. Ex-wife. So he called in a few favors at the local substation. It was a large complex of combined law enforcement agencies, Department of Corrections administration personnel, and a vehicle maintenance yard. He had to show his badge and sign in at multiple desks before they got him to a secure phone line. He called Lieutenant Gilroy, but he was out, so he left a message for him with the duty sergeant. He called again and asked to be transferred to the CRAWL desk and asked about any new requests for assistance in Colorado. While Fort Collins was waiting, maybe he could set up a takedown in a smaller town, or at least let his lieutenant think he was on the job. There was one request from the week before in Steamboat Springs. He didn't know where that was and didn't really care. He jotted down the information and tucked it away for a just-in-case type of situation.

He made some notes, careful to not be too obvious, and then quietly started making inquiries about Susan. He was able to track down her flight information easily but then waited on hold for fifteen minutes before he got her credit card statement and found her hotel reservation. A drive back towards the airport was not what he wanted to do right now, but it might finally put Susan in a desperate enough situation, she might need his help. She might need a law enforcement professional. She might need an ambitious man to clean up her career intentions. And she might need to get laid. And then she might need to shut her mouth and stay at home, like he expected.

Andrew drove the shiny police cruiser to Susan's hotel, parked right in front by the pressure-activated sliding glass doors, and asked for her room number. Andrew was certain he was ahead of Susan's schedule, but he knocked on the door first, with no answer. He located a Hispanic housekeeper at the end of the hall, flashed his badge, and hurried her to unlock the room.

Once inside, Andrew recognized Susan's smell and even spied her regular travel clothes in the closet. A handful of notebooks, folders, and a book on Shoshone traditions sat on the desk adjacent to the television. In the back of the second folder, Susan made some handwritten notes on a typed page on Smithsonian letterhead. Andrew read through the typed page and saw what Susan was so interested in. The series of letters from 1869 and 1870 outlined a pair of wagons traveling along the North Branch of the Old Spanish Trail, and then on towards the Vernal Valley in Uintah County, Utah. He began to sense Susan's growing interest in the letters.

Andrew leafed through the photocopies to the last page and read the last letter in the series. The cursive was elegant, measured, and surprisingly neat for a man's writing. He patiently read through the lines, direct from 1870. This man, the husband, had made a deal with the

Mormons for arms to eradicate the emigrants traveling along the Oregon-California Trail through their territory. And they wanted to use the Indians to do it.

Andrew had never been to Utah, but he knew some Mormons practiced polygamy and would prefer to simply keep their heads down, avoiding confrontation to keep their religion their own. And the Indians, whatever was left of them, had surely been starved, shot, beaten, and moved to reservations as part of that process. They would want some vindication and they would want the proof of the Mormon atrocities and their elitist, racist motives.

Even Andrew had heard of the Meadow Creek Massacre and the possible repercussions of that whole mess. How was anyone supposed to rectify the wrongs of an entire nation of people against a group of emigrants from more than a hundred years ago? And using the Indians to do it. Maybe bringing this episode of history to light was part of Susan's plan. A publicized press event, displaying the original documents, recognizing the decades of mistreatment of the Indians and the crimes perpetrated against the wagon train emigrants. The claims of persecution, prosecution, and systematic fraud by the Mormons. And this was verifiable evidence.

Andrew didn't see the point. The past was the past and there'd be no fixing it. He didn't want Susan uncovering anything and certainly not in front of an audience. He turned back to the typed page. This was exactly Susan's plan. *Susan's success.* He would be humiliated, his lies of a happy marriage exposed. A press-release event, recognizing the wrongs of the past, to propel her career forward, all at his expense. And at the expense of Mormons from over a hundred years ago. How could Susan do this to Andrew so publicly? Susan would humiliate him and the entire state of Utah at the same time. How could she be so cruel, so callous, to her husband?

Andrew jotted down some notes about the photocopied letters, eyed Susan's handwriting in the margins, and then saw what he needed. It was Tom's mother's phone number. Even a punk like Tom knew to call his mom once a week. Andrew checked the peephole, then pulled the curtain back to reveal Susan's view. His police cruiser was just visible under the awning of the hotel's front entrance. He tapped the glass vial in his pocket, did a spoonful, and wiped at his nose just as Susan pulled into the parking lot. She walked with such purpose, those hips clocking back and forth like she was on some kind of mission. He'd have to put a stop to that and maybe climb those hips one last time.

Andrew replaced the folder, put the book back just as he remembered it, and turned to leave. He spied the familiar romance novel on the nightstand as a fire burned in his gut. Like a cold smack to the face, he realized what being divorced would mean to his career path. He recalled the day he graduated from the FBI academy. *His greatest achievement.* Susan had asked for a divorce the next day. *What was she trying to do to him?* Every other supervisor was married, owned a home. A stable home life exhibited tranquility and calm. A happily married G-man was the expectation. He'd never get over it. Enraged, emaciated, and emasculated, he cursed Susan's name, closed the door behind him, and calmly walked down the hall to the fire exit. The black suit disappeared down the stairs just as Susan stepped off the elevator onto the third floor.

***

Susan: Denver, CO, September 1982

Susan was still beaming from her experience in the mountains, still searching her mind for what she could recall about horses. Somehow she couldn't quite connect the dots between the woman on horseback, the mountains calling her name, and the image of the older man fly-fishing in the creek.

Inside the comforts of the carpeted hotel, she strolled with an air of confidence at having opened a new area of her mind. It didn't matter that the lack of oxygen from the elevation at the mile-high city affected most people negatively. She was on an indescribable high. She was on a personal journey. And she wasn't going to let anyone get in her way anymore.

She collected the papers and books she'd been working on when a single sheet caught her eye. She had already read it once before, but this time it struck a chord deep inside her. She read silently to herself:

September 26, 1870

Dearest Sarah Ann,

How I long to see you. Although we are separated by many months and many miles, I can still feel your beauty and a closeness in our hearts. There are hard days ahead and more lonely nights to bear, but my destination is within reach.

Yesterday, we crossed the Gunnison River, a wide but gently flowing current of water. On the other side, a small band of Uncompahgre Utes sought to trade with us and I was able to negotiate a favorable outcome for some in my party. My guide, Ford, speaks some of their language and he was invited back to their seasonal camp for three days of trading. We are awaiting his return and resting the stock animals.

Give your father my assurances and love to the rest of your family.

Respectfully yours,

William Mitchell

Chapter 27

Jack and Tom: Dinosaur, CO, September 1982

Jack and Tom made it to the diner in Dinosaur on Thursday at 3:45 in the afternoon. Jack drove on over to the U-tot-em convenience store and picked up a couple bags of ice. He also bought a pouch of Garcia y Vega cigars just in case his box of Cuesta Rey Caravelles didn't last the trip. The pouch of five cigars fit in his shirt pocket in front of his banded wallet like they were made just for him. Tom and Jack were excited to take the little dory on the river.

"This oughta be fun," said Tom, smiling, then stating the obvious in an agitated tone, "Damn that van is ugly."

Less than fifteen minutes later, Frank rolled up in his fully outfitted jeep. Together again, the three men shook hands, smiling in the afternoon sun, lords of it all, without a care in the world. Within an hour, they were setting up camp at Echo Park, a wide spot on the Green River a few miles below Granite Springs Reservoir. Tom was ready to float the smooth ribbon of river eighteen miles in length. They parked Frank's jeep at the bottom for a shuttle.

***

Tom pulled on an oar as Jack, standing in a foot of muddy water, pushed off from the red sandy shore and piled into the boat. Tom crossed the main channel, spun the boat around like a beetle on its back, and rowed into an eddy, slowing their descent.

Jack unfurled his fly line, the leader dragging under the swirl of the eddy. He pulled clear of Tom's oar and clicked off two arm-lengths of fly line. He gained the advantage with the fly line, most of it tailing behind him, lifted the line from the water and tossed it forward, pausing just above and parallel with the water, and mirrored the flow of the current. Tom eased the oars back, keeping the dory in place, calling out faster riffles, boulders near the shore and deeper pools downstream.

Jack continued wrestling the fly line, attempting to find a pattern, a repeatable motion that covered the water with his oversized wet fly. After five minutes of Tom keeping them in place, he turned a j-stroke deeper alongside the boat, maneuvering them out of the eddy. When they hit the swifter water, the little dory dipped and dove, knocking Jack to one knee. The boat swerved again, nicking an oar on a boulder. Tom lost control. In a split second, the riverboat spun on its axis and he struggled to regain control.

Some swearing, knocking about of gear, and the sun blinding the oarsman caused Jack to halt the fishing and search for the life preservers. There were none. Jack struggled to stand again as Tom continued to fight the current. Recovering trim and flaps control, Tom back-stroked into some slower water at the shoreline.

"Let's do that again," said Frank, relaxing with a spliff.

"Uh, let's not," said Jack.

Exasperated and exhilarated at the same time, Tom said "I'll try to do a little better with the controls from now on. The plan is to find those eddies where we can stay in place for a little while so you can touch a fly on every piece of water." Tom dunked a hand in the cold water, wiped his mustache, and re-gripped the oars. "I'll announce ahead when we're gonna move, Jack."

Tom reached into his fly wallet revealing an army of ants, beetles, spinners, and mayflies. "Retie a big salmon fly on there, Jack, and cut down on the length of leader. Maybe a stonefly nymph." Tom's knowledge from the *Field & Stream* magazines and so much time meticulously spent at Gart's were showing. He felt good displaying it.

Jack did just as Tom suggested, tying a seven-foot length leader directly to a yellow and tan stonefly imitation, grizzly hairs sticking out every which way and disguising the number ten hook. Tom announced his movements, easing the dory back into the main channel and then rowing into a manageable pocket of water between little rapids where the water sought out the easiest path. The water twisted and twirled, fighting silently, beating the rocks with the death of a million waves, creating and recreating itself again and again.

Jack eased into a rhythm, trying to capture some of the river's power. He nestled the fly ahead of at least a dozen boulders, with little success. He tossed the fly line farther ahead, tightened the slack, and watched patiently as the fly grazed past a plate-sized gravel bar. The fly rode the power of the river past, undisturbed. Jack tightened the slack again to throw the fly when the line suddenly went taut. A little surprised, Jack tugged hard on the line, set the hook on a trout in the side of its mouth, and started reeling.

The trout reacted, lept and finned, and swam with the flow of the river. Jack took up the slack and reeled the excess line near his feet. Tom announced a release into the faster current to keep up with the swimming trout. Jack reeled as Tom harnessed the power in the river, gliding over the gentle waves. Frank reached down into the water and netted a colorful, red-banded rainbow trout.

Jack held up a seventeen-inch trout, looked the fish in the eye, winked at Tom, and unhooked the fish, releasing it back to the depths from where it came.

"Not a keeper?" asked Tom, rowing back into the calm.

"The cast-iron skillet is thirteen inches across, so a fifteen-inch trout is the max, plus, there's plenty more where that came from." Jack's face glowed in the afternoon sun. He lit a cigar and concentrated on his surroundings.

After a break, Jack offered to switch with Tom. The two hunched, squatted, and scooted, careful to not upset the delicate balance of the dory with the powerful river or Frank napping. Tom tied on a smaller fly, a hare's ear nymph. Tom immediately started catching. With the sun at his back, Tom could see the trout rise from the bottom, nearly invisible, gracefully turn with the current and capture the fly from behind, just as it drifted by.

After nine catches in barely twenty minutes, Tom offered to switch with Jack again. Jack had a glisten of sweat on his brow, not from rowing in the sun, but from the envious position of watching while Tom reeled in fish after fish. The two swapped positions and glided the dory into the next upturning pocket of water. Jack tied on a similar fly and tossed it into the deepest pool they'd seen yet, a living-room-sized bowl of water with a depth unknowable.

The river seemed to slow, tired of its circuitous journey as Tom lessened the force of the oar strokes. Jack spat the remains of his stubby cigar into the water, a hiss escaping on the wind. In an instant, Jack's rod bent over in half. He pivoted in the little dory, reeled in the slack and tugged on the line. A flash of silver and gold streaked in the depths, the sun seeking the beautiful skin and scales of its opposing life force.

Jack fought as the fish refused to give up the safety of the deep pool. Tom pulled on the oars and the trout revealed its true nature. The trout swam into the fastest, deepest water, fifty yards downstream, seeking another den of safety. Tom struggled to maneuver the boat and keep up with the battle. As he did, the boat neared a cluster of trees, hung up in an overhanging willow, which were wrapped around a stranglehold of rocks submerged just beneath the water. Jack continued reeling. But in the same flash of time as when Jack first hooked the fish, the line broke and the fish was gone.

After an hour with no hook-ups, Jack lit another cigar, bit off the end, and changed seats with Tom. Tom tied a copper john and spun a bit of sheep's wool farther up the line as a kind of indicator, a depth gauge to ensure the hook would just bump along the bottom, skimming over the deeper gravel bars and pockets of still water.

After four or five casts, Tom retrieved his fly and tied on another wet fly, a peacock-bodied, pheasant-tail nymph in a dark gray. The same sheep's wool indicator remained, but he trimmed it with some tiny scissors, leaving the fly five or six inches higher in the water column. The first cast unfurled and Tom expected to unwind more fly line to get more distance, but the hookup was immediate. Over the next twenty minutes, Tom caught nine rainbow trout and three German brown trout, all on the same fly, all in the same manner, not thirty feet from the dory. As they approached the end of the float, Tom netted three more and tossed each in the Coleman cooler. Few words were exchanged.

Tom swapped with Jack again. He attempted to repeat Tom's method. The sheep's wool indicator was a little wetter, the sun a little lower, and the water a little slower. Jack had a strike on two of the first five casts, drifting the fly over similar gravel bars and pocket waters as Tom had. But the two strikes caught no trout. And no more trout were willing after that. With the takeout in sight, Jack cursed the trout and admired the river, even as he smiled at Tom.

Chapter 28

Susan: Denver, CO, September 1982

Susan knew something wasn't right the second she walked into her hotel room. It was Andrew's smell. She was disgusted by it. Disgusted with his attitude. Something sickly sweet with a plastic sort of aroma. Maybe it was the starch in his black pants or the bleach in his white shirts combined with the cologne he insisted on wearing. She wasn't putting up with it anymore. While nothing seemed missing or out of place, she'd had enough of his shenanigans. She called the front desk to ask for another room. After a furious packing fit, she reconsidered. She called Tom's mother and reached her on the second ring. Not wanting to alarm the poor woman and with a delicate sense of professionalism honed from years of careful negotiations, Susan continued with pleasantries and then asked where Tom was at that very moment and how he could be reached.

After the conversation, Susan realized that her ex-husband had already contacted his mother. *Why couldn't he just leave well enough alone?* It bothered Susan, but she was also renewed. The experience with the realtor in Golden told her that there was more to life than commuting on a train and that the West held more promise than she had ever realized. She'd traveled all over the country and had been to Europe twice. The work she had been doing recently might propel her career forward, but it had come at the cost of her happiness. She wasn't about to let it win. And Andrew wasn't going to outsmart her either. Somehow, some way she'd get what she deserved.

With the West and the mountains calling her, Susan canceled the rest of her hotel reservation, and traded in her rental car for something a little more rugged, a Toyota Land Rover, at a cost of over sixty-five dollars a day, plus the insurance at another eight dollars per day. At the first gas station on her side of the road, she stopped and did something slightly out of character.

"Hello?"

"Hi, Kat? This is Susan from the other day on the trail."

"Oh, sure. Ready to see that property in Evergreen? I was thinking of taking Holly in the trailer and maybe letting her wander around the pasture there."

"Uh, no, not yet. I was wondering..."

"Not a big deal, what can I do for you? Interested in a condo closer to town?"

"Want to go shopping?" Susan suddenly wished she hadn't called. She turned into the blue and white cocoon of the phone stanchion and almost whispered. "Is this too weird?" Susan held her breath. Cars from the interstate whistled by, the roar of their engines fading away as the seconds passed and the blood pulsed in her eardrums, the anger rising in her stomach.

"Shopping? Of course," came the stunned reply. "When were you thinking?"

Releasing a breath of angst, she cautiously asked, "Uh, how about now? Or, rather in about twenty minutes."

"Where did you have in mind?"

"I don't know, but I want to get some boots like you have. And I don't want to look like I just got off the bus. I like it here and I want to look like I belong on a horse, even if my riding days are behind me."

Susan began considering her life choices. She could have just as easily moved farther from work and been able to afford an apartment on her own. *Why am I so enamored with the commute? Was it the reading time? The alone time? What would life without Andrew look like?* She ran through it all in her mind on the drive back to Golden. American history and the museum suited her, but the stress from the city left her wanting something different. Something more tangible.

Susan and Kat spent the better part of three hours trying on boots, some western, some not, some practical, some not, and talking about life in the West. She settled on a pair of lace-up Ariats with a western-inspired gusseted tongue and just enough heel to squeeze a pair of spurs onto. Kat wasn't sure if Susan was quite ready for that yet, as she filled her in on horse dos and don'ts. Susan also picked out some round-toe ropers with an eight-inch shaft in two-tone brown. They would take some getting used to and certainly some breaking in. Over the rest of the afternoon, Susan and Kat talked, laughed, and gossiped a little about their husbands. They retired to Kat's back patio and opened a bottle of wine. As Susan revealed more and more about her situation, Kat recognized the drive and ambition in this amazing woman in seductive yet practical boots.

"My husband's gone to the oil field in Wyoming til next month. So I'll set you up in the guest bedroom for tonight. What do you say, we take Holly and Bubbles in the trailer up to Granite Springs? We can make a weekend of it, find your Tom's letters. It'll take some extra time to take care of the horses, but we got nothing but time here. What do you say? Are you in?"

"Uh, I don't know."

"And in the meantime, you can stay here for the next couple days, get some riding in. I might even know a way to finally get rid of that husband of yours. The mountains are calling, and we must go. What do you say?" A clock on the wall of the patio ticked away the seconds, Kat not knowing if Susan got the John Muir reference.

"Sure. I really enjoy your company and riding horseback in Colorado is a dream I didn't think was possible." A big smile formed on Susan's face. She laughed out loud and stated, "If I can ditch that asshole husband of mine at the same time, no telling what I'm capable of."

Kat laughed and mumbled something about 'asshole husband' herself. He had been a good provider, but real estate filled the gaps between oil booms and busts. And now they were just good friends, anyway.

Susan and Kat finished the wine and settled in for the night.

***

The morning of the trip, Kat offered Susan a bloody mary, which she politely declined. Susan would typically have indulged, but the cool, clean air overnight had rested and recharged her. East Coast Susan was fading. They arranged some clothes, found a canvas tent in the basement, and hitched the trailer. Kat was good with the horses, to be sure. It was a little tricky getting Holly loaded up, but once she was in, Bubbles was ready to tag along anywhere. Susan loaded two small bales of hay and a bag of oat feed into the back of Kat's diesel pickup along with the saddles and the rest of the tack. Although Susan was still a beginner with horses, she loved the smell and was certain it was something she could master. If only she had a manual or a book she could read on the train first. And she loved the physicality of it all, sucking the air and wishing she were acclimated to the altitude, whatever that meant.

***

William: Grand Junction, Colorado Territory, October 1870

After fifty-two days, they had nearly arrived. Yet they walked on. The wagon train arrived in Grand Junction two days later. William was that much closer to Vernal. But he was not there yet.

By the early afternoon, the Mexicans were scouting out a place to board for a few days. Dupree was satisfied with camping a few more nights at the edge of town until he could secure further passage west or more permanent lodging. Clarence and his new mountain man mentor went looking to sell their respective wares, a few hides, and the pocket watch he'd carried from Santa Fe. Clarence was intent on getting some boots just like Ford's.

Grand Junction was a small outpost and few travelers stayed for more than a couple days. The Mexicans, along with Dupree, found a wagon train headed farther west and were gone the next day. California fever gripped them all.

At the end of the day, William sat down by firelight in a quiet corner of the hotel lobby and took pen to paper to recount his arrival in Grand Junction to his wife, fifteen hundred miles separating them.

***

Susan: Silverthorne, Colorado, September 1982

Without knowing, Susan and Kat took the same route as Tom, Jack, and Frank, through the Eisenhower Tunnel, then north on

Highway 9, following the Blue River. At the Ute Pass turnoff, they stopped for convenience, and Susan offered an idea for a detour.

"Listen to this letter. It's written from near here, I think." Susan unfolded a photocopy from within her portfolio, turned to the third page, and checked to see if Kat was paying attention. She read aloud:

October 4th, 1870

My darling Sarah Ann,

We have arrived in Grand Junction, a desolate and lonely place on the Grand River, just downstream from the confluence of the Gunnison which we have been following for many miles. Despite the easy crossing and the proximity of the mountains, few settlers remain here. This is still Ute territory and very much on the frontier. One item of note, Ford reminded me again this morning that he and Captain John Gunnison served together in 1853, exploring and mapping the Cochetopa Route that we have been following. The death of Capt Gunnison, at the hands of the frontier, Ford says, and for whom the river was named, is another reminder of the perils of this country. Ford has become a trusted friend, and I will invite him to homestead with us.

The remaining men in my party continue on to California. For most, it is all they can talk about. But rest assured, my cherished wife, that the Vernal in the Uintah was blessed for us. The settling of this land is our destiny and I envision us reuniting soon. My thoughts are with you.

Respectfully yours,

William Mitchell

Susan looked up from the page and saw Kat staring straight ahead, searching the horizon for the right words. Kat mouthed the word, "Wow."

"Do you think we could detour through Grand Junction this afternoon?" Susan felt a lump in her throat at the words. They were pulling the horse trailer, and there wouldn't be a river crossing, but something was coming alive in her being connected to the letters.

"Of course. What an amazing discovery these are. Like history coming to life," said Kat. Without further discussion, she turned the truck around and headed back down the road toward Silverthorne. They continued following the Blue River upstream to Hoosier Pass and then back down to Fairplay, Salida, and Poncha Springs. They turned onto Highway 50, drove over Monarch Pass, and stopped at a roadside park to admire the Gunnison River.

The trip took most of the day, stopping once for diesel and three more times for convenience and a bite to eat, then stopping for the night at a family farm, friends of Kat's from years ago, where the horses could wander around the irrigated fields, graze at their leisure and take in the surroundings. The next morning was cool and crisp, and Kat was eager to get the horses loaded up again. Susan helped water and feed the horses, getting more comfortable with their size and demeanor. And Kat was impressed at Susan's comfort level, a young woman from Washington, DC who hadn't been around horses in twenty years.

They drove most of the next day, arriving at Dutch John on Granite Springs Reservoir around four in the afternoon.

"You're sure Tom's mom said Sheep Creek of the Granite Springs?"

"That's where she said they were going, after floating the Green River. Something about fishing near the mouth of the creek."

"It must be the beginning of the Kokanee salmon run."

"They have salmon here?"

"Well, sort of. They were stocked by the Wyoming Fish and Game in 1964 as a sport fish. They're basically a land-locked red salmon. They eat plankton and tiny aquatic insects. They're delicious by the way, but this is just about their spawning season and that's what is so unique about them. I'm sure that's what the fishing is about."

"Yeah?"

"The fish go through a transformation at four or five years old. Their bodies turn a bright red, their heads a dark green and they grow humped backs and hooked jaws. It has everything to do with the spawn, and then they die."

Susan wished she had a notebook to keep up with Kat's knowledge. She was so busy trying to take it all in, that she missed the herd of pronghorn antelope on the left.

"It's really important for the coyotes, the mountain lions, and the bears, of course. It's the last big meal they get before they start their hibernation. In a few places, you can watch the bears gorge themselves on these beautiful red kokanee salmon and see the cycle of nature in action."

Kat and Susan stopped in town before continuing into the wilds that surrounded Granite Springs. They talked with a nice lady at the Chamber of Commerce building. "My name's Virlie. Like Shirlie, but with a Vee." She suggested setting up camp at the turnoff to Carter's Creek just south of Sheep Creek because there would be more room for the horses. "It's kokanee salmon season, you know."

Susan was impressed with Virlie's attitude and knowledge of the area. She tried to reconcile her knowledge in dealing with small-town museums, men in charge of little, but wielding a large ego, and a small sense of place. And she tried to reconcile the calm character Virlie displayed, unlike the threats, bluster, and emptiness of East Coast big cities.

Kat agreed with Virlie. And that way they could get some riding in, more than riding around the campground in a circle. It was only two miles over the ridge to Sheep Creek, an easy ride along an established trail to start, then across some open sagebrush country. Enjoying the drive, they arrived just after five in the afternoon and set up a taut picket line between the horse trailer and a scrawny pinon pine. Susan spread the tent beyond the pinon pine and Kat helped secure the center post and tie out the sides.

When they were both satisfied with the results, they sat in the grass, in the shade of the only cottonwood above the dirt road, taking in the afternoon sun and watching clouds drift over the lake in the distance. Susan wanted to tell her new friend about the mugging in Philadelphia. But sharing a secret from so far away seemed unnecessary. The smell of sagebrush and the nickering of the horses somehow put her at ease. They were the only two people within a mile or more. Rugged Wyoming lay to the north, about thirty miles or so. To the South, the badlands of the Book Cliffs receded and to the West, the rest of Utah, Idaho, and beyond were waiting to be explored.

For a hundred miles or more, in all directions, fewer than two persons per square mile inhabited the area, at least according to the Wyoming real estate brochure Susan picked up at the Chamber of Commerce building.

They sat in the grass and let the world tick by second after insignificant second. Somehow, the feeling of who Susan was, and where she belonged, started coming into focus. She suddenly felt an empathy for her attacker and wiped a tear from the corner of her eye. There was no mascara to run today. Susan thought about her life, and about horses, and about all the unexplored mysteries of Utah.

"You have to be the mover," Kat started.

"What do you mean, the mover?"

"Look, these horses are bigger than any man or woman, right? But their minds are smaller, like a dog or like a toddler. If you want them to do something, you have to be the mover. They won't willingly do anything without a firm hand leading their actions. But you can't just lead them by the halter. You might have to push their head or push their shoulder, with enough weight and intent that they understand. And if they refuse any command, you can't let that go. You've got to be firmer of mind and stronger of will than they are. That's the only way you'll get their respect and the only way they'll take commands."

"Sounds easy enough," Susan said.

"Don't get me wrong, you don't have to be rough with them. Most of the time, they're willing and gentle, but once in a while, they refuse or turn away from you, or put up a wall. That's when it can be difficult. You might see men being rougher on horses than you would expect. Punching them in the nose, or smacking their ear to take command. I don't think that's necessary, but it's a job not everyone can get the hang of. The stronger mind will prevail. And it's the unyielding will that's important. And when you're being the leader, the stronger-willed of the two, it's no problem. But if you let your guard down, let them take the reins, so to speak, that's when they can kick or bite or knock you down in a second."

Susan continued nodding, eyeing the horses and finding Kat's words a comfort. She wanted to discuss things back and forth with her new friend, but the time just wasn't right.

"The same is true of men." Kat spoke quieter but sensed a bond developing with Susan. While they hadn't talked much of their past abuses, difficulties, and episodes they'd just as soon forget, the two women were similar if only separated by two decades.

"You'd be surprised at how fast and agile these horses are. They have a knack for knowing just where to stomp or kick. And they bite more often than you would expect."

"I didn't get that impression from your horses. Are they safe?"

"Oh, yes. I've spent countless hours with these two. They're pretty gentle most of the time. I just want you to be aware that there are strong-willed horses out there, and there's some horses that aren't ridden regular and aren't cared for like these are. That's when you can get kicked or bucked off even. In time, you'll start to catch on. Just remember that the stronger-willed controls the movements."

Susan dutifully nodded and tried to keep a mental checklist. She wished she had a notebook or a textbook to follow along with the research, but that wasn't going to happen out here. Kat continued talking, explaining the purpose of each tack item to Susan as they saddled the horses and mounted up. Susan tried to willfully control the movements of the horses, but Holly and Bubbles were gentle and used to being ridden. And Susan felt comfortable in the saddle.

She wondered how Kat never seemed bothered by the constant bugs. The mosquitos, the black flies, the no-see-ums, and the biggest of all, the salmon flies that seemed to drop out of the trees onto her neck. Big, ugly, prehistoric-looking creatures, exempted from the evolutionary game of chutes and ladders.

***

William: Grand Junction, Colorado Territory, October 1870

William, Ford, and Nickie continued on northerly towards the Uintah Mountains. From Grand Junction, it was a hundred miles along the Ute Trail over Chief Douglas Pass and down into the White River valley. From the White River Valley, and after two days' rest to gather supplies and fill the water barrels, it was a grueling forty miles up a featureless salt arroyo to the crest. Then another twenty miles downhill to the Green River.

Ford had traveled this route three times before and was surprised to learn that the ferry across the Green River was not controlled by mountain men but was instead now controlled by the Mormons. It was a welcome change despite the additional fee of eight dollars per wagon. In previous crossings, Ford remembered the mountain men being drunk by two in the afternoon and risking emigrants' wagons filled with all their earthly possessions in the sultry, deep water of the Green and under the persuasion of alcohol. The Mormons were a more civilized group, refused to work on Sundays, and treated those using the ferry as a necessary evil, traveling overland through the Deseret Territory. Only occasionally did they gouge the emigrants.

The three men arrived in Vernal, Deseret Territory, on October 26th, 1870. William offered to sell the smaller wagon to Nickie and it only seemed appropriate since he'd driven the beastly thing all the way from Santa Fe. He turned it around in two days and headed out, alone, towards Fort Bridger, almost a hundred miles away.

***

Susan: Granite Springs Reservoir, Utah, September 1982

They set out along the little trail, uphill for a couple hundred yards, then Kat turned off, touched the spurs to Bubbles' flank, clicked her tongue, and said "come on," in a slightly raised voice. Holly reacted, stuttering her hind quarters, then gingerly bounded up the stepped earth to an open piece of ground among the sagebrush and eased into a trot. Susan tried to follow the commands but found herself bouncing up, down, and sideways more than she wanted. Trotting and then slowing to a walk, Kat turned in the saddle and found Susan right behind. She was watching the ground, and watching where Holly was stepping, and focused on the animal's movements.

"Try to be relaxed and enjoy the view," Kat said.

"We're sitting up so high, it'll take some getting used to," replied Susan.

"You know that expression, *my kingdom for a horse*? I sometimes wonder what they really meant." Kat continued up the gently sloping terrain. Reaching the crest of the ridge, they stopped and admired the view.

"I feel like this is my kingdom," Susan replied. "I feel so confident and powerful on Holly here, and the scenery here is amazing. Is this a national park or something?"

"Oh, heavens, no. Let's not do that, it would just ruin the place."

Susan and Kat looked out across the layers of ridges to the west, with Granite Springs in the background. The sun was high in the sky, and a gentle, dry wind blew from the northwest. Susan had difficulty putting it into words, but she felt like the lord of all creation. She had always worn high heels, trying to maximize her height and highlight her slender build. But in this unusual spread-legged position on horseback, nearly six feet higher than her typical surroundings, she felt like a different person. Why had she always been so demure with colleagues? She was just as educated and had a knack for research. Why hadn't she been more demanding of her peers and her superiors alike? She was doing fine in her career, but she had let so many little cuts hurt her professionally. She wasn't going to let that happen anymore. At least if she could arrive at work mounted on a reliable steed. Holly smelled of alfalfa and warm puppies, a smell that exuded strength and freedom. That's what she wanted from her career.

Susan and Kat sat and watched the clouds roll by the soft orange, earthen pottery of Northeastern Utah. The sandstone formations, mounds, and monoliths stretched on in a maze of subtle colors. Kat stood in the stirrups and looked down at the boat ramp at Sheep Creek from several hundred feet above. A handful of folks milled about five or six trucks with trailers. At the far end of the parking lot, one guy in a jeep was relieving himself in their direction. When their eyes met, the man waved at them but continued his call of nature. Kat sat back in the saddle and looked at Susan. "Men," she said, a calm but annoyed look on her tanned face.

"Why is it they always want to show you their most ridiculous feature? Don't they know that's not attractive?"

"Beats me, sis. We're lucky he didn't wave it at us and come running up the hill."

***

Frank finished his business, zipped his pants, and returned to the Jeep to crack open another beer. *Another future satisfied customer*, he thought to himself.

Chapter 29

Susan and Kat: Carter Creek, Utah, September 1982

Susan began to feel more comfortable with Holly. She dismounted, led her to an open spot of ground, wandered away to relieve herself behind a clump of sagebrush, and calmly returned to lead Holly farther afield and remount. It was a rite of passage for every cowgirl, whether she had the blues or not. Even Kat was impressed with Susan's change of demeanor around the horses. It was as if the boots she was wearing had started to define the woman.

Those are nice boots, Kat thought.

When Kat had first met Susan, the pump heels had matched her blouse and skirt ensemble, and her hair was tied up neatly in a sleek, manicured hairstyle. But now, in her rugged Lariat ropers with bump spurs, her hair swung freer, still from a little ponytail, but swaths of unruly strands blew across her forehead, into her eyes, and again back across her face. To Kat, she looked like a cross between something out of a Zane Grey novel and the wild-eyed fillies she raised when she first arrived in Colorado.

But Susan retained some innocence. If Kat were younger perhaps, and if she weren't married to a reliably predictable oilfield roughneck, Susan may have been her type. Those kinds of thoughts would have to stay hidden. Kat stood in the stirrups, stretched, and suggested they head back the way they had come, stopping at a slower, wide spot along Carter Creek to water the horses.

"I'm sore from riding," said Susan, squatting and leaning into the tight muscles.

"You will be," replied Kat, looking away as she fanned the campfire. "Sore in places you wouldn't expect." Kat didn't look up from the fire but knew the uncomfortable feeling of being in the saddle too long, too soon. "Get a good night's sleep and you'll be ready to saddle up again first thing in the morning."

Susan and Kat retired to their tents, falling asleep quickly as the cool night air enveloped them. As they slept, a thunderstorm boomed hundreds of miles away. But despite the distance, it was still visible to the horses, in the immense Utah sky.

***

Susan stirred and smelled the sweet sagebrush that surrounded the tent. The sun was already up and Kat was away at the BLM-provided pit toilet, a welcome respite from the wilds and the fears still swirling in Susan's head. She inspected the horses, saw they were well tended, and walked up the ridge to a cluster of rocks that were waiting for the next millennia to begin.

She sat down in the crook of a rock, collected her thoughts, and put together a plan in her head. Avoiding Andrew was paramount of course, but he was hundreds of miles away now. She'd taken a few vacation days after missing the letters from Mr. Steggeman and missing again with Tom. The time spent with Kat was worth the expense. Maintaining her professionalism in the wilds of Utah was important as well. She still had a job to do. She would make sure to be prepared each morning with whatever caffeine was available and make preparations each morning for the day's ride or the day's hike and she would be certain to keep careful notes about the efforts to obtain the letters, whether the Smithsonian wanted them or not. The letters which Tom was supposed to have in his possession. The same letters that Andrew suddenly seemed so interested in. She would continue carrying her portfolio case, secured in her right-hand saddlebag at the moment, in case she needed to make some notes or with Kat's help, obtain the actual letters. And lastly, she would continue making an inventory of her life. Her career at the Smithsonian Museum had a hold on her and she wasn't willing to let any of that go, but some of her most stubborn personality traits already seemed to have evolved.

She wasn't going to be a wallflower anymore. And she wasn't going to tolerate male chauvinist attitudes anywhere. If it was one man or a hundred, she'd refuse to be silenced and she would speak her mind as an intellectual peer. It was easy, somehow, to contemplate her life among these rocks, the remains of some ancient volcanic eruption. From her perch, somewhat uncomfortable as it was, she could see eighty or a hundred miles Southeasterly towards the Green River valley and beyond that, the LaSalle or Henry Mountains, she wasn't sure which. It was easy and almost magical to contemplate herself in the immensity of the landscape.

She marveled at the tanned skin on her arms and the sides of her face. Only her neck was tender to the touch from the effects of the sun. She would have to make sure to apply some sunscreen each morning as part of her routine. But with the effect of the sun on her face, she didn't feel it necessary to apply makeup like she had on the East Coast. Of course, at night, a moisturizing lotion was essential. But in the morning, a simple eyeliner, a touch of mascara, and a tinted lip gloss with sunblock were enough to set her eyes ablaze and keep her lips moist. Plus, every town in Utah so far had a vast selection of bee products, honey of course, but also a wonderful lip balm called Nephi that was so sweet and satisfying. *Where have I heard that word, Nephi?* And she was satisfied with herself in a way she hadn't felt since she was a young girl. The tanned skin of her face enhanced her more delicate features in a way she hadn't seen in quite a while. A pleasant smile pinched the corners of her eyes and wrinkled her nose, while a stern look included pursed lips and piercing eyes.

She hadn't kissed anyone since that one afternoon with Andrew. But that was two years ago in a moment of weakness. It hadn't progressed anywhere then and didn't change their twisted, strained relationship, but she hadn't given up hope of meeting someone else. Susan had considered a few suitors from the Smithsonian, but the dedication to her career meant they could never work out. A guy at her gym had seemed nice at first, but his possessive qualities and lack of non-gym attire immediately turned Susan off. Maybe if she had a new apartment in a new town, she would have more opportunities. And damn it, she'd make sure her college friends stayed connected. Some friendships are worth cultivating and maintaining, despite the years and despite the miles.

Susan made a few more notes in the journal she kept. It wasn't a diary and it wasn't for work, just some notes about her travels, maybe a sentence or two about the scenery or her conversations with Kat, or a reminder to buy more moisturizer. Susan stood and stretched, feeling her tender parts sore and aching. Yet, she was ready to get back in the saddle, literally, gaining confidence with each ride. She walked back down the hill, picked up a bristle brush, and began stroking Holly's flanks. Kat returned in a few minutes and commented on her gentle nature and composed stance.

"You're a natural with these horses. It shows in how you care for them," said Kat, a little winded from the hike up from the latrine.

"Thanks. I like tending to them."

"When you care for a horse each day and then demand action from them, there's a bond that develops over time that you just can't attain any other way. You'll begin to sense Holly's movements and she'll begin to anticipate your demands. I know I've already said it but you're really good with them."

Susan smiled and waved Kat away, but beamed inside. She finished the rub down, checked the time, and made intentioned preparations for the rest of the day. "Let's ride over the ridge again and down into the campground by the boat ramp. I'll bet we run into Tom here somewhere." Susan could barely believe these were her own words.

"Sounds like a good idea," replied Kat, as she shook the dust off the saddle blankets.

***

By ten o'clock they were on the trail again, this time with a packed lunch and an extra water jug tied over Bubbles' haunches. Susan and Kat topped the ridge, paused at the scene again, and then walked their mounts down toward an empty campground shaded with a handful of ponderosa pines. The horses were calm, already familiar with the ground, and not easily spooked, anyway.

Reaching the flat ground below the hill, Susan saw the man who had waved at them the night before. He was asleep on the ground, under an impressively outfitted jeep. He had a tarpaulin stretched over half the jeep and a sleeping bag unzipped and opened underneath. There was a single sheet covering his midsection and legs and a separate green woolen blanket over his chest and arms. They clip-clopped by as the sleeping man stirred, grabbed his crotch, and pulled the green blanket down off his face. Susan kept her eyes ahead and heard Kat behind say simply, "Morning." They continued past the jeep, avoiding a smattering of garbage and beer cans and the still-smoldering campfire.

When they reached the road, they dismounted, tied their horses to a split rail fence, and walked back towards the sleeping man amid two other tents, the campground otherwise empty. The sun was higher in the sky, at their backs, and the air was calm. It would be another hot day and Kat wanted to be tucked up under a shade tree in the afternoon.

"Hello, sir. We're looking for Tom Sullivan," said Susan. It was a reliable, pleasant greeting that she regularly used. The "sir" gave it a formality and an implied intent.

"He's out there," said Frank, still a little groggy from the night before.

"You mean on the water?" replied Kat.

Frank turned, looked her dead in the eye, and just pointed, with his arm outstretched, towards the middle of Granite Springs Reservoir. He didn't say anything else.

"They're in one of those boats?" asked Susan, remaining pleasant.

Frank looked at Susan this time, and again, pointed toward the lake. He stumbled over to the far side of his jeep and found a jar of peanut butter and the instant coffee. Returning to the women, he sat down on a peeled and polished pine log and offered them a seat. They declined but stepped over to hear anything he might say.

"I got here yesterday. Tom went out early this morning on the water with Jack. They should be back later. Something I can help you with?" Frank sprinkled half a spoonful of the instant coffee into the peanut butter jar, gave it a quick swirl, then licked the spoon.

"You just put instant coffee in your peanut butter," said Kat in a deadpan voice.

"Yeah, so?"

"I've never seen anybody do that and it must taste terrible."

"It's not terrible and there's caffeine."

Kat glanced over at Susan with a knowing smile.

"Please tell Tom I'm here and would like to connect with him this afternoon. My name is Susan Kingsley. I'm with the Smithsonian. He'll know what it's about."

Frank just nodded, wiped some peanut butter off his finger with his tongue, and quietly eyed the two women as they walked away. He had to squint and eventually close both eyes as he turned the canteen up towards the sun and drank deeply.

Susan walked back toward the horses and couldn't help smiling when the fillies shook their manes and stomped at the ground, restless and ready to serve. The two women mounted, walked the horses to the far end of the campground and stopped under the shade of a cottonwood. From there they could see a tiny little boat, bobbing in the water at a distance of maybe a mile or more. It was a windless day, unusual for this part of the country, and already hot. The afternoon might provide more cloud shade, maybe a thunderstorm late in the day.

They waited until they were out of earshot, then discussed their encounter with Frank. The peanut butter and instant coffee confirmed they were dealing with a practical man. And his unusual speech pattern, combined with the pointing, told them he was an idiot. Or maybe he was an idiot savant. Or maybe he was more mechanically inclined and less emotionally intelligent. Although they agreed that was true of most men. They felt like together they knew more about him than perhaps he knew about himself, at least at this time of the morning.

The two women continued talking, formulating a plan for the afternoon. They were more comfortable at the campground on the far side of the ridge and the horses were somewhat protected from the elements. They decided to stay where they were, and then they could check in on the boys whenever they thought it was prudent. They also knew to stay away after four or five in the evening, when the bull sessions would turn to macho drinking that could lead to trouble. Frank didn't seem like trouble, but you just couldn't tell. Susan hinted about troubles with men, and Kat nodded in a knowing glance that reflected the pain and trauma she had once known.

After their discussion, the two women rode the long way around the shoulder of the ridge and along a wooded game trail on the edge of Carter Creek. Kat spied a doe and a fawn lying quietly in the darkest shade of a double spruce tree. The doe crept up the hillside as the fawn instinctively remained motionless. Susan marveled at the instincts of mother and fawn but waited to talk about it with Kat until they arrived back at their camp.

"Ready to try this at a gallop?" called Kat. Susan had mastered walking and a few trots on open ground but a full gallop made her chest seize.

"I don't know, uh...."

"You'll get a real kick out of it," replied Kat, not noticing the pun.

"That's what I'm afraid of."

"As soon as we round this bend up ahead, click your tongue, let Holly have the trot, and give her a little nudge with the spurs on your boot heels. Be prepared, lean forward, and keep a tight hold on the reins. When you feel the horse gather, stand on the stirrups and move with the rhythm of her motion."

Susan patted Holly on the neck, eyed the campground a half mile ahead from the bend, and did as she was told. Holly must have been expecting it because the trot transformed into a gallop at the slightest suggestion of more speed from the trusted rider. Susan gripped the reins, stood in the stirrups, and let the equine beast have her head. The air rushed through her hair and tears flew from the burning wind on her face. She was taken by surprise at the animal's grace and ability.

Holly lunged and bobbed her head forward and back, the horse and rider becoming one. They sprinted forward, galloping along the trail, hooves churning above the pounding earth. The scarf about Susan's neck came unclad and waved in the wind. The wind flew by in waves. Holly's rhythmic streak altered as the campground neared. She turned slightly, expecting more commands to halt as Susan pulled back on the reins and the horse slowed to a canter, trotted around the first set of fence rails, and returned to a walk as Susan sat back on her haunches and turned to see Kat arriving at a gentle trot.

Kat could see the excitement on her face. "How did that feel?"

Susan was at a loss for words but tried to enunciate the sheer joy she had just discovered. "I had no idea they could do that. Why didn't you show me how to gallop sooner? Holly just took two steps, and we were running with the wind."

Kat saw that half of Susan's ponytail had come undone, and the tears from the wind had left a trail of dust cleansed on her skin from the corner of her eye to the edge of her earlobe. And her smile was unmistakable.

PART 3

Chapter 30

William: Vernal, Deseret Territory, October 1870

After the chaos of the past seven weeks, William was relieved to have reached Vernal. He stored the wagons in a warehouse away from the river, corralled some worn-out livestock, and offered Ford three days' rest.

But he hadn't found his homestead yet. So hearing about an opportunity above the town in the Uintah Mountains, he set off alone. It was rumored that an abandoned mine, high up in the mountains, with a large meadow, perfect for a homestead, waited within a day's ride. He rode Lusia north with half his mules into Red Canyon along the Green River. It was still wild country with few other strangers expected on the three-night trip up the canyon. It was about fifteen miles to the mouth of the canyon. From there, he could explore more upriver along the established game trails.

He rode up Red Canyon to the fifth side canyon and arrived at an unnamed creek pouring into the Green River. The stream was littered with sandstone boulders among the gravel bars. At the first bend in the creek, a narrow islet of sandstone stood watch, extending some fifty feet into the air, pinon pines guarding its base. And at the top, a naked knob of dark red sandstone angled delicately over the creek, a stone monolith. The sandstone was stained from age, carved out from some wall of rock eons ago. The Utes called it the Coyote's Tail, but the ranchers around Vernal called it the Devil's Prick. In town, or when ladies were present, they called it the Devil's Thumb. Either way, it was a prominent feature and a sturdy landmark that nobody would misunderstand. William noted the increasing clouds behind the monolith and continued up the nameless creek to his future. His homestead was waiting.

The first mule in line was his best, a dark brown beast with large ears, white stockings on its forelegs, and a dedicated working spirit. He was always the most reliable, even if he was a little harder to wrangle in the mornings in open range. But once he was reined in, whether he had been hobbled or not, the other mules would come easy. It carried two crates containing the rifles, one softer roll of bedding, and a water bag. The second mule, of slighter stature, was also reliable and carried two more crates of rifles. His third mule carried more gear, a tent, and a small food cache.

After only half a mile, William discovered a series of small pools created by boulders blocking the stream. Each pool contained dozens of wild trout, perfect for a change of pace from the dried elk they'd been living on during the previous months. But William had bigger fish to fry, so he continued on, eventually reaching a small meadow littered with gravel spoil piles along the stream. Damned sections of the creek, pools, dropoffs, encircled the discarded mounds of mine tailings. The mine was close by but it was getting late. From this location, it was only a hundred yards up to the top of the canyon on the right bank. The left bank stretched around the bend to the North and extended higher through a series of ledges where the Uintah Mountains reached skyward, above the treeline.

"This land could be the start of my destiny," said William. His lead mule turned its head as if trying to understand the command, then went back to focusing on the next step in line.

The meadow was a shallow bowl shape, perhaps a half mile long, running parallel with the stream. On the far bank was a steep face of granite with some tumbled sandstone and a smattering of basalt and pockets of white quartz. The quartz sparkled in contrast to the dull, lifeless cubes of basalt, the edges worn smooth over time. The sandstone of Red Canyon gave way to the ancient volcanic origins of the Uintah Mountains. It was no wonder why the previous miner chose this spot to prospect for silver or gold. Evidence of mining was piled all around but William could see no obvious mine entrance. Was this simply a placer mine, washing pans of material in the stream? More likely, the mine entrance was hidden, as many were, to avoid discovery.

At about four in the afternoon, a strong wind blew from the northwest and down through the canyon. William walked along the stream until he reached the midway point of the meadow. There, he saw the mine entrance, a dark crease in a slab of sandstone leaning away from a set of juniper shrubs. In front of the sandstone slab was a slightly worn path leading to the opening. But the entrance was only visible from ten or fifteen feet away, hidden by stands of willows along the stream and camouflaged by the juniper shrubs. William peered inside and saw nothing but black. But he could sense the vast open vault of the mine.

Cool, calm air surrounded him, his eyes adjusting to the blackness. This mine may have started as a cave, hidden from the outside world by the slab of sandstone, immovable.

The opening was narrow, descended a slight grade, then made an abrupt climb, forming a vertical S-shape. Twenty feet in, the interior of the mine was warmer somehow than the outside air had been. October was beginning to transform the mountains from summer playground to the frozen environs of winter. Hardship was coming soon. But this location was near enough to fresh water and the timber on the ledges would make an excellent cabin. He would make this his permanent camp for preparations for his homestead just below. And the mine could provide good shelter on the coldest nights when he had to cut timber. Green grass for the mules dotted the hills, and wild game was plentiful.

But William was wary of being discovered lurking about the mine, whether it was known to be abandoned or not. He unloaded his gear and drove the mules farther uphill to avoid discovery. He carried the crates of rifles, the food cache, and water bags to the mine and placed them inside. The darkness was near absolute but a glimmer of light penetrated the S-shaped shaft just enough to allow him to see. And the cave would keep his cache out of the elements and out of sight.

Over the next three days, William made his plans for a homestead, then led Lusia back down the canyon and into town to reunite with Ford.

***

After a brief but awkward reunion in town, William and Ford returned to their familiar ways. They walked over to the public-house, ready for something to eat. Above the door was a hand-painted sign that read, *Closed on Mondays-come back tomorrow.*

"Closed, I didn't know," said Ford, tugging at the loops in his mustache.

"What's that big tent over there?" William turned and squinted. The two continued on while most others were walking away. They strode up to a bench nearest the tent and spied two younger men in blue overalls and matching black flat-brimmed hats in a heated discussion.

"You gentlemen seem to be having a lively conversation. What's all the hubbub about?" William said.

"Sir?" said the shorter man in overalls.

"What's all the commotion about?" asked Ford.

"We were just discussing our next steps. You?"

"I see. Well, we were looking for someplace to get a hot meal."

"Our younger sisters make meals for the stagecoach passengers to take on their journey. They're over there under that blue canopy," said Overalls.

"Thank you kindly," replied William.

"Now, if you'll excuse us, we've got important business that don't concern you none."

"There's no need for that kind of talk, friend. We're just hungry," said William.

"The women-folk under the canopy made ten dollars in three days, but me 'n Jed still can't find what we need." Overalls patted Jed on the shoulder.

"You've been helpful until just a moment ago, what do you need?" said William, trying to be polite.

"It's a personal matter that don't concern you none. See?" Both the Mormons were wearing overalls. They severely resembled each other, but only the shorter of the two spoke.

Ford stood over his feet, unmoving. "Settle down now. An' keep your gossip to yourselves. I can see you're not interested in trade or business."

"I wouldn't say that, but it's a delicate situation and we don't know you fellas."

Ford paused, then made a suggestion, "One of you boys come with me to the canopy. I'd like to get a hot meal and seein' as you know the women, maybe we can make arrangements."

The taller of the two glanced at the other and nodded in Ford's direction. "Let's see about gettin' somethin' ta eat then," he said. Ford walked away with Overalls toward the tent.

"Excuse my younger brother, he can be bull-headed sometimes. His name is Jedediah and mine's Oren." Oren was blond, square-shouldered, and wore farmer's boots.

"I understand, it's a delicate situation to do business most places these days, I'm afraid," said William.

"We've been sent by the elders and the territorial governor to purchase guns but nobody wants to part with theirs and we need more than one or two, ya know."

"Oren, I know exactly what you mean, and I might be able to help."

"Don't see how," replied Oren.

"As a matter of fact, I've been looking to sell or trade a few guns. How does that strike ya?" William stared Oren in the eye and stood, unmoving, in a confident stance.

"I'm guessing you're not a saved soul in the Lord's flock of the prophet Joseph Smith and Father Brigham Young," said Oren, equally confident in his own soul.

"What's that, church group?"

"Yessir, it's the Church of Christ's Saints here in the Promised Land, some people call us Mormon. You been saved?"

"Not recently. What's the church want with guns?"

"Well, you see, mister, I'm not supposed to say, but nobody wants to deal with us too much. They don't like religion I guess and turn us away most times," said Oren.

"I have no quarrel with you, son. What about the guns, though?"

"We need rifles and ammo to defend our land against 'injin' attacks near Provo."

"I see," said William.

"An' against the aggression of the heathen US government. And we need every day huntin' rifles for our growing congregation of believers. You got rifles and ammo?"

"I do, but that's a delicate matter for sure. We'll eat first. Then we can discuss it privately this evening. Don't see as we should do business standin' here in the street."

"Ok, mister. What's yer plan then?"

"Come by the public-house, across from the bunkhouse, at sundown. It's closed, but we'll find a private place to discuss it some more," said William. Ford was walking back from the canopy.

"Alright then," said Oren.

Ford brought back a little cloth bag full of baked bread, sausages, and half of a pie that looked like blackberry. He had a big grin on his face and said, "Those ladies down there are a bit odd, but this here food is like from back east thirty years ago. Plenty of butter and fixin's for sandwiches and what have you. Beats wild game by a sight."

"If you say so," replied William.

"It's on me tonight, boss, the least I can do. Let's settle down in the warehouse, and then I'll show you how us mountain men like to unwind with a bottle of corn mash," said Ford, grinning under his curled mustache.

"Sounds good, but I've got a meetin' with them Mormon fellas at sundown."

They spent the rest of the afternoon in the shade of a narrow-leaf cottonwood, making sandwiches with the bread and sausage and sharing the pie before dozing in the glow of home-cooking. The sun shone through the leaves in the afternoon in a checkerboard of lights and darks in the buffalo grass. The sky threatened rain, but was full of bluster, like so many young men in town and old wives on the farm. As sundown approached, William got up, checked his watch, and walked over to the public-house.

***

"Those Mormon boys just made a deal to buy my rifles, Ford. They've got a box full of twenty-dollar double eagles they're looking to spend on as many rifles as they can get. They can't get no one to trade with them on account of some religious dispute."

"Good for you, Mr. Mitchell. You'll have your homestead hereabouts in no time a-tall," said Ford, wiping his beard and stroking his mustache curls. But you know, you mighta' want to be careful with them there Mormons. Maybe only sell 'em a few at a time. Don't want to start no religious war."

"Religion and war, now there's a topic," scoffed William. He kicked at the dirt, rubbed his forehead, and looked at Ford in the eyes the way few seldom did. They locked eyes, and in an instant, each saw the pain, regret, and scars visible in the other. They looked away. Ford let the topic slide. Slide into the bygone time of generals, captains and corporals, of gunpowder and lead, and of blood and the sense of loss felt by all who touched it.

William returned after dark with his mule, pulled a saddle blanket aside, and sat down with Ford, who poured him a cupful of corn rye. After a review of the deal made with the Mormons, William found a quiet corner and took pen and ink to paper.

Chapter 31

Jack and Tom: *Granite Springs Reservoir, September 1982*

Tom was among friends now. It was quiet in the campground, as Frank prepared wood for a fire. Jack produced a bottle of whiskey, uncorked it, took a draw from it, and passed it to Frank. He responded in kind with two swallows, then handed it to Tom. Tom took a sip, wiped his mustache, and handed it back to Jack.

The air was pleasant, at last, and a cold beer would hide the caustic taste of the whiskey. Tom cracked open a can and threw the aluminum ring at his feet. Frank rolled another joint with care and precision.

"I want to read you guys one of these letters and tell me what you think. I want to hike up the canyon over there. Listen carefully." Tom held up the Ohio package and produced a yellowed letter from near the bottom of the stack and put the package in his lap. "Check this out." Tom wiped his mustache again and felt the whiskey warming his gut. He used his best stage voice:

To my dearest Sarah Ann,

I have news from Uintah. Having arrived just last week, I have struck a deal to sell the goods which has brought me thus, so far, and should bring you to me in the next weeks. The bales of cotton are already on contract and the matter should be resolved tomorrow. The twelve sacks of sugar of which half were lost in the flood, I mentioned in my last letter, are in demand and there are many offers, as it is so scarce here. I have decided to sell only three sacks and keep the rest for your arrival, as I know you will want to bake pastries and such for our camp, while I attend to matters of business and the building of our home.

The best news, as of yet, is a contract to sell the Henry rifles, the munitions, and other assorted arms, which are in excellent condition and will demand a high price. I have agreed to meet with two gentlemen from Provo, Utah, members of a religious sect here called Mormons. They have been ordered by the Territorial Governor to secure weapons against their enemies. They are concerned with indian attacks near Provo but also have a plan to share the rifles with the Utes and Shoshones against the US government. They seem awfully convinced that an army of heathens are headed this way. While I do not understand or support their plan, I must seek out the best price for my goods. They insist that settlers in the many wagon trains headed to Oregon are secretly spying on their religious sect and are as much a danger as the Indians of these parts. I do not agree with their stance, but I have already sold two cases of rifles and intend to sell the remaining four cases of rifles to them soon. My guide and friend, Ford, suggested as such and he has been a reliable confidante and seems to be a very fine judge of character.

I have made arrangements to meet the gentlemen at a hidden and private location in one week's time. It is near an old mine called Bolskar's Folly, where I have cached my rifles and extra supplies. It is a very unusual location but is so well hidden that the remainder of my goods shall be safe from theft and vandals. It is located six or eight miles up the fifth side canyon northward from a prominent rock formation called The Devil's Thumb of the Red Canyon. The upper end of the canyon contains a grand meadow with tall grasses and a superb stand of spruce that will make exceptional lumber.

I have cached the guns and other provisions at the mine and only await the gentlemen Mormons on their return journey with the gold coins in the amount of six hundred dollars. This price should be more than *enough to establish our settlement and last us through a full year while we start a farm and ranching. This will be our home. Until I write to you again, hold on to our dream for a few more weeks. I'll send for you right soon.*

Your loving husband,

William Mitchell

***

Tom looked up and saw Frank staring up at the first star of the evening. Jack was pulling on a freshly lit cigar and nodding.

"You think that canyon is the one over there?"

"Seems reasonable enough. Let's do it," said Jack, blowing smoke up into the azure dusk.

***

Tom, Jack, and Frank spent the morning trying to avoid the headache caused by the whiskey from the night before. Tom only had a couple of sips, but combined with three beers, the washboard road trip from earlier in the day, and not enough water, he was feeling less than a hundred percent. Jack helped Tom launch the dory, easing into the greenish-gray water, the same water that the sun would turn into a brilliant dark blue by midafternoon. The conversation sidled, with few words spoken until they had reached their destination. Tom loved his dory and enjoyed the brief workout in rowing, swiveling in the oarlocks, and tugging on the oars.

He was hesitant to bring up the conversations of the night before. He wasn't even sure if he remembered it correctly. He switched seats with Jack and mentioned the letters. As soon as he brought it up, Jack took hold of the situation. "You want to hike up that canyon, right?"

Tom nodded in agreement and searched for the right words. "This is part of my family history as far as I can tell. I don't know what it means, but I'd like to find out. Somehow stare into the past, ya know. See what this William guy saw."

"Makes sense to me," said Jack.

"We can drop you off right where the Devil's Prick points to the mouth of that canyon."

"Yes," was all Tom could muster. He was still thinking about his great-great grandmother's cousin, Sarah Ann. He didn't know any William in his family and no Mitchells that he knew of. Maybe it was the idea of the homestead that left him longing. Searching for something familiar. He tried remembering the details of conversations he had with his dad. Only a few years in the past, the details were already fading.

"Doubt it's the right place, but I understand wanting to find your roots and know your place in this world." Jack was rowing Tom's little boat. He took shorter strokes and shallower paddles, keeping the dory at a slower pace and letting the conversation take the lead. "If those letters are authentic, I don't see any other place it could be. After the dam was installed, the water backed up and flooded lots of canyons and rock formations and buried the Green River under two hundred feet of water."

Jack paused and spun the dory around seventy degrees with a single j-stroke of an oar to get the sun out of his eyes. He continued: "The drought of the past three years and the avocado farmers in California sucking up all the water have reduced the area of this reservoir by nearly a third. There's canyons being exposed every season and rock formations coming to life that have been underwater for fifty years. That 'Devil's Prick' is the only prominent rock formation I see that matches what you read in those letters."

"It's the Devil's Thumb," said Tom, correcting Jack's comment.

Jack motioned ahead. "Let's drop him off there this morning and we can pick him up in the afternoon. Tom, what do you say? Is five or six hours enough to hike up there and back?"

"Sounds good. Pick me up at, say, four?" said Tom.

"Count on it," said Jack. "Just keep an eye out for bears." He winked and let a broad smile form across his face.

***

Tom cranked up the motor and reached the shoreline in fifteen minutes. Tom hopped out and bounded up the first ledge of sandstone. He turned, waved, and scrambled up a scree slope to the V-shaped opening of the canyon. In less than a minute, he disappeared behind a wall of willows, golden currants, and the occasional pinon pine. Jack looked back at Frank and suggested they get started with the fishing on hand for the day.

"Think he'll find anything up there?" asked Jack.

"Doubt it."

"Me too."

"Not sure we're even in the right county," said Frank.

"We're in the right county. Did you listen when he read those letters? Eight or ten miles out of Vernal along the Green River, fifth canyon to the South, right where the Devil's Thumb is."

"Devil's Prick, you mean, right, Jack?"

"Look at that rock, damn it. Thumb, dick, prick, cock, whatever. It's prominent, that's for sure. I can only imagine some poor homesteader using it as a landmark. Who knows, he may have been calling his homestead the Prick of the Valley Ranch."

Sometimes Jack had a way with words.

***

Tom toiled and sweated, gradually gaining on the drainage that fed into Granite Springs. After an hour, he stopped to check his surroundings and took a swig of the clear water forming in the freestone creek. The sandstone bottom of the stream was giving way to older, more colorful pebbles and the occasional volcanic rock. Purples, browns, greens, and reds sprinkled along the bottom made the water irresistible to walk through, to drink from, and feel like a free man. Tom indulged, soaking his feet, shoes, and socks and all up to his calves at every opportunity. It was harder walking in the water, a gentle current pushing back, seeking the easy path towards the big lake, but every step put him closer. Closer to his goal. Closer to his need for family connection that was growing stronger with each passing day. Closer to the directions in the letter and farther from the stresses of his everyday life.

Along the bank, animals had flattened the grasses, pushed the willows aside, and cleared a path, creating occasional breaks and stops. A game trail. Tom took advantage of these where he could, cutting the corners of the stream. He let the vibrant pine-scented air fill his lungs and concentrated on the rhythm of his steps.

After an hour, Tom saw his first aspen, a series of trees stilted and stumpy along the upper ledge of the drainage. The terrain was rough, but open meadows persisted among the continuing growth of trees. The pinon of the desert gave way to Douglas firs, lodgepole pines, and even the mighty spruce. Clumps of Indian rice grass grew along the rocky outcroppings, but the buffalo grass dominated along the wetter reaches of the drainage.

At just after noon, Tom reached an open meadow unlike any before and below. It was easily half a mile in length with the stream running along one side. A giant stand of spruce stood watch over the meadow. Tom felt a surge of pride knowing he descended from homesteading stock. His inner thoughts were halted with a start. From the corner of his eye, a scrub jay squawked and swirled at a golden eagle perched on the highest pinnacle of a scraggly pine. It suddenly made him aware of the wildness of his surroundings. He had only now become aware of it. A slight panic shot through him. After focusing on the hike, on his breathing, and on reaching a goal, the untamed wilderness encircled him. A fear rose from within him.

***

William: Uintah Mountains, Desert Territory, October 1870

William Mitchell and Benjamin Ford shared a campfire and a pot of coffee on the second to last day of October 1870 and thought about their futures. The sun was just coming up on a clear, blue-bird sky kind of day. Neither had made a commitment for certain, but with each passing day, William got closer and closer to making a decision about a homestead in the mountains above the Vernal valley. He had scouted several areas, some west of Vernal and some to the west of north, but settled on the mine area about thirty miles to the northeast. The meadows around Red Canyon were thick with grasses, which brought herds of deer, and the scrub oak hid rafters of turkeys. The Green River ran a muddy brown most seasons, with hints of red from the surrounding sandstones, but each side canyon had clear running streams, perfect for drinking water and cooking. Populations of wild trout lived in some, geese in others, and even beavers in still others. Beaver fur trapping had boomed and busted some years back, but foxes, bobcats, and minks still brought a fair price for their fur. He intended to raise sheep in the canyon, keep a few dairy cows and raise cattle on the open meadows. But first, he would have to break the news to Ford.

"You know I'm gonna build that homestead in Red Canyon, right?" said William, breaking the silence.

"I know you are, Mr. Mitchell. I've been thinkin' 'bout my future as well. Thinkin' even right now as we're enjoyin' this here coffee, watchin' the sunrise, and gettin' warm. You got a wife headed this way and roots waitin' to put down. I ain't meanin' to stand in your way, sir." Ford rocked back and forth, stood and took a last sip of coffee, then spat the bits of ground beans that had sunk to the bottom. His curled mustache never wavered.

"I've been thinkin' that I might want to see California," said Ford. "Or Oregon, maybe. But I'm no miner, and I ain't lookin' to get rich diggin' in the ground. But a man can see opportunity sometimes. I saw an opportunity in that kid for sure, you know. And I aim to not let any more opportunities get past me. I'm not gettin' any younger, an' my eyesight ain't what it used to be." William sipped his coffee and let the older man ramble on.

"It's hard to know what makes a man, but something tells me part of it is what you accomplish in a lifetime. You know, when you're young, you don't recognize the important things that are happening to you. And when you're older, that opportunity is lost forever. I think what you're doin' right here, right now, Mr. Mitchell is important. It may not feel like it in the short term, but I can see your ambitions. That's what it means to be a man. To make somethin' out of nothin'. Using your hands and using the tools around you, and your knowledge of what you have to make somethin' more than those things by themselves. The sum of the raw ingredients is greater than each part of a thing. The summing, that's what makes a man."

William didn't know how to respond. It was the most he had said at one time since the journey began. He nodded and looked up at Ford. "Thank you." He stood and stepped to Ford and put his hand on his shoulder. "You don't have to get to California today. Want to stay on with me here? Even a week is alright. Or wait until next Spring. Vernal is Latin for spring ain't it? Build a cabin next to mine. Settle in a place."

William stepped back and waited for Ford to respond. For a moment, he thought Ford was going to speak, but he didn't. William continued, "Winter is comin'. Gettin' to California can wait. Think it over."

"I'll think about it." Ford patted him on the back and started to walk away.

"I'm taking some more building materials up the Red Canyon tomorrow, probably a three-night trip to the mine. Those Mormons sure seem anxious to make a deal. Come along?"

"Listen, Mr. Mitchell. I've wanted to say a bit about that. But I've hesitated because of our business arrangement. But now that seems to be finished, and you and I can speak face to face."

"Go on and speak your mind, sir," said William, addressing a peer and a respected man.

"I don't like those Mormons. I don't like how they talk about the wagon trains headed to California and Oregon. People just lookin' for a better life than wherever they come from. And I don't like how they plan to use them injuns in whatever second-comin' and reckoning with the government they got planned. I've known plenty of Utes, Shoshone, Jemez, and Arapaho. None of 'em wanted nothin' but to go on livin' how they been livin' before the white man come an' changed everything. I'm certain there's a stealin' and rustlin' and just plain bad folks on both sides. But when you start throwin' around prophets and promised lands and threatenin' to kill folks cuz they got different gods or make a tee-pee their home, well, that ain't right. I know you got plans, and you're tryin' to make good for yourself, but I don't see this as the best way."

"It's concerning," said William, surprised at how much Ford had to say.

"If you deal with those Mormons, maybe you should do it out of town. You don't want it gettin' back that you was the one armed the crazy church folks. It's none of my business, but you be careful,l my friend."

"...appreciate your concern, Ford, but..."

"I just don't want you to go and make a deal with the devil, you know. Them's the hardest to get out of. And he ain't too forgivin' if you know what I mean." Ford paused and gathered his thoughts. "Now I've said my piece and won't say anythin' about it again. You do what you want, Mr. Mitchell."

"Our business is done, Ford. Please call me Will. And I take it that means you're not comin' along."

Ford looked away. Away from the rising sun and towards the west. "I'm gonna stick around here, uh Will, for a few more days. Maybe see about work on a wagon train headed anywhere. Don't imagine I'll find much, though. Not this late in the year. I'll see you when you get back, we'll talk more then if you like." Ford spat again and walked toward the livery stables.

Chapter 32

Jack and Tom: Granite Springs Reservoir, WY, September *1982*

Jack and Frank spent the day fishing, swapping stories, and eating a lunch of smoked oysters. They had a sleeve of saltines for the oysters, and then they split a three-day-old corned beef sandwich Jack brought from home. Jack brought three beers for each of them. One for celebrating the first caught fish of the day, the second to wash down lunch, and the third for whenever they wanted to drink the last beer. It was Jack who drank his last beer first. But it didn't matter. Frank fell asleep against the gunwale with a big straw hat covering his face.

Alone on the water, with Frank sawing logs, Jack could concentrate on the fishing. After a while, he felt a tug on the line. A fish accustomed to the depths. A fish used to swimming in a school, protected from pike, feeding at will on mysis shrimp, catfish eggs, and tiny aquatic insect larvae, without fear of the shallows, or man, or the light of day. Kokanee.

Jack began pulling and reeling alternately, unaccustomed to the fight of these fish. He saw a flash of silver in the water. With one last effort, he brought the kokanee up alongside the dory, then netted the silver torpedo. It seemed to glow in the afternoon sun, a hint of red and green emanating from its slippery flesh.

With the fishing accomplished, it was time for Jack to let his thoughts wander. He didn't know where it came from, but he thought about his dad. Frank slept while Jack let his thoughts unwind.

That one time. He was havin' a whiskey on the back porch, and I snagged one of his beers, a warm one, from the tool shed and joined him on the porch. Must have been nineteen or twenty. He looked at me like I'd just taken his half-inch socket and used it for a sinker.

Jack opened his last beer. Frank's mouth hung open and the sun was burning his exposed skin.

I thought it was a Keystone can. But Mom swore he only drank Miller, especially if I found it in the tool shed. He passed sometime before I enlisted. Must have been March or April. A blood clot in his lung. All that time working at the tire factory and not wearing the mask like he was supposed to.

The wind began to ripple the water enough to create shallow waves of light dancing off the sides of the dory. Overhead, clouds began to form, threatening their daily popcorn-burst of storms, but most days ended with an empty promise and little rain. This day was no different. A lone eagle touched the ether above, caring not for the clouds or the wind or the fishermen bobbing aimlessly in the blue-green expanse of cold water surrounded by a semi-arid desert landscape on three sides. Mountain peaks flanked with forests rose up farther South and West. Frank slept while Jack raised his can to toast a memory.

***

Tom found a shaded patch of grass near the stream and opened his lunch. He scarfed down a bologna sandwich but savored the tin of peaches, enjoying the juicy-sweet, sunshine-flavored fruit. The meal energized him to continue his walk. Stepping out of the cool shade, he spied a stand of spruce trees just above the ledge of the meadow. Most were twenty-four inches in diameter and reached higher than any of the local rock formations that ringed the meadow.

Tom took a drink from his water bottle and looked around. Remembering the carefully worded letter from William Mitchell, something began to tingle in his spine. Although he had never met the cousin of his great-great aunt in person, Mrs. Kowalski's caring and gentle encouragement on the phone popped into his head. Something seemed so familiar to Tom, even though he had never been here before. A sense of *deja vu*. And the fear. The panic.

He set his backpack down and began searching the outer edges of the clearing. It certainly looked like a nice place to build a home, just like was mentioned in the letter. And the lumber from those impressive spruce trees was more than enough to create an impressive cabin. But the meadow was empty. No ruins, no sign of man at all.

Had a home ever been built? What happened to William?

Following in the footsteps of these letters from 1870 was a thrill for Tom, even if he had trouble articulating exactly what he was thrilled about. He had hiked some during college, but usually as a way to hang out with friends. He continued walking along the outer edge, admiring the spruce trees shrouding the meadow. Midway along the opposite rim, the little stream slowed into a serpentine slough of pools and little riffles. He wandered across a shallow part of the creek, littered with pebbles of every color, and splashed up onto the grassy bank. Large, angular limestone boulders leaned skyward against the scree slope of smaller pink and gray rocks, having slid down and halted in their current location in apparent unison.

Chapter 33

William: Uintah Mountains, Deseret Territory, October 1870

After the negotiation with the Mormons, William was eager to return to the wilds, where he was most comfortable. The meadow with the mine would be his future homestead. And he was anxious to explore the area more thoroughly. He climbed into the saddle of the young colt, Lusia, now a trusted and reliable mount, and headed back into Red Canyon, past the Devil's Thumb where he was to meet the Mormons the day after tomorrow and decided to scout out another side canyon. Perhaps this time, the fates would smile down upon him once more.

He continued upriver until he reached a suitable crossing, a wide gravel bar where a small creek flooded in spring and deposited its alluvial haul. Here, the water of the Green River was flowing gently, lower than the colt's belly, and they were across in less than a minute. Lusia, who had seemed so wild at the beginning, was now one with William. Any ask on his part was a command not to be ignored. They continued on, in search of a dream.

The next side canyon was steeper with fewer open meadows, hemmed in with scrub oak, pockets of aspens, and serviceberry bushes, as tall as twenty feet in some places. Chipmunks were busy feasting on the ripe fruit. But the densest foliage was the Limber Pine. *Poor excuse for a building material.* The low-growing pine was soft and flexible, slow-growing, and not a good choice for construction of any kind.

So he continued on, hoping for an opportunity to reveal itself. Upon reaching a small beaver pond, William dismounted, letting Lusia graze and drink from the clean mountain water as he hiked up above the dam. A beaver was hard at work stripping branches when William cleared his throat and caught its attention. In a flash, the beaver let out a yelp, dove for the water, and smacked the surface with a thwap. Lusia raised up from drinking deeply and pricked his ears.

"Easy, there, Lusia," called William, wandering farther up the canyon. Just above the beaver pond, and around the bend of the stream, a low swell of earth extended away from the drainage, revealing a mountain peak, snow skirting the edges. The stream had produced a smooth-bottomed gulley nearly as wide as it was long. Tall spruces and Douglas firs towered above the meadow, with scrub oak growing along the slopes, wild raspberries sprouting in their shade. William decided to make camp, so he unloaded the mules and gave them water. He hobbled the mules, tying one front foot to one rear so they couldn't do more than shuffle about. William often used this technique to provide free grazing for the animals and freedom to move away from possible predators, but it also kept them close by. A hobbled mule might wander a hundred yards during the night, but it was easy to capture again in the morning.

He took care of the tasks and relaxed. Letting his thoughts wander was his only responsibility for the rest of the afternoon.

I should listen to Ford's guidance, even if it's only a gut feeling. Better to be cautious with these unknown men. Out of sight of the prying eyes of the town.

At sundown, he hiked upstream, near where the mules wandered about, heads down. He assembled the tent and started a fire with some sagebrush twigs and a bit of pine resin. The smell of the campfire lifted his spirits. After the long day, the cool clean air and the sweet-smelling sagebrush created a gentle respite around him. He stoked the fire with a handful of sticks littering the ground and a larger log, torn apart from a stump where an ancient tree had fallen. Satisfied with the day's find, and excited about his homestead, he could hardly sleep. After an hour or more of tossing and turning, he drifted off into a fitful sleep, dreaming of his bride, of plans, and of deals made with the Mormons. Under the Devil's Thumb. And under the devil's eye.

***

In the morning, a light frost covered all the grassy surfaces, the fire was nothing but cold ashes, and a strange smell lingered in the air. William rose, dressed for the frozen air, and walked downhill for a quick drink of water. Lusia was at the far end of the meadow, facing him, ears pricked, and huddled near the rest of his mules. The animals nervously stomped the ground as William approached. He released Luisa's hobbles and led him back toward the stream. But the mules hesitated after being released from their hobbles and tugged back against the lead, so he dropped the rope and let them be, near the water's edge, free to roam.

William walked back up the hill, turned, and saw the mules still eyeing him, ears pricked, slightly agitated, and stomping about. From his vantage point, the meadow was completely hidden from the mouth of the canyon, a good sign. Satisfied with the situation, he turned and walked away from the gently running waters, exploring his surroundings. Reaching the far side of the meadow, he saw several other slabs of granite similar to his own mine entrance. Curious, he checked behind the first two but discovered nothing.

Approaching the third, a curious smell hit his nose. He heard his mules groan and squeal. He turned and was confronted by a beast of a grizzly bear. The massive bear raised up on its back legs and swatted across William's chest. He fell, sprawled on the ground. Bleeding instantly, he was shocked to be facing the cold earth. The bear pursued, closing the gap in an instant, and landed on his left leg. It shattered the bone, sending a shooting pain up his spine. William shouted, writhed in pain, and attempted to turn over to face his attacker. But the bear was already on him. It scraped another set of claws into his shoulder and bit down on his neck, severing his ear, producing a stream of blood, and blurring his vision.

William struggled to free himself, blindly flailing with his free arm and pushing himself away with his uninjured leg. But the grizzly bear raised himself overhead and came crashing down again, opening a wound on his neck and breaking his collarbone. Screams escaped into the air and his hands grasped at the earth, tearing his fingernails.

The bear rose again, launched downward, and clenched its powerful jaws into the bleeding shoulder. Flesh tore away from his body, and his vision started to fade. Blood loss made him unable to fight back or roll away with any strength. He coughed up a mouthful of vomit, the bile churning in his abdomen.

Again, the bear flexed, spinning to the side, plowing up the earth along with a sagebrush bush, sending dirt and gravel flying. The bear spun the bloody prey aside and swatted again at the squirming mess. The clothes ripped away, revealing the soft, white skin along his ribcage. Another claw swipe tore the skin and revealed three ribs as another stream of blood oozed from his abdomen. Unable to scream, he flopped his arm, dislocated from the shoulder, towards the bear's snarling mouth.

Fighting was futile. Light began to fade from William's eyes, blood loss carrying his life away. But adrenaline struck, flashing memories into his mind.

Sarah Ann.

How foolish he had been to leave her. *What had he attained?* There was nothing to show for the efforts he had put into his dreams. Dreams left unfulfilled. His homestead, an apparition. His chest shuddered. His breathing slowed.

He would never hold his wife again.

At that moment, the bear chose its next meal. It paused, eyeing a chunk of flesh, clamped onto a mouthful, and pulled a section of meat into its mouth. The prey stopped moving, and a low groan of breath escaped, creating a fog of steam in the frozen air.

Chapter 34

Tom: The Devil's Thumb, Utah, September 1982

Tom tried to enjoy the time he spent in the meadows, knowing the day was already half-spent and the hike back downhill would be easier. The sun shone down on his shoulders as the wind quieted. The farther he walked from the stream meandering through the grasses, the quieter it got. A damp streak of sweat had developed down his spine and his feet ached. But this might be his only opportunity to explore this land. So he continued on. He reached a point along the woodline of the meadow that gently arced south and faced into the sun.

Satisfied with the effort, but disappointed that he hadn't located any mine, Tom decided to retrace his steps. Closer to the stream, he crouched lower to touch the water and eyed a dark crevice to his left just above the ground level. He stepped toward the opening. An angular slab of limestone, or granite, he couldn't be sure, was lodged against a round basalt boulder. The darkness behind and farther to the upstream side echoed when Tom tossed a pebble inside. *The mine.* A curious smell reached his nose. A cool draft of air touched his skin. It was just as described in the last letter to his great-aunt's cousin. Tom's mind raced. His sweat turned cold and clammy.

A surge of adrenaline hit him, and his head swam with trepidation. His heart surged at the thoughts in his head. This fully intact mine was part of a family history he'd never known. *How could this be? Why am I the one searching? What am I searching for?* He felt the enormity of this still-wild mountain locale and searched his soul for something to compare, something to find familiarity. But he came up empty.

The fear was also present. He was alone. The meadow suddenly seemed bigger than any place he had ever explored. A drop of cold sweat ran down his neck and his vision narrowed into a tunnel. Hidden recesses held secrets. Held promises. Held his fear. Staggering back, Tom bolted from the perch in front of the opening and took huge strides to the streambed, and lunged full force down into the inches-deep water. He bounded across the water, ran toward the center of the meadow. He hadn't had a panic attack in over a year.

Tom wiped his brow and noticed a cut on his forearm. He sprinted in a panicked delirium. The fear was all around him. Yet it was invisible. He saw the faint game trail pointing downhill and plowed toward it. At the first break in the trail, he turned and did his best to calm his racing nerves. His eyes were dilated, and he could feel the blood pumping in his ears. He could feel a tragedy occurring all around him.

Still reeling from the panic, Tom scanned the horizon and recognized important points from the letters. They came to life in his mind, real places and real events, but in a time long forgotten. An image of his father in the hospital shot through him. Fear sent him bounding back down the trail the way he had come. It was six miles back to the open water where Jack and Frank would be. *Six miles. His father. No more.* He put the panicked thoughts away in a corner of his mind and focused on his breathing, on his feet, and on the way forward. Walking downhill helped. As quickly as it appeared, the fear and the panic were gone.

****

Jack and Tom: Granite Springs Reservoir, Utah, September 1982

The waves in the blue-green water picked up, and Jack started the little thirty-five-horse-power Evinrude and motored back toward camp. Jack, the biggest and heaviest, sat in the rear, keeping the dory on an even keel. Tom, the youngest and lightest, sat in the front, facing forward, away from his two companions, and tried to keep the heavy thoughts in his mind from sinking the little watercraft.

Overhead, the eagles had disappeared, and the familiar thunderclouds began their daily dance. It even smelled like rain. Dark and dank rain. Jack increased the throttle as the dory pushed water away from the bow, creating little breakers on either side. The way forward was difficult but passable, pushing aside gallons of water and creating a mound of rollers. Behind, the retreat of the water was almost imperceptible, barely making a sound as the dark liquid swelled back together, fading yet following them. The past would be the past, swept together in tiny domes, then smaller ripples, and finally a nearly undetectable trail on the discolored, upturned sea. But the trail was there, a path discoverable if any of them dared look behind. History.

The three men continued across the water. As they neared the shore, the waves began to pick up, a downdraft pushing them sideways. Jack steered the tiller toward the campground. No one spoke until they prepared for the amphibious landing. Jack twisted the throttle down and applied the grounding bar to the spark plug, ceasing the whirring and winding of the motor. Frank sat up straight.

Jack levered the motor up above the transom line, locked it in place, and grabbed the oars in one motion. Their momentum carried them ashore, gently lodging on the graveled beach beside a clump of willows.

Jack reached for his cigarillos and pulled a new one from the pack. Tom lashed the oars in place, checked the oarlocks, and helped Frank pull the dory farther ashore and away from the increasing waves. Jack cupped his hands, shielding the flame with his back and hiding the smoke with his chin. A warm glow appeared, and two puffs of smoke emerged.

***

On the uphill side of the boat ramp, a dark figure stood motionless, waiting for the men to complete their disembarkation. "I'll need to see some ID from you men."

"For what?" asked Tom.

"For identification purposes. I'm checking for felonious activity, and persons wanted on criminal charges. Have your ID out, and there won't be trouble."

"Seems to me you're the one starting trouble," said Tom.

"I can give you more trouble than you can handle, punk. Get your ass over here. Hands where I can see 'em."

Tom pulled his wallet from his front pocket, opened the side flap, and pulled out a crisp photo card with his thumb. "There's no problem. But I don't understand." Tom was always polite, cordial, and cooperative in nearly any situation.

"Special Agent Andrew Harrison, community liaison, FBI. Step over here, please. I have some questions."

"What's the FBI doing..."

"I'll be asking the questions, Mr. Sullivan. Wait here and don't move. You two, IDs. Now!" Andrew had a commanding presence, and he was accustomed to using it regularly, if mainly in more urban environs. "I said don't move!"

"What's going on?" Tom stayed alert while holding his position in front of the red and white police cruiser.

Jack managed to remain the calmest, the effects of the nicotine soothing his thoughts. He stood near the waterline, smoking his cigarillo and looking the situation over. "That patrol car says, Fort Collins. Let's see *your* ID." Jack remained centered over his feet, squarely looking the suited agent over and sizing up the younger man.

"Don't make me cuff you!"

"There's no reason for all that."

"I'll be deciding what's necessary. Now step forward, slowly, and let me see your driver's license."

Jack calmly reached for the buttoned pocket above his breast. Behind the pack of smokes was a single stack of cards with a driver's license in a banded leather pouch, similar in size to the cigars he always carried. Jack pulled it out and stood at twice an arm's length with the plastic card at waist level. Andrew took one step forward and snatched it from his hand, and placed it in his own jacket pocket without looking at it.

"You didn't even look at it…" said Tom, still standing nervously by the patrol car.

"You, hippie, what's your name?"

Frank shuffled on his feet, kicked a pebble from under his foot, and scratched at his armpit. "Who wants to know?"

Andrew barked a few more orders, keeping the three men separated from himself and any physical location advantage. Frank opened a long-since faded leather wallet chained to his belt, unbuttoned the outside, and opened up the contents. He fished around some loose bills, none more than a ten and a few miscellaneous receipts, a condom, and a card in a manilla sleeve. He pulled it out and handed it to the black suit.

"Las Animas County Public Library. Is this some kind of joke?"

"It's got my picture and full name printed on the face by a recognized government office. It's an official ID." Frank eyed his jeep just beyond the patrol car and counted the seconds to reach it, subtracting the time for law enforcement to reach a radio inside the patrol car. Too close to risk it.

"I'll kick your ass and make you eat this library card, you dope smokin' free-loader. You, with the cigar, don't move."

Andrew slipped Frank's library card into the same pocket as Jack's driver's license and stepped right up to Tom, grabbing his wrist and wrestling it behind his back, and shoving him against the trunk of the patrol car.

"Hey, what are you...." Jack was losing patience.

"This kid's wanted for suspicion of marijuana possession, transporting felony documents across state lines, obstructing a law enforcement officer, and general public menacing. Spread 'em punk."

Jack had enough and stepped up closer. Frank was already circling the patrol car, counting the seconds and eyeing the rolled-down window of the patrol car.

"This is bullshit," said Jack. He tugged one last puff on the cigarillo and tossed it at his feet.

"Stay right where you are. Don't move any closer." Andrew reached for the handcuffs but fumbled the grip, so he just pushed Tom down onto the trunk. "Don't come any closer. I mean it."

Jack and Frank both stopped. The two stood shoulder to shoulder. The black suit pulled Tom's arm up behind him a little farther and whispered into his ear. Andrew pulled him from the trunk lid and shuffled him back a few steps.

"Tom here and I are gonna' take a little walk, no big deal. Stay right where you are. Don't move a muscle. I'll break his elbow off in his ass. Cuff each and every one of you pricks right here in the dirt. God-forsaken hole in the ground they call Utah."

They backed over to Tom's tent, facing the others the whole time. The black suit kicked him in the back of the knee and he dropped like a sack of potatoes in a heap, but the black suit pulled him back up on his knees. Grimacing, Tom listened as the cop whispered again in his ear. Tom nodded and looked away from his friends. Out of earshot, Tom motioned with a nod of his chin and sank down in disgust. Satisfied with the admission, the black suit reached inside Tom's tent and retrieved a green plastic bin with bright red handles. Pulling the handles back, the lid popped open and exposed the insides.

After Andrew retreated, Frank and Jack retrieved their IDs from the ground, covered in dust now, and shook their heads, loathing the shakedown they'd just been the victims of.

"I don't believe it," said Jack. "What just happened?"

Tom sniffled and wiped the snot on his face with his shirt. Frank helped him to his feet, patted him on the back, and scruffed his hair. "First run-in with johnny-law?"

Tom nodded and stepped toward Jack. "My great-aunts' letters, he took them."

"Shit."

"Frank, is this your library card? It doesn't have your name on it. It says ... Ethan J. Elliot. Who's Ethan?"

"That's mine."

"Well, who's Ethan J. Elliot?"

"I dunno," said Frank.

"Oh. OK." Tom didn't understand.

"It got the cop off my ass, didn't it?"

"I guess. Aren't you worried about usin' a fake ID?"

"It's a library card. Who uses a library card as an ID? And besides, I don't have a driver's license. Never saw the point," said Frank.

"I saw you drive up here," commented Jack with increased interest.

"I grew up on a farm. I've been driving since I was twelve. And besides, they didn't care when I drove jeeps in the army. I guess I just never got around to it."

A stunned silence fell over the group, and a subtle understanding began to play out. The three men settled down for the evening, discussed the day's events, and uncorked a bottle of rum. Frank sparked up another joint while Jack kept the fire going with chunks of split white pine and some apple branches he'd felled at home last fall. As the evening wore on, a sense of camaraderie ensconced the men under the cast of stars and among the firelight. Frank didn't mention it, but it reminded him of nights at the front in Khe Sahn and mornings in the rear in Hue. Vietnam.

Sitting around the campfire, Tom repeated that he'd found the mine mentioned in his letters. Jack saw the pride in his family history.

"There's something there. Something inside. I could feel it," insisted Tom. "I'm not leaving here without knowing what. And I'm getting those letters back one way or another."

It was a bold statement. But one that Jack and Frank understood. The cop in the black suit wanted the letters for something nefarious. They just weren't sure what. They'd return to the mine, search the area, and find out what was inside.

Jack chewed on a tiny twig of the apple tree while reviewing the USGS quad and came up with a plan. "Tomorrow morning, we'll motor across the lake to that canyon. Me and Tom'll hike up to the mine. Frank, you're in charge of returning the dory back here and picking us up on top in the Jeep. Think it'll make it?"

"Shouldn't be a problem."

"There's a four-wheel drive logging road about two klicks from this meadow. That's got to be it right here." Jack pointed to the topo map and then nodded at Tom. "Keep a sharp eye out for that cop, too."

Tom looked down at the ground, trying to forget the shakedown.

"You can't miss it," said Tom. "There's an impressive stand of spruce just above the meadow to the south. Right here. You might be able to see it from the road." He paused and looked at Frank. "I want those letters back. And I want to see the inside of that mine for myself. It's part of me, somehow. I didn't mention it earlier, but I had a kind of panic attack up there. There's something alive there, struggling. I could feel it. And I don't want to let it go. Don't want that cop taking it from me either. Whatever it is." Tom glanced up seeking some sort of affirmation.

"I understand," said Jack. "I'm curious, myself. From what you read to us, that was the homestead site and where your great-great whoever, William Mitchell, was gonna meet the Mormons to deal the rifles. Whatever happened there?"

"I don't know," said Tom. "That was the last letter. No more dated after that."

"We'll find out," said Jack. "Frank, plan on picking us up tomorrow afternoon."

"Not a problem. Mind if I take this map with me? What time up there?"

"Shouldn't be later than five or six. Bring the extra jerry can and a gallon of water, just in case," said Jack. "Might be a tougher hike for us old guys." Jack tossed the apple twig away and smiled.

The low light of dusk had faded, the clouds disappeared, and stars began to twinkle in the waves of warmth in the atmosphere above them. The rum was passed around, and Tom replayed the events of the day and repeated what he could remember from the letters. Each of the men recognized the importance of retracing Tom's steps, retracing his family history, and finding the mine entrance. Finding the mine would go a long way towards making amends for having lost the letters. Amends for the wrongs of that phony cop.

"I didn't look at his badge but the car definitely said Fort Collins," said Frank.

"He said FBI. I know that much. And that suit looked like it was straight out of a G-man comic book." Jack continued twisting his full cigar, blowing on the glowing ember and savoring the smoke in his mouth, tracing the smoke around his head, watching it mingle with the campfire smoke.

Illusions of jousting constellations melded overhead. Ursa Minor nudged Cassiopeia with a beam of light. Orion's sword swung about Canis Major's tail into Perseids' elbow. With the right amount of imagination and freedom and just enough rum and smoke, the night sky came to life.

"I'm hittin' the sack. We need to be up early and across the water by sunup. Frank, don't stay up all night smokin' that funny flower. We're gonna need you tomorrow," said Jack. He tossed the remaining stub of the cigar into the fire, spat after it, and wiped his mouth with his sleeve. "We should do this again in the fall."

The men retired to their tents and sleeping bags, watching the stars.

Chapter 35

Jack and Tom: Uintah Mountains, UT, September 1982

The next morning, it was Tom who was anxious to get started. He was the first one up, the first one to have the gear loaded into the dory. Jack wasn't much of a morning person, but he was ready soon enough.

Frank rolled out of bed, took a piss, and looked like he'd forgotten the plans from yesterday. But he insisted he was ready, just had to get a few fishing items together. The three men piled into the dory brimming with excitement. Frank's extra cargo sat under the bench seats. Despite the extra passengers and the additional weight, the watercraft bobbed effortlessly in the now-still waters.

Just as planned and without a cloud in the sky, Frank dropped the men off at the mouth of the canyon. The top of the stone monolith, the Devil's Thumb, protruded from the water, all the while absorbing every little wave. Tom and Jack hiked up into the brush as Frank pushed back out into the water and cranked up the motor.

Midway back towards the campground, Frank took the opportunity to do some fishing. He let the dory drift. From his shirt pocket, he pulled out a knock-off Zippo lighter with his army unit insignia, a sword with a thunderbolt for the blade. Signal Corps.

From the inside pocket of his rucksack, Frank withdrew a stick of the ANFO 55% extra dynamite. He checked his surroundings and used the lighter to start the fuse. It hissed and sparked, one, two, three seconds. Frank dropped the weighted dynamite package into the water and paddled away. The fuse on the dynamite bubbled and smoldered a glowing orange even as it sank. It grew smaller and fainter until it disappeared in the blackness. And then, *ka-blam*. A concussive blast from under the water, perhaps thirty or forty feet down, rippled and shocked outward in a perfect oval. A tiny bubble of smoke and water droplets escaped the surface as he stood and grabbed the long-handled net.

Concussed fish began floating to the surface, gills open, eyes fixed, yet still alive. Frank checked his surroundings again and poked through the fish, finally eyeing a fifteen-inch lake trout, silver-streaked and topaz-spotted. He scooped it up and tossed it in the ice chest. The half-sticks of dynamite sucked the oxygen out of the area momentarily but returned to normal in as few as five seconds. In the water, it was the blast that stunned the fish, and most times, a healthy fish would recover and swim away in thirty seconds.

Lighting the fuse on another stick, he waited, one, two, three, then dropped it over the side. *Ka-blung*. Frank stood with the net, selected an eighteen-inch kokanee salmon with a pronounced hook jaw, and tossed it in the ice chest.

Frank continued "fishing" for another half-hour, repeating the process like a tired old grandfather clock striking five in the afternoon.

Satisfied with his catch, Frank collected his gear, rearranged the fish in the ice, put his fishing tools away, and started up the Evinrude motor. It was still early, only ten-thirty, and the day promised to be another scorcher.

***

Susan: Uintah Mountains, September 1982

Susan and Kat woke early, a few stars still visible along the bluest part of the horizon, as the sun was cresting over the La Salle Mountains to the east. The horses were calm, flicking their tails while Susan snuck past on her way to the pit toilet. Returning, she paused to enjoy the crispness of the morning. She patted Holly on the neck and stroked her head. Susan pulled the blanket off the filly and hung it over a slat in the horse trailer. She unwrapped the last bale of hay and tossed two big handfuls into the rope stockade. She tried to imagine what she would be doing today back on the East Coast if she hadn't made this journey. Nothing came to mind. Nothing except the commute. She tried to imagine the city without her in it. It was a meld of images, rushing past like subway cars, in a blur of alarms, bad coffee, unfulfilled ambitions and heartaches suffered.

Susan stoked the fire and started a pot of cowboy coffee and sat on the ground, legs crossed, by the horses with her journal and the last pages of a research paper she'd been reading. She surprised herself by diving right into the journal, writing about the cool morning, the smell of the horses, and how much she enjoyed being alone. The thought of living in the West one day popped into her mind, but she tucked it away for later.

She enjoyed Kat's company and the wide-open spaces here were intoxicating and revitalizing in a way that was difficult to explain to someone who hadn't seen it. Susan was never a great writer, but jotting down notes was a regular task. She attempted to unshackle herself from her work in the journal, but the flowing cursive and short pen strokes always reminded her she was meant to be a researcher.

Kat wasn't feeling well and asked Susan if it would be all right if she stayed put.

"Of course. Anything I can do for you?"

"No. Thank you," replied Kat.

"OK. I'll ride Holly back over to the campground. See if I can talk with Tom."

"OK. We'll catch up this afternoon."

***

Susan put herself together, gave Bubbles some extra attention and oats, and mounted Holly for the ride over the hill. This wasn't the first time she'd ridden by herself, but it was still a fresh experience she tried to enjoy each time she swung a leg over. Susan circled the campsite, then started up the trail to the place where it angled away, and the open country led up to the boat ramp on the other side. Susan noticed the hoofprints from the past few days, and Holly seemed to understand. They were becoming inseparable: horse and rider.

Susan reined in Holly at the crest of the hill and took in the view. The reservoir was as blue as ever, and the surrounding shores were dusty brown and yellow where the water had receded during the drought. Boulders littered the shoreline, and Susan could only make out a single boat on the water. The campground remained motionless. No activity. The same vehicles as yesterday.

Susan clicked her tongue, and Holly responded with a few eager steps down the hill. The hoofprints from the days before were fainter and less evident to Susan on the downslope, but Holly knew where to go, confidently yet cautiously descending. At the bottom, Susan wandered the campground, searching for Tom and his friends. There didn't appear to be anyone around. Holly perked her ears and slowed to a walk as they approached.

Susan dismounted and tied Holly to the nearest split-rail fence behind them. She walked up to Frank's jeep and shouted, "Hello?"

There was no response, so she continued on. "Hello?" she shouted again at a nearby tent. Susan circumscribed the whole campground, ending up at the boat ramp, then turned to walk back towards her horse. Holly was hidden from view, shrouded behind some scraggly Gambel oaks and a pair of cottonwood trees.

She stopped in her tracks when the red and white police car swerved into the campground and came to a screeching stop, sending dust into the air and choking the scene. Andrew stepped out from behind the wheel. "Hello, darlin'. You miss me?"

Susan stood motionless, in shock at the sight of him in his black-on-black uniform in the oasis of the desert environment where she now found herself. "What are you doing here?"

"Just checking up on my wife. Keepin' the peace, kickin' ass, and takin' names, sweet-cheeks. Now tell me what *you're* doing out here all alone."

"Ex-wife. And nothing that concerns you." Susan was trying to collect her thoughts.

Andrew popped the trunk and took out a kids-size green baseball bat. Susan recognized the Louisville Slugger logo and stepped back. Andrew turned his back on his ex-wife and headed straight for Tom's tent. He swung at the top tentpole, ripping it from the nylon eyelet but not causing any destruction. Without hesitation, he marched towards the van, flipping the bat around, and plunging it into Jack's passenger side tail light. The red shards tumbled onto the sandstone gravel and rolled down a slight incline. Andrew continued to the other side, stepping over the tongue of the boat trailer and smashing the driver's side taillight. Flipping the bat around again, he stepped sideways, crow-hopped, and took a massive swing into Jack's driver's side mirror, breaking it off the vehicle and smashing the glass into a thousand pieces.

"What's your problem? Oh my god, what are you doing?" screamed Susan.

"There's not a problem. Just fixin' a little situation that needs taken care of," said Andrew, returning to the front of the patrol car and within earshot of Susan. "Tell me where these guys are."

"I don't know. Out fishing, I suppose. What's it to you?"

"Official FBI investigation, honey. And not any business of yours."

"What? Just leave them alone." Susan took a step too close and paid the consequences. Andrew popped Susan across the back of her leg with a closeup swipe of the bat, and she fell to her hands and knees. Andrew grabbed her wrist and twisted it up behind her back, forcing her back to her feet.

"Stop this. Stop!"

Susan struggled against the weight pulling on her wrist, but Andrew was too quick. He slapped her face and grabbed her by the neck, pinching her skin and yelling in her face while still controlling her by the wrist.

"I'll do whatever I please. And shut your face. You're under arrest for impeding a law enforcement officer."

Andrew spun her around and grabbed her other elbow and pinned it behind her. He wrestled her wrist into a handcuff and clutched her by the back of the neck. He pulled her arm back and locked it into the half-dangling handcuff, securing her arms behind her back and forcing her forward towards the patrol car.

"You can't do this. I didn't do anything. What's wrong with you?" Susan's pleas fell on deaf ears and a silent campground. Holly's ears were twitching as she stamped about nervously, but the lead rope held her to the split-rail fence. Andrew didn't take any notice and opened the passenger side door of his patrol car and pushed Susan inside and slammed the door. He returned to where he'd left the bat, scooped it up, and returned to the still-open trunk.

Andrew tossed it inside and reached for his vial of white powder, snorting up two spoonfuls and retrieving a shotgun from the trunk. He spun wildly, fired a shell at Tom's tent, and stepped forward while pumping another shell into the chamber. Closer, he fired again, splintering Tom's tent, sending it flying and peppering it with pellets. He turned, pumped the action, and fired into Jack's van, breaking the back windows, as dust and sunlight filled the interior.

Susan couldn't believe her eyes. Sitting upright in the backseat, she watched as Andrew fired the shotgun wildly into the air. She swallowed hard when Andrew returned to the trunk, but sighed a breath of relief as he wandered off towards the beachhead. The sound of a boat distracted the black suit from his path of destruction. Susan wrenched and pried at the steel that held her wrists and pondered the mesh cage that imprisoned her body. Confined. *Has he gone mad?* Susan's nerves were frayed, but her resolve was steady.

***

Andrew strode confidently toward the sound of the motor. Rounding the beachhead, he spied Frank unloading his cargo and wrestling with the dory.

"Hold it right there, hippie," said Andrew, lowering the weapon.

Frank reached his hands skyward. "You're harshin' my high, man." He stepped back, away from the water, and slouched his shoulders as if to say, *"You can beat me all you want, but I'm not resisting."*

"Where's Tom and the others? They're wanted. Obstruction of justice and impeding a law enforcement officer. That academic broad is under arrest, and you're next unless I get some cooperation."

"What do you want, fuzz?"

"I'll ask the questions here, you dope-smokin' punk-ass. Where are they?"

"I just dropped them off by the marina. They had some 'shrooms they was lookin' to sell, and I don't know"

"The marina? What? Mushrooms? I hate punks like you."

Frank dropped to his knees, bent forward at the waist, and put his hands behind his back. "I don't want no trouble, sir…"

"Which way is the marina? I'm taking your boat, freak."

Frank pointed and helped the black-on-black suit get into the dory as the motor cranked back to life. Frank pushed the boat out into the rippled water, pointed towards the eastern shore, and mumbled under the sound of the motor struggling against the waves. "They're over…Nixon, past the second inlet…roof of the Whitehouse…beyond the third rail… dope… and then me and Timothy Leary… draft-card…"

***

Frank: Granite Springs Reservoir, UT, September 1982

Frank had never said so much at one time without saying much of anything, aside from his Libertarian mantras and Vietnam-era jungle gibberish. The black suit turned the tiller and throttled the motor into the waves, cursing Frank and eyeing a trio of buildings harboring five boats along the eastern shore.

With a grin permanently affixed to his face, Frank waded back through the graveled shallows and scooped up his rucksack. Rounding the corner, he paused to spark up another doobie. Shielding his eyes from the sun and turning to avoid the wind, he saw a red and white police car parked in the middle of the dirt road with the trunk open. He stumbled up the slope toward his waiting jeep and saw Susan silently pleading with her eyes in the locked backseat.

He walked towards the police car, then veered away, up the hill to the plateau of the first campsite, ringed by cottonwoods. He caught his breath, ashed the joint, then relit the tightly wrapped herb. Frank took a deep draw on the joint and held the smoke, and looked directly into Susan's eyes. He exhaled, glanced up the hill, coughed once, then slowly turned back towards the black suit motoring away. Expressionless, Frank turned his back on Susan and walked back towards his camp. Her heart sank.

Arriving at his Jeep winded, at what seemed like ten minutes later, Frank unlatched the back tailgate and swung the hinged door to the side. He adjusted his pack, reached far into the passenger-side wheel-well storage locker, and pulled out an olive-green ammo can. In the bottom was a nylon cord coiled in tight loops. He grabbed the coiled mass and shook free some leaves, a clump of bed-rust, and a wad of road debris revealing a jangle of keys.

Frank pulled up his drooping pants, ashed his joint, pinched the burning end out, and tucked it behind his ear. He looked around again at the empty campground and silently walked back over to the police car. He eyed the open windows and pulled the coiled nylon cord up to his teeth. Susan sat upright, desperately wanting to shout, but not knowing what to say, and grimaced at the pain of her anchored wrists.

Frank opened the driver's side door and found the perp-lock mechanism to release the backdoor. He'd never been in the front seat of a cop car and wasn't impressed. There weren't any donuts, and there sure wasn't a lot of room. It seemed like the perp cage took up more room than was necessary, and the passenger seat was filled with spiral notebooks, Ziploc evidence bags, zip-ties, and a few miscellaneous forms and envelopes labeled *Priority, Outside Jurisdiction Only, Evidence, Fragile/Do Not Bend, Booking Detail,* and the like, along with a file folder box on the floorboard.

Frank pushed aside a pile of papers, discarded a white powder-filled baggy the size of a tennis ball, and picked up the radio mic.

Clearing his throat, Frank let a smile escape the side of his mouth as he winked at Susan and held the receiver down. "Fort Collins unit 45 to dispatch, respond, please. Ten-one-oh-six."

Crackling over the speaker came the response. "Unit 45. Secure, received."

Frank keyed the receiver and put the mic up to his mouth. "Thank you, dispatch. I'll be ten-seven until tomorrow morning at eight. Have a good night. Out of Jurisdiction Fort Collins Unit 45, ten-forty-two. Out."

"Thank you, forty-five. Good night and see you at the ten-forty-one. Out."

As the sun disappeared behind a solitary cloud, Frank stepped out from behind the wheel of the police car, opened the back door, and helped Susan step out into the lonely scene. Astonished, she didn't have anything to say and couldn't help but notice the peculiar, skunky smell emanating from the unusual Good Samaritan.

"How did you...?"

"Turn around, please." Frank held the coiled nylon cord out as a jingle of three keys slinked down the cord and dangled loose. He pulled the first key up to Susan's handcuffed wrists and examined the gauge.

"Nope." Frank grasped the second key, a stainless circular solution, and twisted the mechanism loose, releasing Susan's left wrist. Released from her constraint, she automatically pulled her arm forward, wiped the hair from her face, and extended her arm in a soothing motion. Frank opened the second lock and tossed the handcuffs back into the car.

"Thank you. How do you... "

"Let's not get into any details. We gotta go."

"You're probably right. My ex-husband has gone rogue and ..."

"Your ex-husband? We really gotta go now. Here take this."

Frank handed Susan a padded manilla envelope stamped *Fragile/Do Not Bend* and closed the back door of the police cruiser. He motioned for Susan to walk forward to his Jeep and the shade of the cottonwoods behind. From his shirt pocket, Frank retrieved the lighter.

"Better just keep walking."

Frank unholstered his backpack and retrieved a single dynamite stick, then checked over both shoulders. He held the lighter to the fuse and tossed the hissing dynamite in the open window of the patrol car and stepped away. One, two, three. *Ka-blong*. The back windows of the police cruiser shattered and exploded in a muffled percussion of smoke. The rumbling echo faded before Susan even recognized what happened. She turned and saw the police car smoldering in a pile of broken glass and resting under a cloud of papers parachuting back to earth.

"What did you...?"

"Your ex is getting the joke just about now, ma'am. We gotta make ourselves scarce. And I'm due to pick up Jack and Tom in a few hours."

"What joke? Where'd Andrew go?"

"He was headed east to the marina, but I'm supposed to meet the guys over the west side, up above the Devil's Thumb. Up the canyon."

Susan looked down at the manila envelope and peered inside. To her astonishment, the letters, two dozen of them, still folded neatly in their envelopes and yellowed from years in an attic trunk, bore no sign of additional damage. She picked one up and recognized the handwriting immediately. They were all from William Mitchell. Come back to life and ready to be preserved under glass at the Smithsonian.

"But how did you...?" Susan couldn't find the right words.

"Let's not get into that. Come with me to pick up the guys? Your ex is gonna be pissed about his car."

"I don't care about that prick or his car. Set the fucker on fire if you want." Susan rubbed her wrists and paced in the dirt.

Frank tossed the keyed nylon cord in the back of the jeep and returned to where Susan was pacing. He lit the joint again and offered Susan a toke. She declined, but the offer had the intended effect. She stood in her place and looked up at Frank, a slouching, long-haired, and mustachioed loner. He had just freed her from the incarceration of a police car. *Who is this guy? What am I doing here?* Susan kept her thoughts to herself, but she could feel her ears burning, and Frank's eye's on her, despite his blissful, sleepy vibe.

"Let's go," said Susan.

"Where?"

"To get the guys."

"Ok. Hop in," said Frank.

"Wait. I've got Holly," replied Susan, standing firm, but still unsure of the marijuana smell emanating from her long-haired rescuer. "How far is it? You know where to pick up the guys?"

"I don't know. Prolly two hours, at least. It's eighteen miles of four-wheel-drive road, then two miles of open country to a spot within two klicks of the head of the canyon."

"I'll take Holly and meet you there. I don't wanna' stay here because, you know, I don't wanna' be arrested again or whatever." Susan shuffled her feet, passed Frank, and untied Holly from the split-rail fence.

Frank scoffed, took another hit from the joint, and spoke as the smoke swirled about. "You can't ride there. You're a girl, and it's like ten miles. You don't even know where to go. Hop in, and I'll show you."

"I don't think so." In a flash, Susan pivoted in her boots and led Holly in a semicircle. She hunched a foot up into the stirrup, swung herself over the horse, and spun Holly around to face Frank again. "I'm a woman, not a girl, you long-haired piece of dog shit." Susan kicked Holly in the low belly and felt her stifles gather and spring the two of them forward. She gave a yell and took up the slack of the reins. Holly advanced into a gallop in two strides and swung her tail to and fro at the dock. Susan reached the end of the campground and the road that wound back up the hill. She stopped, turned Holly around to the right, and slowed her to a trot, then a walk, returning to the campground. She walked Holly right up to Frank, sat her horse, and waited.

Frank didn't speak, having finished the spliff. He was distracted by the complexity of the tailgate of his Jeep but hesitated to watch Susan ride up and speak.

"I'm sorry," she said. "I don't even know what a long-haired piece of dog shit is. That's not like me." There was a pause, but Susan sat up in the saddle, standing on the balls of her feet in the stirrups. "Thank you," Susan said, casually.

"For what?"

"For, uh… you know, the police car problem I was having." She felt the blood rushing into her cheeks.

"Sure," said Frank. "Anytime."

Susan spun her mount around, gave Frank a nod, and took off in a gallop up the hill and around the bend. At the same time, the 5:20 train at Washington Union Station left the station. The seat in the third row of the second car was empty.

"Damn," said Frank.

***

Susan slowed Holly to a trot at the first fork in the road and then stopped to catch her breath. Riding hard was fun but exhausting somehow, and the exhilaration always caught her off guard. At the top of the hill, she could see back to the campground and the views off to the north. She didn't know exactly where she was going, but any direction away from Andrew seemed like the right way. Frank had said the guys were hiking up the canyon on the west side of the reservoir. And she remembered from the letters about the prominent monolith guarding the mouth of the canyon. Finally catching up with Tom had been her ultimate goal. She had the letters now, but it didn't seem right to retire back to her campground with Kat and leave Tom hanging. So, she decided to find Tom too.

From her vantage point, she could just make out the tip of an orange sandstone formation two or three miles away–she couldn't be sure, along the shore. With the sun at her back, the sandstone seemed to glow, revealing hints of red and gold. She didn't know how the reservoir came to be. And she knew even less about the geology here. The exposed cliffs along the reservoir had a base that looked darker, an almost purple hue, clearly different than the rest of the red sandstone above it. At one point, the sandstone cliffs and sheer rock walls gave way to a gentler, mountainous terrain, with larger trees growing skyward like spikes on a desert plain.

From the first prominent hill above the South shore, Susan could see Frank preparing to leave the campground. He closed the tailgate, filled a plastic jug with a gallon of water, and discarded other items in the bushes behind Jack's tent. She'd have to make this decision on her own. With the speed and agility of her horse, she'd already gained almost a mile between her and the campground. A tiny red and white sliver of a boat appeared at the far extent of her view, picking up speed and leaving a white-fringed wake of turquoise water behind. *Andrew.*

Susan weighed her options and made a decision. She'd make her way along the ridgeline around two, three, four canyons to the fifth, she estimated, where the sandstone monolith was peeking above the water. Turning west, she should intersect the four-wheel-drive road somewhere four or five miles upland.

***

Andrew: Uintah Mountain, September 1982

Andrew arrived back at the beach in a rage. His sunburned face was tinged with anger, and his eyes stung from the dry air whipping over the water. He jogged up to the patrol car and found Susan gone, papers strewn about, and a slightly sour smell escaping from his smoking car. A tennis-ball-sized baggy was broken open, and the white powder clumped in a pile in the open trunk. He scooped up a pinch with his fingers, snorted, and licked his fingers clean, numbing his mouth and amplifying his rage. Blood pumped in his veins like a fire-hardened machine. His ex-wife was gone, somehow exploding the patrol car and luring that long-haired hippy into helping her escape. *Where are they? I'll rip that peace lover a new asshole.* The jeep was gone, but the patrol car was still operable even if the side and back windows were shattered and open to the elements.

Andrew pinched another bit of the cocaine and snorted, flooding his brain with dopamine. He pinched his nostrils shut and squinted into the sun. The effect was at its maximum, like a laser beam of light digging into his brain at midnight. His focus was never better. He could just make out a dust cloud from a vehicle billowing into the air to the west. *Susan. And that library-card-lovin' flower child, Ethan J. Eliot.*

Andrew grabbed the shotgun and closed the trunk lid. He secured it upright in the Jotto rack and started the engine. A cloud blew from the exhaust as he put the car in gear and punched the accelerator. A rolling, ever-expanding cumulus of dust showered the scene. He spun out of the campground, gaining traction and picking up speed as he hit the dirt road. He touched the lights-and-siren knob but then thought better of it and picked up the microphone.

Bouncing along the dirt road, fifteen over the posted speed, Andrew barked orders, alternating between the gas and the brake pedals, swerving around the tight turns. "Yes, *bleep, chaaarrr...*" The radio cut out, and gravel spewed. "... support immediately... *bleep...*" Screeching wheels tore into the turns as the car leaned against the increasing momentum.

Andrew gained ground on the swirl of dust ahead of him as he continued his tirade. "West of the resev... *bleep... scchhhheee.*" The car lurched and bounced off a rock sending more shattered glass raining down in the backseat.

"Copy, forty-five. Bleeek.... in the air... confirm, forty...." The radio squelched and crackled over the airwaves in a blur of pops and pisses. Andrew replaced the microphone, drifting onto the edge of the road, slammed the wheel back, overcorrected, and slid sideways through a long curve. The cloud of dust from the jeep ahead of him topped a rise and disappeared from view. Andrew punched the gas and shortened the distance.

***

Frank: Uintah Mountains, WY, September 1982

Frank continued on his merry way at five under the posted speed of the dirt road. At the top of the rise, he took a long look at a sign that read "Raw Honey," then figured he could stop on the way back or maybe when they left on Monday. He took the first right, crossed a dry creekbed, and swung back left within a stone's throw from the main road paralleling the canyon rim. The jeep came to a rolling stop as Frank released the clutch and found the nearest bush to drain his bladder. Dry-mouthed, he took a swig from a gallon jug, letting the water spill down his chin, and drip onto his chest. The smell of dynamite lingered on his hands and in his hair. Refreshed, Frank continued on.

Chapter 36

Andrew: Uintah Mountains, WY, September 1982

Andrew topped the same rise and suddenly saw the sign. A five-way intersection dead ahead. He pumped the brakes and held himself against the steering wheel, daring to avoid a collision, hoping against hope it would stop the speeding patrol car. He skidded to a stop, veered the rear end of the car into a mailbox, and crashed into a metal sign. "Raw Honey," it read, but now pointed into the air, broken off at the base. The sheared-off aluminum signpost held jagged between the sandstone rocks and the rear tire's tread, puncturing the tire and holding it fast.

Andrew exited the driver's seat and examined the scene. Air was leaking from the tire, and the bumper dangled on the ground from a broken bracket. He kicked it and banged a chip of paint loose. But the bumper held. The spare in the trunk was available, but Andrew wasn't having it. He bent the honey sign over, stomped it, and got back in behind the wheel. Air continued leaking, and the tire began losing its shape.

***

Jack and Tom: Uintah Mountains, WY, September 1982

Tom and Jack continued hiking up the canyon. Tom was a dozen years younger, had already completed the task the day before, and had more stamina. He tried to take it easy on the older man, pausing at each ledge or mark of elevation gain.

In just under an hour, Jack was sweating through his shirt, sweating through his pants in an offputting pattern, and sweating through his hat. It was continuously lifted to wipe a pale pink and furrowed forehead. He had long since given up his cigar and promised to smoke less if he could trudge farther and faster than Tom. His large frame carried more weight and he wished he hadn't drunk so much water so early in the climb.

Together they had climbed more than two thousand vertical feet over a distance of almost five miles. They had only rested once, in the shade of a cottonwood, on an overturned log from an elm tree that had recently given up the ghost. They admired the view of the little stream, multi-colored pebbles holding firm against the constant downpour of snowmelt from high up in the Uintahs.

It was just after one in the afternoon when Tom commented on the changing terrain and hinted the half-moon-shaped meadow was just ahead. He waited at a narrow break in the trees for Jack to catch up, not wanting to spoil it.

"Here's the meadow."

"I'm gonna quit smokin' as soon as we're done here." Jack resisted the urge to cough, knowing it would only make his breathing worse. "That was one helluva climb, Tom." Jack wiped his forehead again and smeared the sweat on the seat of his pants.

"Look up there. You can just start to see the stand of spruce trees mentioned in the letter. Coming to life right before our eyes. Just another hundred yards or so."

The two men strode on into the meadow, slowing to an easy walk and admiring how the little stream meandered through to the other side and out of sight as if it were tired from the uphill climb, too. They spread out, walking through the tall grass and in between the sage and rabbitbrush until the stand of spruce was in full view. A cathedral of serrated spruce trees stood motionless. They reached high above the ridgeline like a row of hooded monks standing sentinel between the gates of heaven and some forbidden land the men had just entered. They stood in awe at the spectacle, yet each secretly yearned for a time and place when securing a homestead was the ultimate goal. Somewhere along their path, on the east side of the reservoir in Utah, they had crossed into Wyoming, a sparsely populated land of still-wild places none had dared explore. A land of mountains, rivers, mines, and few people.

Jack took the initiative and calmed Tom's frayed nerves. "Mighty fine view and a great place to build a homestead." He waited two beats, not expecting any response, and continued. "Tom, this is part of your family history, no matter how distant it may feel. There's something alive here. Can you feel it?" Jack spread his arms and opened his palms like a preacher. "There's a history here that everybody's forgotten except what's in those letters. Something special here. Hard to describe, though. I've traveled all over, and one thing I'm certain of, it's not often you get to experience a place like this. It's as if this meadow was silent and hidden from view for a hundred years, just waiting for us to stand in this spot at this exact moment. I've got goosebumps. Can you feel the energy?"

Tom glanced up and admired Jack's calm. They stood with the sun on their backs, the sweat drying on their skin, evaporating into the clearest blue sky either had dared circumscribe in their mind's eye. Tom felt just as Jack said. He got a tingle along the back of his neck and stood silent, not wanting the moment to end. It wasn't a panic attack. It was the opposite from what he'd felt yesterday. It was as if they were the only people alive. The only people to have seen this meadow, these spruce, and these mountains, cut by a perennial flow of water unnamed and unknowable. And yet it was theirs. And it belonged to no one at the same time.

"I wandered around this way, crossed the stream down there, and walked along the far side of the yellow and gray rocks. See?" Tom pointed but remained in his place, firmly planted where he stood, now confident in his place in the world, even if he had to gain it alone in the wilds of Wyoming. The stress in his shoulders melted away into a carefree bliss.

Tom walked forward, calmly strolling over to the stream, stripped off his shoes and socks, and waded into the water. Jack thought about it, then just walked across the stream in his hiking boots like he expected to walk on water.

"Tom, you said a big rock hid the opening to what you think is the mine entrance, right?"

"Yeah, it's just up ahead," said Tom. "On the right."

Jack retrieved a cigar from the pouch and lit it.

Tom was still grinning from the near-religious experience they'd just shared, despite the feeling of dread, anxiety, and general uneasiness from the day before. Something magical was happening.

The two men neared the granite slab. It was triangular, at least from their vantage point, and seemed to hold back an entire mountain of bowling ball-sized boulders, some would call it a scree field, that had tumbled down and come to rest where they lay at a time when none could hear, and none could write it down, and none could fathom a homestead.

Arriving at the darkened crevice in between the largest stone and the rest of the mountain, Tom peered inside and knelt down, partly in reverence and partly to see better. No light emanated from the inside, but the unmistakable smell of cool air and an open cavity was evident. Tom blocked the sunlight as Jack duck-walked two or three steps, then stopped.

"It's big in here, but I can't see anything."

Tom pulled a pair of silver-chrome flashlights from his pack, ducked his head in, and handed one to Jack. Jack took another three short steps, feeling his way along and waving his arms in front of him, and then he switched on the light.

It was a massive opening in the earth, a single support against the far wall. A knee-high trench ran the length of the room and turned right into a squarish hole of black so dark no light reflected back. Looking around, Jack could see the room was big, so he continued on to the back wall, checked the opening, and examined the space on the other side.

"Looks pretty solid. Tom, come on in. There's plenty of room. You'll get a kick out of this. Tom hunched over, clicked on his flashlight, and crawled inside. He had to shield his eyes as Jack pointed his flashlight right at his face.

"Easy. Christ," said Tom.

"Sorry."

"I'm not crazy about tight spaces," muttered Tom. "I don't like it here."

"Relax," said Jack, still casting the beam of his flashlight around the space. "There's plenty of room for a family of ten, Tom. And there's cool fresh air coming from someplace. I can feel it."

Tom seemed to calm himself, all while keeping a dedicated eye on the light coming from the entrance back into the meadow. It was dry inside, and graveled on the stone floor. Jack peered around the bend and into the shaft that led deeper into the mountain. Taller and older, he had certain responsibilities that were expected. He disappeared from view for a moment and Tom reacted.

"Where're you going? Don't do that. I'm gonna step outside if you're gonna go farther. I just don't like this." Tom's breathing was short and his voice was staccato and halting. It wasn't fear, it was self-preservation that evolved from generations of men escaping close quarters.

"You gotta see this," shouted Jack from the next chamber. Jack reappeared in the hallway-like opening and waved Tom forward.

The hallway was narrow but not as narrow as the mine entrance. Stooping down was enough for Tom to walk into the open chamber. No one had been here in a long time. There was a single oil lantern hung above the floor at the far end. Below it, five wooden boxes sat frozen in time, darkened with age and stamped on the end with a faded ink that shined when viewed with the artificial light from Tom's flashlights.

Tom was already looking over the crates, at the craftsmanship of the boxes, the worn but secured condition they appeared to be in, and the meticulous nature of the second mine room. It was nearly the same size as the first, but no light from the outside world made its way inside. The temperature was cool, approaching constant, and the air was fresh, almost moist.

Jack admired the scene. "What is that?"

Tom tried to open the lid of the first crate closest to him and found it stuck shut by several rusty nails. Feeling the closeness of the mine, Tom couldn't take it anymore. "I'm gonna step outside, get some fresh air."

Jack continued poking around the remnants of the mine, Bolskar's Folly, and tried to imagine William Mitchell. He sat down on one of the wooden crates when Tom's voice shattered the quiet.

"Hey, get out here. Someone's coming!"

Chapter 37

Susan: Uintah Mountains, WY, September 1982

Susan rode along the dirt road until it started to veer off to the south at a point where she could see the first canyon and its ancient, circuitous route up the mountain. She reined Holly in, steered to the right and spurred her into a trot at an opening in the brush. Holly responded in kind and sent dirt and gravel kicking up behind them. Slowing to a walk at the first bunch of trees, Susan had to duck, then turn Holly again to stay in the right direction. Angling westerly, but advancing ahead of the sun's path, they continued walking through the trees, trotting through the lower brush and arrived at the head of the first canyon in fifteen minutes.

She dismounted, checked Holly's bridle for debris, and pulled an apple from her saddle bag. She fed Holly the snack and checked her surroundings. The head of the canyon was just a low spot in a sea of sage, open to the winds, preventing any evergreens from growing. The next chasmed canyon opening was slightly farther west and only a half mile or so. Susan walked Holly towards a patch of grass and let her graze for five minutes before remounting and riding on. At this point, Susan felt like a grizzled veteran with Holly. She confidently covered the half-mile in a few minutes. She was pleased to see a pool of water dripping from the sheer wall on the south, mostly shaded side. So Susan dismounted again and let Holly graze while she hiked up to fill her canteen and a canvas waterbag for Holly.

She returned, climbing up a steep slope to find Holly munching on grass a quarter mile away. But with a quiet confidence, she calmly hoisted the water bag over her shoulder and trudged cross country to where her horse was wandering on the shoulder of the mountain. Susan knelt down and placed the waterbag at Holly's feet and checked her route again.

As the crow flies, she was less than three miles from her estimated destination. It may have been foolish to take off like this, but she was confident in her decision-making skills. She was free of Andrew and free to continue on this journey, wherever it led. Finding Tom was important. The mine mentioned in the letters was not a priority. The safekeeping of the letters themselves was paramount. They'd become part of her now. They were a roadmap through the wilds to a specific location. And she was near the terminus. It was this thought that gave her pause. It was the letters that had led her here, to this spot, alone, upright yet changed.

The thoughts in Susan's mind started racing. But the view from the second canyon calmed her irritated nerves. It was three more canyons farther North to where Frank was supposed to pick up the other guys. *Why am I counting on a funny-flower-smoking explosives expert for my well-being?* She never would have trusted someone like that in the city. She put that aside and climbed back up into the saddle. It gave her a better view, as she clicked her tongue and guided Holly forward.

The sagebrush of the desert gave way to pines of varying shades of green and olive reaching skyward. Susan continued, despite the lack of a clear path, putting the sun at her back and the desert behind her.

Satisfied with her progress, she led Holly along a game trail and entered a wooded section littered with ferns and willows growing along a small stream. But the going was slow. It took almost an hour to steer up, over, and around the maze of willows and ponds created by the little creek.

By mid-afternoon, Susan was hungry, and the destination was still unknown. She wasn't lost, she just didn't know where she was. She shared the last of her apple with Holly and drank the rest of the water from her canteen. If it was an emergency, she had a packet of peanuts from her plane trip three weeks before, buried in the bottom of her portfolio. *Such a long time ago.*

Susan continued northerly and, when possible, westerly or uphill, not wanting to be forced to backtrack from the edge of a cliff. After another thirty minutes, she crossed a dry drainage that dropped off to the east in dramatic fashion which she considered the head of the third canyon. She rode on, keeping the sun at her back, but now stopped more frequently to check her surroundings, look for any signs of the road or civilization. It had been nearly three hours since she'd seen another person. And that hadn't exactly gone according to plan. *What am I doing out here?*

Susan dismounted and took Holly by the lead rope to give her a rest and to stretch her aching legs and backside. Her wrists still hurt from the handcuffs. She'd applied sunscreen in the morning, but the back of her neck was burnt, and her skin was scratchy with dust. Her pant legs were littered with sagebrush leaves and wildflower seeds encapsulated in white fluff, dried blooms, and western detritus. Her allergies had not been an issue as of yet, thank god. Her boots were starting to show wear but felt appropriate out here in the brush country of Utah. *Or was it Wyoming now?*

Susan led Holly up to a stand of aspens and let her graze for a few minutes while she grabbed her journal and took an account of her situation. *I'm alone. Wait, I've got Holly. I'm out of water. Andrew is somewhere.* She paged backward through the journal's pages of the last two weeks. She hadn't written as much detail, but there was change. Entries that mentioned mountains and deserts and streams. She thought about life without Andrew. She thought about Kat and the West.

Time to get movin', Holly.

Susan made careful decisions, based on reason, with her available resources, and with Holly. They were a team, anticipating each other's moves as Kat had suggested. *Kat must be worried.* Susan continued estimating her location but couldn't be sure exactly one way or the other. *Lost.* Susan kept Holly at an easy walk, dodging clumps of golden currants and myrtles bristling with thorns. Tall ponderosas and other pines she couldn't identify surrounded her every step of the way. *At least Andrew's not around. I'll have to talk some sense into that creep. Maybe I'll report him to Lieutenant Gilroy. Arresting your own ex-wife? Ridiculous.*

Susan topped a low rise and turned north at a steep grade. At first, she'd been so careful about watching where they were riding, watching Holly's path for obstacles or other impediments. But now, she was confident. Confident in Holly's gait. Confident in Holly's sure-footed steps. And confident in her riding ability. *Fuck Andrew.* She was free to look up now, look ahead. They rode on.

She and Holly ventured farther afield. *Is this the fifth canyon?* Susan replayed the day's ride in her mind, fully expecting Frank to be a no-show, or to have missed the road altogether.

Susan adjusted her seat in the saddle, patted Holly on the neck, and reined her to the east, down the slope, following a little stream. In less than a mile, they entered a grove of spruce trees like Susan had never seen before and she marveled at the height and breadth of the biomass. After a few fits and starts, creeping their way through, Susan emerged from the wood and found herself in an open meadow, crescent moon shaped, and saw a man waving at her, then ducking behind a massive rock. Two men emerged. She'd found them!

Susan clicked her tongue and brought Holly to a trot, riding up the far side of the stream. When she got closer, she slowed to a walk and reined Holly into the running stream and across to where Tom and Jack were standing, dumbfounded. She sat her horse and stood up in the stirrups, giving her a commanding view while she stretched her back and shoulders.

"Afternoon, gentleman. I'm Susan Kingsley with the Smithsonian Museum."

Chapter 38

Susan: Bolskar's Folly, WY, September 1982

"I'm Tom. Very nice to meet you." He shielded his eyes from the sun and looked up at the woman on horseback.

"Good. I think we spoke on the phone."

"Oh, uh, yes. What are you doing out here?"

"I've come to, uh, apologize." Susan was a little surprised at the word. "Is Frank here?"

Jack stepped away from the mine entrance and attempted to take center stage. "Frank's gonna pick us up in an hour or so. What's the emergency?"

"That crazy FBI agent, he's my ex-husband. He's gone off the rails and has been following me and Tom for the past week. He's after your great-aunt's letters for some reason, and, uh, he arrested me earlier this morning. I'm terribly sorry for the difficulties he's caused. Frank filled me in on the shakedown you men received. He's deranged, and I don't know what he'll do next. I just want you to know I have your letters, and I think they're worth professionally preserving. Is this the mine mentioned in them?"

The men stood motionless and silent, taking in everything this impressive woman said. It was unusual to see a woman on horseback lecturing you about your recent scrape with law enforcement in the middle of nowhere. They were at the north edge of a half-moon-shaped meadow, its beauty as impactful as any could have imagined, and from where they stood, the closest paved road was at least twenty miles. And the nearest police station or community outreach center was at least fifty miles away.

"What's he want with the letters?" asked Tom.

"If he thinks the letters are valuable, he'll be impressed with what we've just found," said Jack. "Come on, check this out."

Susan hesitated and stopped Jack before he could lead them back inside. "Listen, if you've found something related to these letters, I need to inform you... I need to be present and make careful notes about what you think you have. The provenance of any historical or archaeological finds is more important than you realize. If this is an intact archaeological site, everything must remain *in situ* until it can be processed."

Jack paused, still ogling the attractive woman dominating their position from the saddle.

"No problem, babe," said Jack.

Susan touched Holly with her spurs and stepped right up to where Jack was standing, suddenly more alone than he would have preferred, and towered over by Susan. "Don't call me babe. You can call me Mrs. Kingsley. Or Assistant Acquisitions Manager Kingsley. Or ma'am, I suppose."

"Of course. Yes, ma'am. No offense meant." Jack backed down, backed away, and found a new respect for horses. And for this woman in boots and spurs.

Susan turned in the saddle and addressed Tom. "Like I was saying, I spoke with you on the phone. And I also talked with your mother and your roommate. Nice man. Part of my job is to retrace the history surrounding artifacts like these. And again, I want to offer my sincerest apologies for my ex-husband's actions. And for getting you into this mess. Pursuing history involves a lot of travel, but it's exceedingly rare to actually do any field search on this scale." Susan couldn't help but break eye contact with the men to scan the meadow again.

"Yes, ma'am," said Tom cautiously.

"Please, call me Susan. Now that must make you Jack."

"Yes, ma'am, uh, pleased to..."

"What is it you gentlemen would like to show me? Let me get my journal."

She was all business, in boots and spurs, six feet above her audience and riding an impressive chestnut steed. Susan backed Holly two steps, then spun her toward a small willow growing from the bottom of the scree field. Some loose gravel sprayed over the scene where the men stood. They were still in awe of the impressive figure. Susan climbed down, loosely tied Holly to the willow, and stepped up to where Holly had been standing. She was the shortest of them now. But she had already won their confidence.

Over the next thirty minutes, the men showed Susan the mine and the wooden crates they'd found, as she made careful notes she kept to herself. She made measured suggestions about their care and any identifying features, making sure they remained undisturbed. Taking inventory of the events was paramount to preserve the provenance.

Jack showed Susan the first box, identified as *R-T double knotted*, as these were two of the more prominent letters visible in black paint and the only box secured with two overhand rope knots. He had foolishly pried open the first box before Susan had arrived. A dozen Henry Repeating rifles were wedged in wooden racks and tied in place with green canvas. Pine wood shavings filled the box midway and released a pleasant smell as Susan peered inside.

R-T, double-knotted wooden crate opened by Jack, on Saturday, September 5th, 1982. Contents include manufactured Henry rifles of antiquity.

On top of the second crate, Susan found a leather-bound journal which she carefully inspected. Underneath were four slips of paper folded neatly. One was the bill of sale from the Henry Arms Company, clearly printed with New Haven, Connecticut. The second was a receipt from the Atchison and Topeka Railroad for freight delivered on September 4th, 1869. The third was a deed to the mining claim, Bolskar's Folly signed with William's signature. The fourth was a promissory note between two parties, brothers Oren and Jedediah, and William Mitchell, of Vernal, County of Uintah, in the Territory of Deseret.

Susan recognized the penmanship, the elegant cursive instantly. It was the same author as the letters.

She delicately opened the leather journal. Its pages were filled with the same elegant cursive and dated on every other page at the top. Susan's insides were in knots. The letters she had read and which had driven her change were now accompanied by an entire book of journal entries and verifiable proof of events spanning four hundred miles of the North Branch of the Spanish Trail. An audible gasp nearly escaped from Susan's lips. But her professionalism persisted. She carefully closed the journal. Together, this was something the Smithsonian would want.

"The date on this freight receipt was yesterday," stated Susan.

"Yesterday?" said Tom.

"Yes, yesterday's date in 1869. One-hundred-thirteen years ago, nearly to the day." Susan was smiling in a way that made the men uneasy. They could see she was in charge of the situation and the right person for the job, preserving this piece of living history.

"I don't understand."

"We'll need a full team to process this site. Search the grounds for other artifacts and make a detailed survey of the mine and preserve these rifles. I'll keep the journal and the three slips of paper with me in my portfolio. I've made notes relating to this and listed each of you as witnesses to the event, including the date and time. I would expect I could have a full team here within a week or so and have this site wrapped up in three weeks. And I appreciate your help on this, I won't forget what made this happen. Tom, which way is the road where Frank is supposed to pick you up?"

"Uh, I'm not sure, upstream, I suppose. Jack, what do you think?"

"Yeah, it's supposed to be about half a mile farther up thataway to where Frank should be waiting for us." Jack shuffled on his feet, looking down, then glanced up at Susan. "I've got to say, uh, Mrs. Kingsley, you certainly know your history preservation. Are you certain you want to leave all this here?" They stepped back outside and into the sun. A few clouds intimated wind and rain.

"It's been here, perfectly preserved, for over a hundred years. A few more weeks won't hurt." Susan replaced the portfolio in the saddlebag, untied a half hitch in the lead rope, and threw the reins over Holly's ears, giving her a gentle nose rub and a pat on the neck. She hitched a boot into the stirrup and launched herself upward, throwing a leg over the saddle. She adjusted her hips in the seat while holding onto the saddle horn with both hands and felt the men eyeing her every move.

"Ma'am, Jack didn't get it right, so I'm gonna say it. You're a real pro, an' anytime you need help getting right with that FBI ex-husband of yours, you just let us know. As you know, we've had a run-in with him before. And by the way, you were the best thing that ever happened to that piece of shit. Pardon my language. And I'll just add on a personal note, you look like you belong on that horse. And on the cover of one of those trashy romance novels. I mean that in the most respectful way possible." Tom retreated and made a sort of bow, and stood next to Jack.

"You're a knock-out, lady. And you can be pissed at me all day, but I'm gonna say it anyway. A woman on horseback in boots and spurs is impressive and makes me hot under the collar. And I respect that." Jack just couldn't help himself.

"Thank you. I appreciate that. But this is my job and I have work to do." She walked Holly back across the stream, circled, and pointed her upstream and back towards the spruce grove where she came from. All the men could do was watch in wonder.

Waiting for the moment and relishing in the admiration, Susan took off her hat, wiped her forehead, and tucked some loose hair behind her ear. "What are you waiting for? Let's go." She let a little smile escape as she replaced her hat. The knots that had been churning in her stomach had been replaced with a steely ball of fire.

PART 4

Chapter 39

Susan: Uintah Mountains, WY, September 1982

Susan waited while Jack and Tom gathered their belongings and waded back across the stream. She estimated it would take them an hour to walk to where she had turned down the drainage and maybe another thirty minutes to where Frank was supposed to meet them. So she took the lead and acted as scout, marching Holly ahead and over the deeper brush to find the easiest route for the men on foot.

After half an hour of walking, Susan dismounted and faced the men. They were tired and needed a rest.

"Listen," she said. "Andrew can be charming when he needs to be and combative when he needs to be, too. So don't cross him. He's had a bunch of complaints against him for police brutality. He sees it as a badge, so don't get cocky with him. He'll leave you out here with an eye swollen shut and a ruptured spleen and not think twice about it."

Jack and Tom watched curiously, noting Susan's small frame and serious tone.

"Don't get in his way, alright? We'll get this cleared up soon."

Jack shook his head in disgust, remembering the beatdown Tom had taken the day before. He wasn't planning on getting in Andrew's way anytime soon.

***

Frank: Uintah Mountains, September 1982

Frank arrived at a wide spot in the road and noticed a faint two-track trail off to the east, so he put the jeep in four-wheel low, a task that required getting out, and turning each of the lugs into the locked position. Although sometimes they didn't want to turn. The gears didn't always align with the wheel hubs for easy manipulation. It took Frank a few minutes to lock one or two lugs, roll the Jeep forward or back, then check to see if the other lugs would slip into place. It took three minutes to complete the process, but it was enough time for the patrol car to catch up.

Andrew rolled up on Frank just as he locked the last lug in place, the Jeep still idling. He was stunned to see the same black-on-black suit in such a remote environment.

"Well, well," said Andrew. "If it isn't that library card punk from earlier. I don't know how you managed to..."

Before Andrew finished his sentence, he slugged Frank on the side of the head and threw him onto the ground. This time Frank reacted.

"You can't arrest me. And I'm not resisting." Frank rose to his feet and tried to put the jeep between him and the black suit. But he wasn't fast enough. Andrew tackled him from behind, as the pair rolled into the grass beside the road. Andrew reached for his handcuffs and placed a well-timed elbow into Frank's neck. The shock to his neck and the change in blood flow was enough to make Frank woozy. But Frank wasn't giving up that easily. He pulled his arms in tight to his chest, face-down in the dirt, hoping the cop would tire and leave him alone.

"I'm not resisting," shouted Frank again, between clumps of grass and breaths choked in dust and debris from the ground. Frank's head was spinning.

"You're gonna get a beating for this, you dirty hippie." Andrew continued wrestling with his perp, trying to get an arm behind Frank's back to lock a cuff in place. He thought about pulling his piece and shooting him in the leg, but that wasn't necessary yet.

"Give me your arm, Ethan."

"Who's Ethan?" came the reply. Susan's voice was strong and steady.

"This book-lovin' deadbeat is Ethan. Ethan J. Eliot. Now get down here and help me cuff this ass-clown."

In his clouded anger, Andrew still believed Susan was his wife. Still expected Susan's assistance. Still owned Susan.

***

Susan: Uintah Mountains, WY, September 1982

Susan jumped down from Holly and ran to where the two men were still wrestling. She decided right then she'd had enough. With a quick thrust of her foot, she kicked Andrew's arm away. Frank tucked his elbow under his chest and turned his head to see Susan deliver a swift kick to Andrew's groin. He flinched and took a direct shot to the inside of his thigh, missing the delicate parts.

"What are you doing, you bitch?"

"What I should have done years ago." Susan gathered herself, gave Andrew a quick rabbit punch in the kidney, and recoiled like a prizefighter. Andrew turned to protect himself as Susan swung a boot at Andrew's head. It was a glancing blow. But the spur on her boot heel caught his lip and ripped open a gash. It tore the flesh from the corner of his mouth all the way up the side of his face.

Andrew slid off to the side, holding his cheek, his mouth hanging agape, and his eyes filled with rage. With his right hand, Andrew took a wild swing at Susan, connecting with her shoulder. Andrew rose and hurled himself at his new prey. They stumbled and wrestled down the hill and into the grass. Blood began to leak from in between Andrew's fingers, as he held the left side of his face together. The wound bled crimson and dripped onto Andrew's black coat, glistening in the afternoon sun.

Susan twisted free of his clutch, retreated, and readied herself as Holly stamped and reared, kicking in the air and whistling. The black suit reached into his coat pocket and pulled out the chrome nine-millimeter. Frank swung with all his might and struck Andrew with the pipe-arm from his floor jack, connecting with bone. His head snapped sideways, the gun slung away into the bushes, and Andrew collapsed in a heap.

Susan picked up the handcuffs lying in the dirt on the road and clicked one ring around Andrew's right wrist. He wasn't unconscious, but he was close. The wound on his face continued to bleed, soaking his shirt. His other hand, drowned in blood and tissue, slunk helplessly into the grass and dripped blood onto the hard ground below. He wasn't the first to bleed in this drainage. Susan did her best to calm Holly as Frank put the patrol car in neutral and pushed it back off the side of the road. He opened the driver's door, pulled the radio mic, and called in.

"Fort Collins car forty-five. Officer needs assistance. Over."

"Uintah County Dispatch. Forty-five. What's your twenty?"

"Six or eight miles west-northwest of the Sheep's Creek Campground, where that piece of shit tried to arrest me. Over."

"Identify yourself, forty-five. Confirm."

Frank got out of the car, pulled the radio mic to its full length, and gave Susan a wink. "Ethan J. Eliot, Animas County Library asset-protection unit. Officer needs assistance. Over and out." Frank took two more steps and gave the mic a firm yank, severing the coiled cord.

Susan stood speechless, holding Holly's lead rope in one hand and the open ring of the handcuffs firmly locked onto Andrew's wrist in the other. She gathered Holly in close, tied a quick-release knot onto the handcuffs, spun a loop around the saddle horn, and grabbed Holly by the halter. She clicked her tongue and walked Holly to the road, pulling a semi-conscious and mostly-limp body behind her. One of Andrew's shoes came off, and his belt gave way next. Dragging the bloodied mass to the patrol car, his pants stretched, then ripped, revealing his underwear, white cotton briefs, trailing in the dirt and scuffing his bare ass.

Frank had seen enough and stopped Susan from coming any closer. "Any more of that, and you'll be in a world of trouble."

"You haven't seen trouble yet."

Susan ran her hands along Holly's neck, patted her shoulder, and whispered in her ear. *Good girl.* She tugged on the knot, broke it free from the handcuffs, and tossed the lead rope back toward Holly. With both hands she pulled Andrew to the front grill of the patrol car and latched the ring of the handcuffs around it, clicking it locked on Andrew's other wrist. As she did, Andrew started to wake from his slumber and tried reaching for his face, grimacing and grunting on the ground.

"You awake, dear?" Susan gave him a gentle nudge with her boot.

"Wha, grr," was the only sound Andrew made.

"We're done, you hear me? And you're done harassing my new friends. Got it?" Susan stood up straight and looked at Frank, reeling from the scene unfolding in front of him.

"We should be going. Soon," said Frank, an urgency in his voice, rather uncharacteristic of him. The effects of the marijuana were fading.

"In a minute. Give me one of those dynamite sticks."

"For what?"

"Don't argue with me, uh, Ethan." Susan winked back at Frank and tucked her hair behind her ear.

Frank calmly opened the tailgate of the jeep, grabbed a drab-olive ammo can marked, canned fish, retrieved a half-stick of dynamite, inserted a fuse into the blasting cap, and handed it to Susan.

"Ready to meet your maker, asshole?" Susan grabbed the dynamite and gave Andrew a quick kick in the balls, only protected by his tighty-whities. "You're a sorry excuse for a man, you lipless prick."

Andrew squirmed on the ground, covering his cheek with his shoulder, feeling for his lip with his tongue, and waiting for the pain from his testicles to reach his liver. Susan grabbed the waistband of Andrew's underwear. She tucked the half-stick into the band and asked Frank for a lighter.

"Whaii. Bon't. Uugga." Andrew gurgled as he reclined back trying to extricate his groin from the rest of his body.

Frank pulled the lighter from his shirt pocket and handed it to Susan. She flicked the steel wheel against the flint. A spark erupted and a tiny flame rose up.

"Careful of the flame." Frank backed away and took cover behind his jeep. He wasn't sure what to say next, so he just blurted it out. "Careful of the package in his pants, too." It wasn't something he'd ever said and couldn't think of another situation when he'd need it again, so he didn't wait for a reply.

"Got it," said Susan, smiling. She leaned in close and spoke softly, right into Andrew's eyes. "This is gonna be fun."

Andrew writhed and snarled in his place, drooling spit, dripping blood, and attempted to spew obscenities from where his lower lip used to be. Susan lit the fuse as it sprayed sparks onto Andrew's squirming torso.

"You're gonna' leave us alone from now on, one way or the other. And you're gonna' do it as a eunuch."

"What's a eunuch," asked Frank, mortified at the site of Andrew with a half-wad of fifty-five percent extra dynamite in his drawers.

"It's a person who's been castrated, Frank. Uh, I mean Ethan."

The fuse continued burning, scorching Andrew's thighs despite his best effort to squirm away. Susan began to back away as Andrew struggled to form words. All he could muster was a weak, "No, no, no. Oh, no."

Susan ran and placed a boot on Andrew's neck, holding him in place against the bumper. She grabbed the dynamite in her fist. The sparks burned her wrist as she growled into his face.

"I never want to see your mangled face again." Susan clutched the dynamite in her fist and ripped it out of Andrew's underwear band, and punched him in the nose all in one motion, showering his hair with sparks. He let out a moaning murmur and dropped his head into the blackness of unconsciousness. Susan spun around on her heel and slung the flaming half-stick into the open door of the patrol car, and dove for cover. *Ka-blam!* Glass shattered, and smoke burst into the air as Susan covered her head on the ground. Clouds of smoke billowed out of the now windowless car and into the air. The blast left Susan in a chasm of ringing ears and blurred vision.

Frank ran to check on his rescuer as Holly reared, screamed, and galloped away down the drainage, frightened by the blast. Frank helped Susan to her feet.

"You ok? I've never seen a woman do anything like that before."

Susan just smiled, dusted the dirt off her clothes, and tucked a strand of hair behind her ear. "You've never met a woman from Tennessee, then. We dynamite-fished all the time when I was a kid. My uncle worked in the coal mines. You think I didn't know what I was doing?"

"That fuse was getting really short," shouted Frank.

"Don't sweat it, they're just half-sticks. It just makes a little bang."

Frank tried to fake a smile as he reviewed the situation. "We really should be going. The police take those "officer needs assistance" calls pretty serious. What should we do with him?"

As the smoke cleared, Susan took a last look at Andrew. He was bloodied, and he was beaten, but he was alive. Susan noticed something else wrong with him. As he began to regain consciousness, a foul odor emanated from him, and a large brown stain pooled from between his legs.

"I guess the threat of having his balls blown off scared the crap out of him." Frank winked at Susan and then continued. "We need to get going." Frank helped Susan back up onto the roadway. "And I see the guys coming up the hill with your horse. The fuzz are gonna be here soon with plenty of backup."

Chapter 40

Susan: Uintah Mountains, WY, September 1982

Susan checked her surroundings and stepped up to the top of the escarpment above the wide turnout in the dirt road. Tom and Jack were walking up the hill with Jack guiding Holly by the lead rope. She saw Frank turning the jeep around to face downhill by way of the southerly hill. She saw her ex-husband crawling in the dust and dirt, shocked at the soiled and flowing excrement between his legs. She remained calm. Holly's eyes continued to dart left and right amid the tumultuous scene. Above it, the blue of the sky illuminated the players in the arena, and the burnt sienna of the sandstone captured all in an amber glow.

Holly whistled, then neighed, as Jack struggled to keep hold of the filly. She spotted her companion near the ridgeline and struck out, snapping the man's grasp on the reins, and surged forward.

Susan shouted an audible yawp at Holly with such exuberance that even Frank, in all his grump and slightly stoned grip on reality, paused to watch. He saw the earth, the animal instinct alive in all of us and the epitome of womankind in only the select few, united in a dance of flying hooves, swaying hips, prancing manes and flailing scarves, captured in a moment of glee, oneness, and oblivion.

Holly responded with a shrill whistle. The two ran toward each other, then circled as Holly nickered, her big brown eyes darting and blinking. They were reunited again.

Frank turned the jeep around and did his best to make room for the rest. Tom jogged up the last hundred feet of open country, reached the two-tracked road, and saw the smoldering police cruiser. "What happened? Is that the... What the hell?" He saw Andrew, handcuffed to the front bumper, with his pants around his ankles, mumbling an incoherent refrain of curses and sobs.

Jack arrived on the scene, incredulous, and insisted it was time to get moving. He was speechless for a change and relied on Tom to make sense of it all.

"You guys climb in. Susan can follow us with Holly. Can you trot her three miles back to the first fork?" Frank was making more sense than usual.

"It shouldn't be a problem. We'll be right there." Susan mounted Holly in two steps and swung her around to face Andrew. "See ya' later," was all she said.

Andrew spat, kicked at the ground, and wrestled with the handcuffs. His ass was wet and dirty and bore the marks of being dragged across the rough ground. His wrists hurt, and his shoulders ached from being restrained. His brain was losing its cocaine-fueled brilliance and his face was bloodied and scarred. His suit jacket was torn, and he was eight miles from any paved road, not that the police cruiser was drivable. The car was mangled, the gear shifter was broken off, the radio was busted, and the windows were smashed. The vinyl seats had rips, tears and burn marks in a typical blast pattern. The front windshield was shattered, and shards of glass littered the dash, etching the dirt and debris blown around. But the trunk release still worked. Jack hit the button, and the trunk popped open, revealing a half kilo of cocaine blown out of its shrink-wrapped packaging, twisting and twirling in the air like a powder puff of balloons blown about by an invisible hurricane.

"Whoa. That's a lot of coke," said Frank.

"That explains a lot," replied Susan.

"We should be going now." Frank started the jeep and popped the clutch, jerking the four-wheeled metal machine forward beside the disabled cruiser. Jack got in the front beside Frank, and Tom climbed in the back.

"Take it easy, Frank. You're liable to toss me out of this death trap." Tom tried to wedge himself into the lowest center of gravity and still have two handholds on the roll bar above his head.

Frank eased the three of them into a manageable fifteen miles per hour until they reached the first jumble of rocks. They slowed, steered, and sputtered up the incline, avoiding the grasp of the rough and rutted four-wheel drive track. The going was slow, but Holly and Susan maneuvered through the rough patches like a sure-footed champion. Holly overtook the weighed-down Jeep and was only too happy to gallop ahead over the open portions of the mountain landscape.

***

The fork of the road was approaching. It was almost twilight when Susan slowed Holly to a walk and saw the wall of police cruisers, lights flashing, and a small army of various law enforcement officers, complete with a Bell 206A helicopter. Susan stopped in the road, just out of reach of the amplified bullhorn squawking in the air. She adjusted her seat in the saddle and spoke kindly to Holly. She waited for Frank in the jeep to catch up, just a few minutes behind.

"That's a lot of cops," said Tom, still trying to assess the situation.

"Let me handle this," said Jack. He got out and confidently walked up to Susan and patted Holly on the shoulder. "I'll see what the problem is, and then we can decide what to do."

Jack walked up the road, waved at the spotlight operator, and casually raised his palms. He continued walking, shouted something at the bullhorn, and stopped. The conversation was just out of reach. Jack turned to Susan, nodded, and pointed at the guys in the jeep. More instructions came from the wall of law enforcement as Jack walked forward, then stopped again, spun slowly around, and raised his sweat-stained shirt to reveal he wasn't armed.

He continued walking forward, then pointed again at the spotlight. An older, potbellied sheriff's deputy strode forward, breaking ranks from his roadblock, and met Jack in the middle of the road. Only the two of them were privy to their conversation. After a few moments, Jack turned and began walking back towards Susan and the guys in the jeep. When he got about halfway, he stopped and shouted.

"Frank, come on over here for a minute. It's Ok."

Frank turned the jeep off but left the headlights on and did as he was told. He walked up the road casually, nodded at Susan, and joined Jack. Jack patted him on the shoulder and spoke quietly into his ear.

"Whatever," from Frank, was all Susan could hear. Holly stammered on her feet, not entirely comfortable with all the flashing lights and particularly alarmed at the spotlight.

Frank stumbled forward along the road, just as Jack had done previously, to within earshot of the sheriff. He continued complying and showed the deputy he wasn't armed, the same way Jack had done. He and the sheriff walked toward each other and spoke quietly for a few minutes. At one point, the sheriff let out a little laugh, then nodded and patted Frank on the shoulder. They talked for a few more minutes.

Frank finished up with the sheriff's deputy, returned to where Jack was standing, and then the two walked back to Susan.

"It's gonna be ok," said Jack. "They'd like you to dismount and show some ID. I think we can be on our way after that."

"I'm a little worried," said Susan.

"They're not concerned with us." Frank let his shoulders droop and teetered back and forth on his feet, thinking about the quarter ounce of weed in his front pocket, and if Johnny Law would mind if he rolled another joint.

"OK, if you say so." Susan got down, rubbed Holly on the nose, and gently gave the reins to Frank. "No sudden movements, please."

Frank nodded and stood at Holly's head, holding the reins down by his side. Susan walked toward the sheriff and suddenly felt small and not as important. But as she reached the sheriff, she turned and looked behind her. Three men were waiting patiently with her horse somewhere in the Uintah Mountains, west of Granite Springs, Wyoming. *Or was it Utah here now?* She wasn't even sure which. The thought gave her pause. She calmly strode up to the sheriff in his tan-on-brown uniform.

"Hello, sir. I'm Susan Kingsley with the Smithsonian Museum. What can I do for you?"

"Well, ma'am, you can tell me where your husband is, for starters."

"Ex-husband."

"Of course. That's what I meant. I've just spoken with your friends here, and we'd like to locate him as soon as possible. We're responding to an 'officer needs assistance' call but haven't been able to locate him. Any idea where he is?"

Susan confidently explained his location, casually omitting the part where she assaulted his face and humiliated his manhood. It didn't matter. Andrew's movements were being tracked by Lieutenant Gilroy, who was waiting impatiently at the tailgate of a police truck. Andrew had become the target of an investigation after some questions had arisen from the Washington Park police department. Evidence tampering and witness intimidation were the most serious charges. The hunter had become the hunted.

"Ma'am, you and your friends are free to go. I've just had a word with Jack and with Frank there. Both Vietnam veterans, you know. I've got three more with the county department. Reliable is what you'd call them. All honorable discharges, just like your friends there. Hard to find men who want to put their lives on the line these days."

Susan nodded and considered a reply but waited.

"Even if Jack, there, only saw the enemy on a radar screen from two hundred miles away in a bathtub in the Pacific. Navy guy."

Susan looked down at her feet, trying to avoid the rambling comments from the local sheriff. She tried to put some words together but she wasn't sure where to start, so she just nodded.

"I got trench foot one time in the jungle, an' they sent me to the navy hospital with a bunch of sailors, and the corpsman, there, said I was the only guy he'd seen that day that didn't have a venereal disease. That corpsman treated penis-rot all day long. Wonder what ever happened to that guy. Prolly still checkin' peckers for polka-dots somewheres."

Susan had stopped looking at her shoes, but she wasn't sure there'd be an opportunity to respond, so she kept nodding and trying not to look out of place. It was difficult to do, considering she was the only woman among forty men, more than half wearing a holstered gun and her friends behind her holding secrets.

"I'm sorry, ma'am. Not sure you needed all that information. You're free to go. Just promise me you'll extricate yourself from Frank, there, and his dynamite. I don't even know what to charge him with. Fishing without a license is all we could come up with. The US army was his initial authorization, and he's kept up his explosives license every year since."

"Thank you, officer, uh. What is your name?"

"It's Sheriff Fulsom. Owen T. Fulsom and I'd appreciate your vote this November."

"I'm very pleased to meet you, sheriff. Thank you. I'm not registered to vote in Wyoming but I appreciate the kind words you said about my friends."

"This is Utah, ma'am. Pleasure to meet you."

***

Susan continued the ride back down the road and arrived at the campground to find Kat and Bubbles talking with a BLM ranger. Kat ran and hugged Susan, letting her concern fade into a warm embrace. Frank idled the jeep to a stop and Jack and Tom got out.

Susan didn't let them get two steps before announcing, "Give me fifteen minutes, and then I'll give you my opinion. Don't go anywhere."

Susan retired to the far side of the campground and talked with Kat for a few minutes, then sat down at a picnic table and made some notes in her journal.

The sun was just beginning to set when she assembled Kat and the men. The emotions churning in her stomach had subsided and she casually addressed the small group. She attempted to sound as though the past events were an everyday occurrence.

"Thank you, everyone, for the adventure of the past few days. It's just what I needed. Frank, thank you for helping with that other matter." She didn't let the least bit of a smile show on her face. "Tom, as far as I can tell, these rifles, the journal, and the letters belong to you and your family. The deed to the mining claim and its contents would have been inherited by Sarah Ann Griggs, his wife. When she remarried and started a family, these items were unknown but intact. The genealogy will need to be confirmed all the way to Mrs. Kowalski. The journal and letters, together with the rifles, make a significant find. At first, the letters themselves weren't historically significant, but combined with the journal and today's discovery, the Smithsonian would be interested in their recovery and preservation. Also, I think you'll find that the rifles will be quite valuable. Somewhere in the neighborhood of three to five thousand dollars, a piece. And the journal appears to shed some light on the Mormon Church's impact on the Native Americans and their interactions with the settlers along the wagon trail. It's a consequential discovery. The North Branch of the Spanish Trail was a major emigrant and trade route for many years. Few traces of it remain. That makes these letters even more material."

"As you know, as part of my research, I finally contacted Mrs. Chapman in Ohio and she shared with me the probate ruling making Tom, here, as the sole male heir, and Mrs. Linda Kowalski's wishes, the rightful owner of the remainder of her possessions. That makes the letters, the journal, and the rifles yours to do with what you wish."

A stunned silence fell over the group. Jack, Frank, and Kat stopped and stared at Tom.

Susan continued in her calmest voice, looking directly at Tom. "Your best bet is to loan these items to the Smithsonian. They can provide cover for your discovery and protect your interests. And the Smithsonian has affiliate museums throughout the country–a place where they can be securely housed. In particular, the Cody Firearms Museum has a very impressive display. It's at the Buffalo Bill Center of the West in Cody, Wyoming. And these rifles would make an excellent addition. The cataloging process would continue, and the museum there has specialists familiar with preservations of this kind. In addition, the letters, the journal, and at least one of the rifles would make a wonderful exhibit at the Smithsonian's History of the American West wing. The rifles would continue to be yours but on a semi-permanent display. They have value beyond what a gun collector might offer."

After acknowledging each of the men, Susan continued. "As a representative of the Acquisitions Department of the Smithsonian, we would be pleased to offer you the title of Diamond Benefactor, which includes lifetime admission to any Smithsonian Museum and its affiliate partners."

"Whoopee," said Jack, in his best deadpan voice.

"It also comes with a ten-thousand-dollar benefit paid on the first anniversary."

"Oh." Disbelief and shock filled the onlookers as all eyes returned to Tom. He nodded in agreement. "Let's do it."

"I think you'll find that the rifles will appreciate in value as news of their relevance comes to light. The journey from Connecticut to Santa Fe, then along the Spanish Trail, is all documented in the letters. The consequential arrangement made with the Mormons indicated in the journal comprises an effectual narrative. Not to mention the plight of the indigenous peoples that are part of that history. This will be impactful to Native Americans. It's important when discussing history and race."

Susan took a deep breath, shifted her weight and continued speaking. "In five years, the rifles will be worth double what you could get for them today. And if you'd like to move them, or sell them, or loan them to a reputable collector, I'm certain it would pay dividends. I'll have a team here within a week. I'll be in touch with you regularly, but I would appreciate you keeping this discovery private until then. Gentlemen, can I count on your discretion?"

"Sure."

"Of course."

Only Frank seemed disinterested and failed to respond in any meaningful way. The excitement from the afternoon was fading, and it was finally time to roll that joint.

"Frank, can we count on your discretion? We'll need to be in unanimous agreement." Susan's loose strands of hair blew in the wind as she looked Frank in the eye and asked the direct question. She didn't look away.

"On one condition," replied Frank, thinking the situation over.

"What's that?"

"We all swear we found your ex-husband handcuffed to the front bumper of his exploded patrol car, with his pants around his ankles. That we just found him that way."

"Seems reasonable enough," said Jack, grinning.

"It's a little unorthodox, Frank, but I'm agreeable." Susan felt the blood rush to her face as she recalled the incident with her ex-husband just a few minutes before. She kicked the dirt and felt her spur graze the ground as a feeling of empowerment swept over her.

Chapter 41

Susan: Denver, October 1982

Susan sat down near her gate and pulled out her book, *Hearts Aflame*, and opened it to the first page. While she enjoyed reading the words, the story seemed flatter, less complete, and farther away. She put it away and wandered over to a newspaper stand. She quietly perused the paperbacks until she found something more suitable, Edward Abbey's *Desert Solitaire*. It was time to make more changes. She decided to put away the romance novels. And even if the environmental eco-warrior bio wasn't her ideal genre, it provided a link to Colorado, Utah and the West that was now a part of her. She wore boots.

Jack and Tom: March 1983

Tom loaned most of the rifles to the Cody Firearms Museum, reserving three for the Smithsonian, one for the Golden History Museum, and five he kept at his Mom's place in Denver in a gun safe he got from Jack. Jack had a brass plaque made for the gun safe. It reads:

Bolskar's Folly, Devil's Thumb above the Green River,

Deseret Territory, 1870-1982.

Until I write to you again, hold on to our dream *for a few more weeks. I'll send for you right soon.*

Your loving husband.

William Mitchell

Jack, Tom, and Frank remain friends to this day.

Chapter 42

Andrew: 1983

Andrew recovered from his injuries in Salt Lake City after being helicoptered out. He served a thirty-day suspension from the FBI for mishandling evidence. He was never charged with the drug possession, evidence tampering, or witness intimidation. He was busted back down to trainee through the end of the year. After that, he worked a desk job in the check fraud department for six months, then transferred out, and rejoined the Baltimore Police Department as a Detective. He retired in 1985 after a nineteen-year-old street dealer shot him in the foot. He moved to Miami the same year and drowned in his girlfriend's bathtub on New Year's Eve. She was questioned in his death but never charged.

Chapter 43

Susan: 1983

Susan returned to the Smithsonian and moved out of her apartment before the end of the month. Nothing would ever be the same. The following year she bought a condo and challenged for the Assistant Director's post in the Acquisitions Department. When she was passed over for the promotion, she resigned her position. At the exit interview, she voiced her opinions about discrimination in the workplace, women working for less pay, and the lack of women in supervisory positions. It fell on deaf ears but planted a seed. She sold her condo for a small profit and put the proceeds down on a twelve-acre horse property in Evergreen, Colorado.

Kat returned to Golden, continued selling real estate, and eventually helped a friend from back East buy a twelve-acre horse property in Evergreen, Colorado. She greeted her old friend with a housewarming present, a ten-year-old dark brown filly with a white star on her forehead, Holly Go-Lightly. Susan and Kat remain friends and go horseback riding every weekend.

The End.

Acknowledgements

This novel would not have been possible without the input, suggestions, and support from numerous people. Thank you to my early readers and editors, Danielle Dudak and Ash McGuffey. Taking your suggestions in stride amid a major rewrite helped my story come alive. Without your edits, this novel wouldn't be what it is today. Thank you.

To Marty Cavanaugh, Ethan Elliot, Jody Myers, Cisco Estrada, Alan Felyk, Drake Scott, Tess Duck, and Vaughn Johnson, and the rest of the fine folks at DWW, and the cast of characters they are, I'm so appreciative of the knowledge I've gained and the friendships cultivated. Additionally, I owe a debt of gratitude to Chris Chinchilla and Kaitlin Sclafani for helping me to polish this manuscript into its final form.

Without the encouragement and guidance of my parents, Sonja and Jerry, I would not be the writer or the man I am today. Despite the ups and downs of everyday life, books were always around and a part of my life. Thank you.

Thank you to Rachel, whose writing inspired me so many years ago and continues to be a bright spot in my life.

To my friends and colleagues, Craig and Diane, Bob and Emily, Dan and Laura, Jim and Terrel, Dick and Bob, Neil, Gordon, Troy,

Mallory, Dave, Kent and Cynthia, thank you for your enduring patience as this book unfolded. There were so many times a conversation, a humorous anecdote, or just a moment hurried me back to write. My sincere hope is that each of you see a little bit of yourselves in the characters and their motivations amid the wonderful setting we call home. We are all so lucky. Thank you.

And last but certainly not least, thank you to my partner in life and supporter at every turn, Robin Wiggs. Without your invaluable input, Susan Kingsley would not have been bold or fierce.

One final note to my readers: I sincerely hope you enjoyed reading this book. They say you write the book you'd like to read. As an author, the goal is always to engage, inspire and entertain. If you were entertained, inspired by the settings, found yourself rooting for a character, or discovered a deeper motivation or meaning in the words, then I would ask you for a favor. Tell someone. Leave an honest review on Amazon here.

huffmanmatthew@yahoo.com

www.MatthewLHuffman.com